*He was in love with a woman almost two hundred years old....*

*She was virgin and innocent and totally inexperienced....*

*He found her inexperience wholly endearing and not a little exciting. She had thought he had a fever.... And then her embarrassment at realizing the truth had been almost palpable.*

*He undid the buttons that held her nightdress closed to the throat and opened back the edges. He touched her breasts one at a time, stroking them lightly.... And while he did so, he leaned his head back from hers so that he could watch her face in the faint light from the window. She looked back until her eyes fluttered closed and she made soft sounds of pleasure....*

*He wanted to give her pleasure, and more than pleasure. He wanted her to feel herself loved and cherished and worshipped and—married.*

"The Heirloom"
by MARY BALOGH,
National bestselling author of *Heartless*

**Timeswept Brides**
also includes

"A Dream Across Time"
by Constance O'Banyon
Bestselling author of *The Flamme*

"Man of Her Dreams"
by Virginia Brown,
Bestselling author of *Jade Moon*

"Bride's Joy"
by Elda Minger
Bestselling author of *Baby by Chance*

P9-BZU-462

# ROMANCE COLLECTIONS FROM
# THE BERKLEY PUBLISHING GROUP

*Love Stories for Every Season...*

**LOVE POTION:** Four breathtaking tales of fantasy, ecstasy, and true love inspired Cupid's Magical Elixir, by Rebecca Paisley, Lydia Browne, Elaine Crawford, and Aileen Humphrey.

**A HOMESPUN MOTHER'S DAY:** A heartwarming collection from the heartland of America—featuring your favorite Homespun authors: Rebecca Hagan Lee, Jill Metcalf, and Teresa Warfield.

**TIMELESS:** Four breathtaking tales of hearts that reach across time—for love, by Linda Lael Miller, Diana Bane, Anna Jennet, and Elaine Crawford.

**SECRET LOVES:** Passionate tales of crushes, secret admirers, and other wonders of love, by Constance O'Day Flannery, Wendy Haley, Cheryl Lanham, and Catherine Palmer.

**HARVEST HEARTS:** Heartwarming stories of love's rich bounty, by Kristin Hannah, Rebecca Paisley, Jo Anne Cassity, and Sharon Harlow.

**SUMMER MAGIC:** Splendid summertime love stories featuring Pamela Morsi, Jean Anne Caldwell, Ann Carberry, and Karen Lockwood.

**SWEET HEARTS:** Celebrate Cupid's magical matchmaking with Jill Marie Landis, Jodi Thomas, Colleen Quinn, and Kathleen Kane.

**LOVING HEARTS:** Valentine stories that warm the heart, by Jill Marie Landis, Jodi Thomas, Colleen Quinn, and Maureen Child.

# TIMESWEPT BRIDES

*Mary Balogh*
*Constance O'Banyon*
*Virginia Brown*
*Elda Minger*

**J**
JOVE BOOKS, NEW YORK

If you purchased this book without a cover, you should be aware that this book is stolen property. It was reported as "unsold and destroyed" to the publisher, and neither the author nor the publisher has received any payment for this "stripped book."

TIMESWEPT BRIDES

A Jove Book / published by arrangement with
the authors

PRINTING HISTORY
Jove edition / July 1996

All rights reserved.
Copyright © 1996 by Jove Publications, Inc.
This book may not be reproduced in whole
or in part, by mimeograph or any other means,
without permission. For information address:
The Berkley Publishing Group, 200 Madison Avenue,
New York, New York 10016.

The Putnam Berkley World Wide Web site address is
http://www.berkley.com

ISBN: 0-515-11891-5

A JOVE BOOK®
Jove Books are published by The Berkley Publishing Group,
200 Madison Avenue, New York, New York 10016.
JOVE and the "J" design are trademarks
belonging to Jove Publications, Inc.

PRINTED IN THE UNITED STATES OF AMERICA

10  9  8  7  6  5  4  3  2  1

# Contents

*ABSOLUTELY DELIGHTFUL*

I find a tender
sweetness in
these stories —

endings a bit
abrupt as in most
short stories

wish they were more
developed — but love
the tone of them !!

# The Heirloom

Mary Balogh

"THERE IT IS," he said, easing his foot off the accelerator, partly because they were at the top of a steep slope and partly because he wanted to savor—and wanted *her* to savor—the sight below.

"Mm, wild," she said. "But lovely for a week's holiday away from the rat race." She stretched her arms above her head and her legs out ahead of her, and yawned.

He did not want to admit that the mildness of her reaction disappointed him. "The Cartref Hotel," he said, moving over to the far left of the road so that faster traffic could pass them. He pointed to the large whitewashed building at the foot of the hill. " 'Cartref' means 'home' in Welsh, you know."

"Yes." She laughed. "You have told me so a million times, John—and that many moons ago it was one of your family homes. It is no more than a cottage in comparison with the others, though, is it? And it is so remote from civilization that I wonder anyone ever came near it. And they would have had to come by carriage, wouldn't they?

It must have taken *days*. Ugh!''

"Everything was sold off or given over to the National Trust by the beginning of the century," he said. "This was the last to go—my grandfather sold it in 1920."

"Probably because everyone had forgotten all about it until then," she said, laughing again.

He pulled right over onto the shoulder of the road and stopped the car. It was not the safest place in which to do such a thing, even though he put on the hand brake, but it was something he wanted to do. Every time he had been here as a boy they had zoomed down the hill, glad to be at the end of their journey, eager to be at the hotel and relaxing in its old-fashioned but luxurious rooms.

To him it had always seemed the loveliest place on earth. He had never minded its remote location on the coast of Cardiganshire in West Wales. That had been its main charm, in fact. And there was an added seclusion to the particular location of the Cartref Hotel because it was located at the bottom of steep hills rising to either side of it. Across the road from it were grassy dunes, a wide golden beach, and the ocean. Behind it was a high fern-covered hill. The hotel itself, once a family home, was a small and elegant mansion.

It had always hurt him to know that it might have been his one day if he had lived in a previous age. It was something he did not feel for the other ancient homes and estates that had once been in the family. Just this one.

"Can you understand why I wanted to bring you here for this particular week?" he asked, reaching for Allison's hand and holding it tightly. "Is there a lovelier place on earth?"

"Oh." She laughed. "I am sure I could think of a dozen without even having to try too hard. But this is very picturesque and I know it is special to you. And I suppose there will be no chance to feel boredom. Not *this* week.'' She turned her head and leered at him, waggling her eyebrows.

He lifted his sunglasses and dipped his head to kiss her, despite the fact that one passing motorist leaned on his horn—with the hood down on the car, they were in full view, of course. No, this week there would be no boredom. This week, they had both agreed, would be spent largely in bed, with the occasional walk or drive for relaxation. This week was for themselves. He was to forget his law practice, knowing very well that all his outstanding cases were in quite capable hands for the coming week, and she was to forget her thriving boutique, which had been left in equally capable hands.

This was the week of their engagement.

He released the hand brake, flicked on his signal light, and pulled out onto the road before continuing on the way down the hill. At the bottom he made a sharp right turn onto the horseshoe driveway that led up a slight slope to the front of the hotel. There was parking off to either side, but he stopped in front of the doors. He would park later, after they had settled in.

It was over twelve years since he had been here last. He had come with his parents at the age of sixteen, despite their assurances that they would understand perfectly if he did not wish at his age to go on holiday with them. He probably would have remained at home or gone to stay with a school friend if they had been going anywhere else but Cardiganshire. But their destination had been irresistible to him.

''Mr. Chandler?'' The owner of the hotel and his wife were both in the foyer to greet him and Allison, even though there was a receptionist behind the desk. Huw Jones held out his right hand and smiled broadly. "I would have recognized you anywhere, though you were just a pip-squeak the last time we saw you. Hasn't changed at all, has he, Blodwyn?"

His wife laughed. "Only that he has got taller and darker and handsomer, Huw," she said. "How do you do, Mr. Chandler?"

They had long memories, these people from one of the more remote areas of Wales. Not only memories of his last visit with his parents, but the memory that his family had owned Cartref for two centuries.

"This is my fiancée, Allison Gorman," he said, setting an arm loosely about her shoulders. "Mr. and Mrs. Jones, Allie."

They were upstairs in their room ten minutes later, their suitcases and bags just inside the door. Huw Jones had gone himself to park the car. It was a front room at the center of the house, the one John had specifically asked for, the one he supposed had been the master bedroom in a former age.

Allison plopped down on the bed after kicking off her shoes. It had been a long drive. They had come all the way from London with only one meal stop. She sighed with contentment.

"Wake me for dinner," she said.

He strolled to the window to look out. It was a perfect view. The slope of the hills on either side of the valley was almost geometric. Whoever had built this house had taken great care with its exact placement. There were masses of flowers in beds between the horseshoe driveway and the road. The tide was half in, but there was still a fairly wide expanse of sandy beach. The late afternoon sun made a shimmering band of light across the water. There was an old lighthouse on a small island beyond one of the head-lands. He remembered that one could walk out to it at low tide.

He hunched his shoulders. If he could just ignore the hotel sign and the traffic on the road . . .

There had always been a funny feeling about the Cartref Hotel. Perhaps it had something to do with the name—*home*. And yet it was not entirely a feeling of homecoming he felt here, though that was definitely a part of it. He had always had a feeling of—nostalgia. He was not quite sure that was the right word. He had it now, powerfully strong. He felt the ache of tears in his throat.

Maybe it was merely curiosity, the desire to look back in time to see it all as it had been. Though he never had that feeling when he visited any of the other former family properties. Mr. and Mrs. Jones must be close to retirement age. He had found himself wondering lately—it was what had made him bring Allison here, perhaps—if they would be interested in selling. It was a foolish idea when his life and Allison's were so much bound up with their careers in London.

Sometimes he wished . . . Oh, sometimes he hated modern living. He hated the global village idea. He hated computers and instant communication, though, as Allison had pointed out when he had said these things to her, he would probably scream to have it all back again, if deprived for only a day.

"Wouldn't you like to live here for the rest of your life?" he asked now without turning. "Forget about the rat race? Bring up children close to nature and the ocean, away from the ugly pull of civilization?"

"Telephones, television, modern transport," she said after yawning, "they are all here, John. You cannot escape them. And, no, I would not like to live in a country back-water, picturesque as it may be, thank you kindly. I am not the back-to-basics type. Don't get any ideas.''

She spoke lightly. There was laughter in her voice. But he felt a twinge of something he had been ignoring ever since accepting her proposal a month before—yes, it really had been that way around. They had known each other for a month before that. And ignore it he must. He supposed it was natural to feel qualms about taking such an enormous step as marrying. To him it was an enormous step, even though his best friend had commented half seriously that, after all, marriage was not a life sentence these days as it used to be. If it did not work out, then they could bow out of it and try again some other time with other partners.

That was another thing he hated about modern living—its basic cynicism.

He loved Allison. Certainly he lusted after her. She was tall and blonde and sleek. She was poised and articulate and ambitious and successful. Of course there were differences between them. Many of them. It was natural. They would work through the differences if they wished their marriage to be a success. That was the challenge of marriage.

He turned to look at her. She was lying with her hands locked behind her head, her legs crossed at the ankles. She was looking at him and smiling.

''It was a funny party, wasn't it?'' he said, grinning. ''An engagement party without a ring.'' It had taken place at his flat just the day before yesterday.

''Who needs a ring?'' She shrugged her shoulders. ''And everyone was told about the family heirloom. It will be something to show when we return. Are you going to insure my finger for a million pounds or so?''

''I think you are a little more valuable than the ring,''

he said. "Why not insure all of you?"

"Gallant John." She smiled at him. "Or mercenary John?" She opened her mouth to say more, hesitated, and then spoke anyway. "Do we have to wait until this evening? I know you have arranged a special candlelit dinner downstairs. But do we have to wait?"

He had the ring in his wallet. He had driven to Reading yesterday and got it from his father. His mother had died eight years ago. The ring was for his bride now. Not many of the family wives during the past three centuries had had the ring in time for their engagements.

He had always had strange feelings about the ring. His mother had not worn it a great deal, as she had had another engagement ring—the family ring had not come to her until fifteen years after her marriage. So he had not seen it much himself. Whenever he had, he had felt—how had he felt? It was almost impossible to put the feeling into words. Breathless? Nostalgic? Excited? Afraid? None of the four words, except perhaps the first, really described his feeling.

And the feeling had returned yesterday. He had thought perhaps it was the value of the ring and the knowledge that now it was in his keeping and that soon it would be on Allison's finger. But it was not so much the monetary value that had affected him as the historic value. Though that word was too cold, too clinical.

He had put it carefully in his wallet. He had checked and rechecked ever since to see that it was still there, even though the wallet had never left his person. But he had not unwrapped it or touched it. There was something about touching it—well, something that made him breathless. He could put it no more clearly than that. And he did not have to. He had never tried to explain the feeling to anyone else.

"No," he said now, reaching for his wallet. "There is

no reason to wait. And I would rather do it here in private than in the dining room where someone else might notice and somehow intrude.''

"I have not even seen it," she said, sitting up.

He took the velvet bag out of his wallet and the tissue paper out of the bag. He unwrapped it. He had not yet touched the ring with his bare hand. His father had wrapped it yesterday.

He sat down on the side of the bed and held out his palm to her. "You see?" he said. "It can be the something old and the something blue for our wedding." *He had said that before.* Déjà vu hit him like a hammer blow, catching him somewhere low in his stomach. He must be very tired from the long drive.

It was a large sapphire in a heavy gold setting. His father had had it cleaned just last week and sized for Allison.

"Mm, very nice," she said, warm appreciation in her voice.

Yet for some reason the words cut him. *Very nice?*

"Well?" She was laughing and holding out her left hand to him, the fingers spread. "Are you going to put it on me or am I going to have to do it myself?"

He did not want to touch it. It was absurd. And he knew now that two of those words about his feelings were correct—he was both breathless and afraid. But afraid of what? Afraid of dropping it? Of losing it? Of sharing his family heritage and therefore himself with a stranger? Good Lord, Allison was not a stranger. She was his fiancée. They had been together for two months. Intimately together.

He picked it up. It felt warm, as if it had been worn recently. The heat from his body had warmed it through his wallet and through its wrappings. He slipped the ring onto her finger.

"There." He smiled at her. "The deed is done. You are mine, body and soul. I love you, Allie."

"I love you too." The tears that brightened her eyes were unexpected. She was not an overly emotional person. Passionate, yes, but not emotional. "I do, John. I know we do not see eye to eye on everything. You half meant it a moment ago when you suggested coming here to live for the rest of our lives, didn't you? And I would die of such an existence. But we do love each other. We will make this work. Won't we?"

Allison did not usually need reassurance. She was abounding in self-confidence. She sounded anxious now, endearingly so. Sometimes, treacherously, considering the fact that he was living through the 1990s, he wished she were a little more dependent. But that was certainly something he would never utter aloud.

"Yes," he said, releasing her hand in order to wrap his arms about her. "Of course we will. We will adjust to each other's needs. Because we love each other."

He kissed her and lowered her back onto the bed. He followed her down until he was lying beside her, his mouth still against hers. Surprisingly, though, he found that it was not desire they shared but tenderness. Passion would come later, in the night. Now was the time for love—in the moments following their official engagement. He reached one hand down to hers, to take her ring between a thumb and forefinger and twist it.

He was not sure at what precise moment he felt the other ring. At first his fingers merely brushed against it. Then they moved curiously to it and felt its smoothness. It was a plain band, like a wedding ring. He stretched his hand out along hers, palm to palm. Hers seemed smaller than usual. It was as if the ring had dwarfed it. Her lips had softened to exquisite gentleness. For the first time he noticed her perfume—subtle and unobtrusive, but unmistakably lavender.

The drive had tired him far more than he had thought. He doubted that he was going to be able to get up for dinner. He even doubted—alarming thought—that he was going to be able to make love to her tonight. He was so tired he could hardly exert any pressure against her hand and against her ring—her rings.

And then, before he opened his eyes, he realized something. He realized that it was not Allison he held in his arms at all. It was another woman. And in fact it was he who was lying in *her* arms.

Perhaps the most disorienting realization of all, though, was that *he knew who she was*.

"Adèle," he murmured, and opened his eyes. Even doing that took great physical effort.

She had dark eyes and dark hair, worn rather formally in a topknot with wavy tendrils at her temples and neck. She wore no makeup. She was wearing a dress of some flimsy stuff, low and scooped at the neckline, drawn in by a wide ribbon beneath her breasts. The sleeves were short and puffed. Empire style, he thought. Regency.

She was looking at him with such naked love in her eyes that his heart turned over.

*Adèle?* How did he know her name? How had he known he would open his eyes to see her? How did he know he loved her more than life?

"John?" She released her hand from his and lifted it to his face. She set the backs of her fingers against his forehead. They felt cool. He saw the ring on her finger—the rings. They both looked very shiny and new. "You slept for a while. The fever seems to have cooled a little. Would you like a drink? Water? Lemonade?''

He did not want her to have to leave the room. She could fetch water from the bathroom. Had he had the flu? ''Water, please,'' he said.

She sat up and got off the bed and reached out to pull a strip of silk beside the bed. Of course, he thought, his eyes following her movements. One of the servants would bring it. And, yes, definitely Regency. Her dress—it was made of muslin—fell soft and straight to the floor from beneath her bosom. She was small—he knew that he had to raise his chin only a little to be able to rest it on the top of her head when they were both standing.

His eyes roamed the room, seeing with a curious mixture of surprise and recognition the ornate canopy above the bed, the finely carved bedposts, the velvet curtains, which were pulled back so that he could see the rest of the room. He could see the ornate Adam furniture, the gilding on the high ceiling.

He must have dozed again for a few moments. She was taking a glass from a tray held by a maid—the same maid who had removed the blood-spotted cloths some time ago.

Flu? *He had been coughing blood.*

She turned back to the bed with a smile. He had never seen such luminous tenderness in anyone's face as there was in hers. She half knelt, half sat beside him and lifted him—there seemed to be no strength in him at all—until his head nestled on her shoulder. The water tasted good, though it was not very cold. He half expected to feel it burn his throat, but it did not. He drew a deep and careful breath, expecting to feel a burning in his lungs, but he did not.

''Thank you,'' he said. ''You are an angel, pure and simple, Adèle.''

"You will feel better for the rest," she said. "The journey was a long and rough one, John. It was madness to come so far. But I know now what you meant about this place." Her cheek was resting against the top of his head. "It *is* the loveliest place on earth. And I am glad we came. I think you will get better here."

He could tell from the bright warmth of her voice that she did not believe her own words. He was dying. He had come here to die.

"I already feel better," he said.

What he did feel was strange—a massive understatement. A few minutes ago he had been lying in this very room with another woman—with Allison, his fiancée. Both room and woman had changed. Even he was different. He could see his legs encased in tight pantaloons with silk stockings instead of in jeans and socks. He could see his waistcoat. He had seen the ruffles of his shirt cuffs when he had lifted his hand briefly to the glass—and his hand was thin and emaciated. Yet he knew he was not asleep. And he knew he was not mad. He *knew* all this though his mind was sluggish on the details.

He saw her rings again when she set the glass down beside the bed. She was *his wife*. He held out his hand to her on the bed and she placed hers in it. He raised it to his lips and kissed the sapphire of her ring. Damn, but he was weak.

"But I should not have done this," he said.

He was not quite sure what he meant by the words, but she knew, all right. He could hear the tears in her voice when she spoke. "John," she said, "please do not. Please do not keep on saying that. I *know* that it was I who asked you to marry me. It was unpardonably forward of me to do so, and I never would have done it if I had not thought that perhaps you needed me.''

''Adèle,'' he said.

''No,'' she said. ''Talking takes your energy. Just rest. Please rest, my dearest love. John, I *wanted* to marry you. More than anything else in this world. I love you so very dearly. I have always loved you, from the moment you lifted me down from that stile when I was four and you were eight and the other children were jeering because I was stuck and frightened.''

He smiled at the memory of the infant with the soft baby curls and huge eyes.

*The memory?*

''This is what I have always dreamed of,'' she said. ''Being your wife, John. Being with you like this. I do not care for how long—'' She broke off suddenly and he could hear her distress in the silence. ''But you are going to get better. I know you are. I feel it. I am going to make you better. They said you needed a dry, warm climate and so you went off to Italy for a whole year and came back worse. I do not care what they say. This place will be good for you. And I will be good for you.''

He pulled on her hand until she was lying beside him again. He turned onto his side to face her.

''You *are* good for me,'' he said. ''You are all I could ever need, Adèle. How foolish I was to go to Italy and waste a whole year I might have spent with you. But no matter. We have the rest of our lifetimes together.''

Her eyes were bright with tears, brimming with love. The rest of a lifetime. How much longer did he·have? A few weeks? A few days? And yet, weak as he felt, he did not feel *ill*. He should, shouldn't he? He had tuberculosis— consumption. Didn't he?

"How long have we been married?" he asked her.

She looked frightened for a moment. Perhaps she thought he was delirious. Then she smiled. She had a dimple in the middle of her right cheek. It had been there since she was a child—*How did he know that?*

"For shame," she said. "Have you forgotten the number of days? But it was a long journey for you—four days, with the wedding just the day before we set out. It has been five days and four hours, sir. We are an old married couple."

Yes, he knew how long they had been married. He had remembered as soon as he asked the question. He knew, too, that the marriage was unconsummated, that she fully expected it would forever remain so. She had married him anyway.

"I love you," he whispered to her.

Her eyes filled with tears again. "Yes, I know you do, John," she said, "even if not quite as you would have loved a bride if you had had more opportunity to choose. But I know you love me. I am content."

Had he ever given her the impression that he did not love her totally, to the exclusion of all other women? He knew he had. He knew it as soon as he asked the question, silently this time. He had always loved her as a friend. He had loved her, too, as a woman, though there had always been a niggling doubt. Was it just habit that made him believe that he loved her? Did he really love her? Was he prepared to give up all other women in order to spend the rest of his life with her?

Finally the question had become immaterial. He was dying. He had come back from Italy to find her still unmarried at the age of twenty-four, still waiting for him, still loving him. And so he had married her.

But looking at her now, he could hardly believe that he had ever doubted the depth of his feelings for her. There was something about her just a little too soft, a little too dependent, he had thought. He might prefer someone rather more forceful, someone with a more vivid personality. He could not understand why he had never before fully appreciated her strength of character. She had remained true to a dying man. She had married him, knowing that there was no future with him—because she loved him.

And yet—his mind became dizzy with disorientation again. It was not *he* who had doubted. And it was not he who now loved her with all his heart. That was another man, the one who usually occupied this weak, thin body. *He*—John Chandler—could have no feelings for Adèle at all. He was in love with Allison Gorman. He was engaged to her. He had just placed on her finger the ring that Adèle was now wearing.

He knew what had happened, of course. He accepted it with a calm that puzzled and amazed him, as if it were an ordinary, everyday occurrence, or as if he finally understood the feelings he had always had about the house and the ring. He had slipped back into history. When he could set his mind to working rationally, he would even be able to work out exactly who in history he was impersonating. He had a smattering of knowledge about the family. And this was a Regency man. He should not be difficult to trace.

"If I had had an opportunity to choose my bride at leisure and in full health," he said, "I know whom I would have chosen."

She closed her eyes. He knew she was steeling herself against pain, though she showed no other outer sign than that.

"The Honorable Miss Adèle Markham," he said softly,

"now Adèle Chandler, Viscountess Cordell. How could I ever have chosen anyone else when my heart was given to her?"

Her eyes opened again. "How kind you are," she said. "Kinder than usual." She touched his lips with her fingertips. "And you are talking too much. You will tire yourself and start coughing again."

During their journey into Wales he had sometimes been made irritable by her fussing—though that was an unkind word to use. By her everlasting patience and consideration for his well-being, then. *Kinder than usual.* It had not escaped her notice, then.

"I shall leave for a while," she said. "You will be able to rest better if I am not here."

But he set his arm about her and held her against him. "Don't leave," he whispered. He was afraid that if she left she would never come back, that he would never see her again. It was an unbearable thought. And dizzying in light of the fact that he had just got engaged—to Allison. "Kiss me."

He knew that the joy that lighted her face had always been there when she was a child and a girl. Beautiful, joyous Adèle. He knew, too, that it had not been there a great deal in recent years—only the soft, gentle look of love.

"Kiss me, my love," he whispered again. "Don't leave me. Don't ever leave me."

Her lips were soft, gentle, slightly pouted—quite different from Allison's wide, sensuous mouth. Adèle kissed as a child kissed, but with the added dimension of womanhood. She kept her lips sealed to his. He parted his lips and licked at hers. So warm and so sweet. He prodded his tongue through the seam to the softer, moister flesh within. She moaned.

He was too tired to become fully aroused. Which was just as well, some sane but distant part of his mind thought. He was kissing someone else's wife. He was kissing someone who was not Allison. But she was *his* wife. She was his love. The only, eternal love of his heart. He was not normally given to such poetic flights of fancy.

"Oh," she said when he drew back his head a few inches. "Oh, John." Her eyes looked rather dazed.

He did not feel ill, he thought. Just very weak and very tired. He needed food and air and exercise. Lots of all three. He was not going to die. People of the 1990s did not die of tuberculosis—not in First World countries, anyway. He had been vaccinated against it as a child, just like everyone else in his class, when a schoolfriend had developed the disease. But he was not in the twentieth century at the moment. Somehow he had been transported back into the early nineteenth. Something told him, though, that he had brought part of his old self with him, as well as his mind. He had brought his resistance to the disease that had been killing John Chandler, Viscount Cordell. *He knew the name of the man in whose body and mind he found himself.*

"I need food and air and exercise," he told Adèle. "What is for dinner? Do you know?"

"John?" she said. "Are you sure? You know how—how upset you become when you cannot do what you try to do. Perhaps if you rest for a few weeks your strength will come back. I am going to see that it does."

Yes, it had been a trial to him, his weakness. He had never resigned himself to his fate. He had always been a man of high energy, someone who wanted to accomplish a great deal in this world, someone who could never sit still and let the world go by him. He had raged against his illness. It seemed hard to believe now that he had been such a high-powered man. Why waste life on busy living? Allison would approve of him as he had been, he thought, and felt the dizziness again for a moment.

"And when my strength does come back," he said, "we will live here forever, Adèle, and never return to the hurry of modern life. We will raise our children here where it is quiet and beautiful, where we can be close to nature and to God."

She hid her face against him. He knew she was crying. His words must seem cruel to her. "Forever" to Adele was probably only a few weeks, at the most. She knew there would never be children.

But he thought of something suddenly as he held her close to him. He remembered now. There had been an eccentric Viscount Cordell of the Regency era who had come to Cartref with his bride for their wedding trip and had never returned to England. They had lived here until a ripe old age, the two of them, with their children. He could not remember the exact date of their deaths and he could not remember how many children they had had. But he could remember one other thing clearly—two things.

That viscount had been John. His wife had been Adèle.

John Chandler, Viscount Cordell, certainly had not died of consumption within weeks or even months of his wedding.

It seemed to her that she had loved him all her life. When he had lifted her down from that stile, he had lifted her into his life. He had always included her, guarded her, listened to her, and talked to her after that, though a mere four-year-old girl had seemed nothing but a nuisance to her brothers and sisters and to his and to the other children with whom they had played. He had seemed so grown-up, so tall, so handsome, so—oh, so wonderful to her infant's eyes. And he had remained so ever since.

She had loved him with a woman's love for years and years. She had resisted all of her parents' attempts to find a suitable husband for their youngest child. If she could not have John, she would have no one. She had decided that when she was sixteen, perhaps earlier. If he had not cared for her, perhaps she would have forced herself to turn her eyes, if not her heart, elsewhere. But she had always known that he loved her. There was a special gentleness, a special tenderness in his treatment of her.

Not that he would have married her. She was a dreamer with a streak of realism. He was an older son, heir to a viscount's title and fortune. More important than that, she knew that he did not love her as she loved him. He loved her, but she was not that one love of a lifetime, of an eternity, as he was to her. He loved her, perhaps, as he would a beloved sister. Maybe a little more than that. He had kissed her on her seventeenth birthday. . . .

And then he had become ill. No one, at first, had been willing to admit what it was that was striking him down, robbing him of flesh and color and vitality. But *she* had known from the start. She had watched her handsome, strong, vital, beloved John begin to die. And something in her had started to die too.

All her dreams became focused on one single impossible goal. She wanted to be the one to nurse him out of this life, the one to love him over into the kingdom of love so that there would be no darkness for him between the two moments. The dream had seemed even more impossible when he had left for Italy in the hope of some miracle cure. She had expected never to see him again.

But he had come home. She had gone with her mama

and papa to call on him. She preferred not to think about her first sight of him. Death hovered over him, very close. But her dream had lurched painfully into focus again.

She had found a way to be alone with him for a few minutes just two days later and she had asked him to marry her. He had protested, of course. For the first time he had spoken the truth to her.

"I am dying, Adèle," he had said gently. "I do not have long left. I have nothing to give you, dear."

Somehow—she was not normally a bold woman—she had persuaded him that indeed he did. That he had the power to enable her to be with him all the time, making him more comfortable.

"I cannot stay close to you if I am not married to you, John," she had said. She had taken both his thin hands in hers and had kissed them repeatedly. She had not known quite where her boldness had come from. "I can think of no greater happiness than being close to you."

And so he had married her just one week later. He had decided on some impulse to bring her here, to his home in Wales, for their wedding trip. Everyone had thought him mad. It was such a long distance over roads that were notoriously rough. But she had not tried to argue with him. She had known it was a dying man's wish—to die in the place he considered the loveliest in the world. In the place that had the loveliest name she knew—*Cartref*. Home.

She had come here with a strange hope in her heart. It was the hope for a miracle. It was strange because she had never had hope, not since the moment she had realized he had consumption. Even when he went to Italy, she had had no hope. When he had come home and when she had begged him to marry him, there had been no hope beyond the dream to be his wife and to have the privilege of comforting his last days.

But throughout the journey, hope had built, even as his body became weaker with exhaustion and as the coughing spells became longer and more frightening. By the time they reached Cartref that new and strange inner part of herself knew that he was going to recover, even while the rational, practical part of her was certain that it was impossible. She must not buoy herself up with false hope, she had told herself repeatedly.

Besides—the thought had saddened her—if he recovered, he would find himself trapped in a marriage that was not entirely of his own choosing.

During the three days following their arrival in Wales, then, she watched the changes in him with a bewildering mixture of hope and cold reason. He was rallying after the exhaustion of the journey. He was rallying from the pleasure of being in a place he loved. And from the knowledge that no further great effort would ever be required of him. They had both known, though it had never been spoken between them, that he had come here to die, that he would never have to make the return journey to England.

It was not unusual, she knew, for patients to rally and even seem to recover from serious illnesses for a short while. That was what was happening to John. She tried to believe that and to be grateful that she was to have a little more of him than she had ever expected, especially during that dreadful journey. She had even doubted once or twice—or the part of her that had not been borne up by that strange hope had doubted—that he would get as far as Cartref.

On the first day he dressed for dinner—his valet had looked at him in amazement and then at her in inquiry when he demanded it—and came down to the dining room with her. He even ate. Not a great deal, it was true, but then since their wedding it had seemed to her that he existed on air. He had eaten no solid food.

"I have to eat," he told her with a smile, tackling the fish course. "I just looked at myself in the looking glass, Adèle, and I am nothing but skin and bones. I do not know how you can bear to look at me."

She would have wept except that there was a twinkle in his eye. "You are John," she said. "I could look at you every moment for the rest of my life and not grow tired of doing so."

He chuckled—and her heart turned over with joy at the sound. "And I am so weak," he said, "that I fear I made a dent in both the banister and your shoulder coming downstairs."

They had taken the stairs one at a time, with a long pause on each one. The butler had watched anxiously and incredulously from the foot—John's valet had carried him upstairs on their arrival.

On the second day he insisted on taking each meal in the dining room, even breakfast. And he forced himself to eat. She could tell that it was an effort and part of her wondered if it was worth torturing himself when . . . But there was the other part of her that hoped and did more than just hope. There was a part of her that *knew*.

He would not go back to bed except for one hour in the afternoon—he had her promise to wake him after an hour, provided she was awake to do it. He insisted that she lie down with him, and he held her hand, twisting her sapphire ring, until he drifted off to sleep.

For the rest of the day he *walked*. It was incredible to see. He would not sit down to conserve his energy. And he would not allow her to close the downstairs windows after he had thrown them all open, even though the air coming off the ocean was brisk. He walked all about the house, slowly and doggedly, her arm drawn through his, though he assured her that she must not feel obligated to trudge her slippers to shreds on his account.

"I would trudge my slippers and my boots and the soles of my feet to shreds to be with you," she told him, rubbing her cheek against his shoulder. "But do not exhaust yourself, John. And do not catch a chill."

"Sea air and exercise are good for a person," he said. "Once I am stronger, I am going to be marching along the beach and running up and down the hills to build an appetite for breakfast."

She laughed against his shoulder. Helpless laughter that bordered on tears. "Will I be able to keep up to you?" she asked. "Or will I have to trail along half a mile behind?"

"I shall match my strides to yours," he said. "But we will have to get you fit enough not to pant and wheeze as we run."

"Up hills?" she said, still laughing. "*Hills*, John? Have mercy."

He even went outside on that second day and strolled very slowly with her along the graveled paths between the flower beds that stood between the house and the rough trail that descended the hill to one side of the house and ascended on the other side to the village of Awelfa, just out of sight over the crest.

He stopped frequently to draw deep breaths of the fresh salt air. She was terrified that he would bring on another of the coughing spells. He had not had one since just after their arrival the day before.

And then once, before they strolled on, he dipped his

head and kissed her. He kissed her the way he had kissed her yesterday—and never before that—with his lips parted and his tongue stroking over her lips and even pressing through. A shocking, wonderful kiss. One that made her knees turn weak. A fine prop she would make for him if he kept kissing her like this.

And that was the biggest change in him, she thought, and the one she had been most trying to ignore, because she had accepted the way he was and had thought to be happy with it long after he had gone. She had accepted that he loved her but that there was no magic in his love.

Since their arrival, since that coughing spell and the short sleep of exhaustion that had followed it, he had been different. There had been something in his eyes, something in his voice, something in his kiss . . . And something in his words, too, though she guessed he was speaking them out of tenderness and gratitude to her. He knew that she loved him more than life and he knew that she was going to have a leftover life to live very soon. He was being wonderfully kind to her as he always had been.

But there was something in his eyes. The eyes cannot deceive as well as the voice can.

On the third day he decided that they would go walking on the beach.

"John." They were in the dining room at the time, having just risen from breakfast. "Is it wise? You are so much better. Would it not be wiser to rest today? To get your strength back gradually?" She stepped closer to him and framed his face with her hands. "There is even a little color in your face today."

"Perhaps in time," he said, "you will even have a halfway handsome husband, Adèle."

His face blurred beyond the tears that sprang to her eyes.

"You are the most handsome man in the world," she said.

He laughed—oh, how she loved to hear him laugh. "Did you not know," he asked her, "that the most sure way to build strength and energy is to use them?"

He had some strange ideas, this new John who had appeared just the day before yesterday. "How absurd," she said.

"They are just like love," he said.

She smiled at the idea. Yes, it was true. The more love one gave, the more there was to give. But strength and energy? She was not at all convinced by the analogy. She could see, though, that he wanted to walk on the beach, that he wanted to believe his strange theory. She could see that he was happy here at Cartref. Why should she try to curb his happiness merely so that she could guard his little remaining strength and keep him with her a few days longer? She had married him so that she could love him into the next world.

"Do it, then, you foolish man," she said. "I shall even come with you. But do not expect me to carry you home."

"Soon," he said, "I'll be able to do that for you, Adèle." His eyes softened, filled with that look again, the one that made her breathless because it was new and unexpected and undreamed of. "I want to be whole for you. I am *going* to be whole for you."

She had expected nothing of this marriage except a fulfillment of her own dream. She ached with sudden longings that she did not want to feel. She did not want to have more pain than there was going to be anyway.

And yet there was the hope. And the *knowledge*.

"To the beach," he said, taking her hand and leading her to the door. "No more procrastinating."

"To the beach, sir," she said, trying to match the lightness of his tone.

He had only one real fear and it was a fear that puzzled him at best and made him feel guilty at worst. He feared being suddenly projected forward into his own life again—though there seemed nothing particularly alien about this life. He feared every time he woke up from sleep that he would be back in the Cartref Hotel in the middle of the 1990s.

It was a fear that puzzled him. Could he *want* to be trapped in a former age, cut off forever from the life he had known for twenty-eight years? Could he want to live without the trappings of late-twentieth-century civilization? And without the conveniences—electric lights and shavers, central heating, running water, zippers, to mention just a few. And without his red sports car?

And it was a fear that made him feel guilty. Could he be content never to see his father again? Or his other relatives and friends? Or Allison? He had just become engaged to Allison. She was the woman he loved, the woman he had decided to spend the rest of his life with.

And yet he feared having to go back. He feared having to leave Cartref and his sense of belonging there. He feared—oh, he feared more than death having to leave Adèle. How would he ever cope with the grief of being separated from her by the insurmountable barrier of almost two centuries?

He did not fear having been projected back into the body of a desperately sick, dying man. He could be deceiving himself, of course. He knew that it was possible to be very ill and not even realize it until a chance medical checkup revealed a problem. But even so he felt convinced that he was only weak, not sick. All he needed in order to get back his full health and strength was food and rest and exercise. He was certainly in the right place for all three, despite the horror Adèle and his servants felt for his insistence on exercising.

Perhaps what cheered him most of all was that memory he had from his studies of family history. The memory of John and Adèle Chandler, who had begun their married life in the Regency era but had lived on with their children well into the Victorian age. Sometimes he wished that he had learned more about them and that his memory was sharper. But then, he decided, he did not really want to know exactly when they had died or who had died first. And he did not really want to remember how many children they had had—though he did know that it was more than one. If he was to live the life of the Regency Chandler, he did not want to know any more about his future than the fact that it was to be a lengthy one, with Adèle at his side.

He put a cloak on over his coat and his waistcoat and his shirt to go to the beach, despite the fact that it was a warm day. Adèle would have been too upset if he had refused. And he wore a hat, though he was afraid that it might blow away in the wind. It was probably wise to dress warmly anyway—his emaciated body felt the cold. It would do him no good to catch a cold in his weakened state.

Adèle looked remarkably pretty with a yellow spencer over her matching dress and a straw bonnet trimmed with blue flowers. He had always felt a treacherous preference for the femininity of female dress of a century and more ago, though Allison's clothes were always chic and elegant and sexy.

But the prettiest thing about Adèle was her face. Despite her anxiety that he was going to tax his strength too much, there was a glow of joy in her face that he knew he had put there in the past two days. He knew that he had aroused hope in her—it was another cause for fear if he should have to go back and take his tuberculosis resistance with him. And he knew that he had surprised her by the depth of his need for her and his love for her. He knew that the John she had married had never felt more than a deep affection and tenderness for her.

She deserved more. She had devoted all of her love for all of her life to him. He knew that she would go on loving him for the rest of her life, even if he should die tomorrow and she should live on to be eighty or ninety. He knew that her love for him was that deep.

"Are you ready?" he asked her, offering his arm. "Though this is a deceptive gesture, is it not? It seems that I am offering you my support when in reality I am begging for yours. I hope you noticed this morning, though, that I paused on each stair for only five seconds instead of five minutes."

"Yes." She smiled wistfully at him. "I noticed." He wondered if she was fighting hope or if she was beginning to give in to it. "I do believe you have put on weight, too."

"All of half a pound, I daresay," he said. "Though I believe it is the cloak that makes me look voluminous. Wait until it is filled by the wind on the beach. You will be putting me on a reducing diet."

It irked him to have to descend the stairs so slowly, to have to walk so slowly from the house and around the cobbled driveway to the road—or track would be a more suitable word—and across it to the grass and then the beach. There was just not the strength to stride along as he wished to do. But when he remembered how just the day before yesterday every step had taken almost all his strength, he decided that he must make a friend of patience for the coming days and weeks.

She chattered to him—mainly to try to keep him from using precious energy in talk, he guessed. Though he could remember that she had always liked to walk and chatter with him. Only him. Other people knew her as a shy, quiet, not particularly interesting lady. It was as if she saw him as the other half of her soul and could talk with him as freely as she could think.

He drew her to a halt when they were on the beach and shaded his eyes against the sun sparkling on the water. The tide was almost out. The beach was wide and flat and golden.

"The beginning of eternity," he said. "It is a wonderful place to live, Adèle, close to the ocean. One is constantly reminded of the vastness of life and eternity. And of God. And yet it is an awareness without fear. One feels a part of it all, a part of eternity. I never fear death when I am here."

He could never speak thus with Allison, he realized. She would either think he had taken leave of his senses or she would plain not comprehend.

The brim of Adèle's bonnet touched his shoulder. "You are right," she said. "It is a very good place to be. I am glad we came here, John. You could not have brought me to a better place."

He drew his arm free of hers and set it about her shoulders. After all, they were on the beach and some of the proprieties could be allowed to slip away there. Besides, he had brought some of his twentieth-century lack of inhibitions with him. She looked first startled and then very pleased indeed. The wind and salt air had already whipped color into her cheeks.

"I am not going to die," he said. "Not yet, anyway. I am better, my love. All I need is to regain my strength. I know you will not quite believe it yet—perhaps not for a long while. But it is true."

Pray God—he closed his eyes to make it a real prayer—that he could stay with her, or that at the very least his own health would stay with the man who would return to her. And pray God that that man, if he must return, would love her as she deserved to be loved.

"I believe it," she said softly. Her voice was trembling. "I do believe it, John. I knew when we were coming here and even more so when I saw Cartref and the valley and the beach and ocean—I knew that a miracle was going to happen."

"It has," he said. "A greater miracle than you realize, I believe."

He took her hand in his and began to walk with her toward the water. Through her glove his thumb and forefinger played with the ring on her finger. This was what he had imagined doing, he thought, when he had suggested a week at the Cartref Hotel with Allison. He had imagined quiet walks on the beach, rambles in the hills, browsings in the village of Awelfa. Long afternoons and nights of lovemaking. He was not at all sure that Allison would have enjoyed any of it except the lovemaking. She needed the hectic pace of city life as a constant stimulant, he realized.

He did not.

He felt the now familiar dizziness for a moment. How could he be doing this, strolling inside someone else's body with someone else's wife two hundred years ago, and not be feeling either alarm for his own sanity or panic at having slipped through some time warp? But it was not someone else's body. It was his own. He recognized himself in the mirror even though he did not look quite identical to his usual self. And he recognized himself inside. He had all of Viscount Cordell's memories, though some of them were coming back to him slowly. And Adèle was *his* wife, his beloved wife, even though their marriage was unconsummated.

The sand was becoming damp and spongy. The pressure of her shoes and his Hessians was making wet indentations. Finally they came to the first trickle of the receding tide and they stopped. He set his arm about her again.

"Now if I had all my strength back," he said, "I might pick you up and carry you in and make you pay me all sorts of forfeits to persuade me not to drop you."

She giggled—what a joyful sound it was. He realized that he had not heard it in a long while. His illness must have saddened her for a few years even before he went to Italy. "And if you think *that* is going to make me say I am glad you do not have your strength back, sir," she said, "you are very mistaken."

"What?" he said. "You would not mind being dropped into the ocean?"

"Of course I would." She giggled again. "But it would not happen. I would pay all the forfeits."

"Would you?" He drew her a little closer. "That is something I must keep in mind. I shall put it to the test— sooner than you realize."

She was crying then, noisily and unexpectedly, and hiding her face against his chest. He set his arms about her and rested his cheek against the flowers on her bonnet. This must be very bewildering for her, and rather frightening. She must expect that he would have a relapse at any moment.

"John," she said eventually, choking back her tears.

"Oh, do forgive me. What a goose you will think me. It is just that I never expected—Oh, I—I don't know what it is I am trying to say."

"You expected to come here to nurse a dying man with all the gentleness of your love," he said. "You did not expect to be teased and threatened. And you did not expect to get your shoes wet in the tide."

She lifted a wet and reddened and very beautiful face to him and smiled. "How good God is," she said. "How very, very good."

He tried to imagine Allison saying just those words. But he did not want to think about Allison, and he pushed guilt back out of his conscious mind.

"Yes," he said, and kissed her. His body, he realized after a mere few seconds, was already beginning to respond weakly to the desires of his emotions.

He handed her his handkerchief after a couple of minutes and she dried her eyes and blew her nose. He started coughing at almost the same moment, as a gust of salt air caught his throat. It was just a harmless cough, over in a moment. But he noticed the quickly veiled terror in her eyes and then the gentle tenderness that had been there when he opened his own eyes two days ago to find her instead of Allison on the bed with him.

"Nothing," he said. "Look, it is over. No blood."

She smiled at him and stood on tiptoe to kiss him again.

"But," he said reluctantly, "if I am not going to have to demand that you sling me over your shoulder and carry me back to the house after all, Adèle, we had better make our way back there. At a very sedate pace. You may even persuade me to lie down for half an hour or so when we get there, provided you will lie down at my side."

"You know I will," she said, taking his hand. "You

know that is why I married you, John. To be always at your side. You cannot know how happy it makes me just to be there. All my life I lived for the times when you were home and when you would come to play with the others. I tried not to cling and I tried not to be demanding or to be a nuisance—"

He squeezed her hand. "You never did and you never were," he said. "You were always the joy in my life, Adèle."

"Oh." She sounded breathless. "What a lovely thing to say."

"Our house," he said, looking up the beach to the manor in the distance. "Our *Cartref*. Shall we stay here forever, my love? Forget to go back to England? Live here and love here together, close to all that matters in life? Shall we bring up our children here?"

"Yes," she said softly. "Oh, yes, John. Let us do that."

Beneath the brim of her bonnet he could see her face. He could see the soft, joyous, wistful dream in it.

*And we did it, too*, he told her silently. *We lived happily ever after here.*


She tried to hold on to the cold reality of her sanity. She tried to tell herself that a man who had had consumption in such an advanced stage, a man who had appeared so very close to death just a week ago, could not recover his full health. Miracles did not happen in the mundane times of the early nineteenth century.

Soon this last burst of strength and vigor would go and he would go—out into the beyond that did not frighten him, into the kingdom of love where she would follow him one day. When the time came, she must let him go and be grateful for this precious and wonderful and unexpected week.

In many ways it would be harder to let him go after this week. She had glimpsed the joy of married life this week, as she had never expected to do, and she knew that the bleakness that would come after would be almost unbearable for a long, long time.

But she knew, too, that she would be grateful, that she would live on the memories of this week for the rest of her life.

She tried to be sane and sensible. She tried to keep herself steeled inside just as she had been from the moment she first saw him after his return from Italy. She tried to keep herself prepared, to guard herself from total collapse when it was over.

But it was difficult to do. She felt almost as if after their wedding, after their departure for Wales, they had traveled into a new and different world, a magic, wonderful world where miracles happened, where love was to be loved and life to be lived, where death was not to be feared, where death was not imminent, anyway.

It was not just hope she felt as the days passed and his health showed every sign of recovering. It was knowledge, certainty. It was faith.

And so faith warred with sanity in her mind. And faith was winning.

Every day he was stronger. Every day he ate a little more heartily. He was still very thin, but some of the gauntness, the skeletal look, had gone. There was a suggestion of healthy color to his flesh. Every day he walked a little faster and a little farther. Every day he talked a little more and laughed a little more and teased a little more.

On the last day of the week they walked all the way up

the hill—though they stopped several times to look down at the view and recover their breath—to the village. They were greeted with vociferous Welsh cheer at the tavern, where they stopped for lemonade. She knew that word would quickly spread that Viscount Cordell was not lying at home dying but was up and about and apparently recuperating from a long illness. She knew that they would now have callers and invitations. The tavern keeper had already mentioned an assembly that was to be held soon in the rooms above the tavern.

John had said they would be there and would lead the first waltz. Absurd man.

The thought of waltzing with him had made the tears spring to her eyes and she had had to blink and fumble in her reticule and wonder aloud if it was an insect that had flown into her eye and set it to watering.

The walk back down the hill had been less strenuous than the climb. But he had been tired enough to lie down—with her at his side—when they returned home. But only for half an hour. He seemed unwilling to lie down for longer during the daytime.

Yes, faith was overcoming sanity. She had almost relaxed totally into it. She had almost stopped doubting and fearing. He was getting better. It was not just a respite. The disease had gone.

It was with a sick lurching of the stomach, then, that she awoke one night to the sound of his coughing. She sat up sharply. He was standing beside the bed, holding back the bedclothes on his side of the bed.

"I woke you," he said. "And in the worst possible way. I just had to get up for a minute. The cough was nothing. But I know it puts terror into your soul every time you hear it. Forgive me."

She knew he was right. The few coughs she had heard from him in the last week were different. They were not the deep, racking, gurgling coughs she had heard too many times during the journey from England. They were symptoms of nothing. They were merely coughs.

She lay back down and turned onto her side as he climbed back into bed. Life had been so very joyous for the past week that it was difficult to pick out one single thing that made her happier than any other. But perhaps it was this. This lying beside him in bed, feeling the warmth of his body next to hers, hearing his breathing. This knowing that she was his wife and had the right to lie here. She was glad she had lain in his bed the very night of their wedding and every night since. She had not asked permission to lie there. She had wanted to be near when he needed her. It was why she had married him.

He had never told her to go away, to lie in her own bed. She would never go away unless he asked her to. Yes, this was the greatest joy. She smiled when he turned his head toward her, though they could not see each other very clearly in the darkness.

"I disturbed you," he said. "You were sleeping so peacefully."

"I am happy," she said. "You cannot know how happy I am, John."

He turned onto his side too, and slid one arm beneath her head. With the other he drew her closer so that her body was against his. He felt less angular and fragile than he had felt in the nights after their wedding, when she had held him in her arms.

"Are you?" he said. "Are you, love?"

She lifted her head hopefully. She loved his kisses. Especially when she was lying down and her knees were not so badly affected.

He smiled at her and kissed her. She experimented. Instead of waiting for him to prod with his tongue through the seam of her lips, she parted them for him. And when she discovered the pleasure of moist flesh caressing moist flesh, she opened her mouth. His tongue came sliding hard and deep inside and she was very glad indeed that she was lying down. She would have disgraced herself utterly by crumpling into a heap on the ground.

And then she felt alarm and pulled her head back sharply. One of her hands shot up to touch his forehead.

"John," she said. She could hear her voice shaking. "You are fevered. You should have told me."

His chuckle seemed to mock her terror. "My love," he said. "My own little innocent. I am the big bad wolf in your bed, I am afraid."

She understood instantly. She lowered her hand and was glad of the darkness. She felt mortified.

"Adèle," he said, "you married me to nurse me to my death. I know you love me, sweetheart. I know, too, that you did not expect this ever to be a normal marriage, a consummated marriage. Perhaps you never wanted it to be. And if you still do not, I will respect your wishes. I will be forever grateful for the selfless love you showed in marrying me. But if you do not want it, you are going to have to remove yourself from my bed now or sooner—and stay away. You do understand me, do you not?"

She felt such a deep stabbing of longing that she did not believe she would be able to speak if she tried. But she did try.

"Yes," she whispered.

"Or I can move to another room," he said. "There is

no reason why it should be you, is there, merely because this is called the *master* bedchamber?''

"Don't go," she said, clutching his nightshirt. "Stay with me. Make me your wife. Oh, please, John, make me your wife."

She was frantic with need then. She had expected to die a maid. She had thought about it and accepted it as a consequence of her devotion to him. She would never marry again after he had gone. She had decided that and had never felt any doubt that it was a decision she would never want to revoke. There could never be anyone else after John. Never.

And now—there was to be John?

When his mouth came back to hers, she opened her own eagerly and waited for what was to happen. She knew— even the cold reason in her knew—that it was going to be the very happiest night in her whole life.

He had woken up wanting her—and knowing that he was now strong enough to have her. But the matter was not as simple as merely reaching for her and taking her. He was not quite sure he had the right. Was he really her husband? In body certainly he was and in mind he half was—more than half. As the days went by he found himself thinking more and more as the Regency John. But the other one— the twentieth-century John Chandler—was still there. Which one was he, exactly? Which one would he be for the rest of his life?

He had just become engaged to Allison. He had had a number of women between the ages of seventeen and twenty-eight, but he had committed himself to fidelity when he had agreed to marry Allison. Was it right to sleep now with Adèle?

But she was his *wife*.

And he knew that if he had to go back to the twentieth century he would not be able to marry Allison after all. He thought with grim humor of the reason he would have to give her if he was going to be honest. He could not marry her because he was in love with a woman almost two hundred years old.

Adèle was a virgin. With his Regency self he had no doubt of that, even though his other self might have taken for granted that at the age of twenty-four she must have had a few lovers. Was it right that he be the one to make love to her first? Who would be doing it? But he knew the answer to that. It would be her husband. He was her husband.

But what if the other John came back as sick as he had been? Would it be better for her not to have known the consummation? And what if he left her pregnant?

But he *knew* that John Chandler, Viscount Cordell, had not died so soon. And he knew that the two of them had had children. Was it his own history he had learned? Or was it another man's? He felt dizzy again, realizing that he was seriously considering such a question.

It was his desire and his indecision that had driven him out of bed to pace for a while. He had decided to wait, to let more time pass, to be more sure that he was here to stay. But then he had had that brief coughing spell as he was about to slip back into bed, and she had woken up.

She was small and well-shaped without being in any way voluptuous. Every part of her was nicely in proportion with every other part. He had noticed that with pleasure since the first time he woke up to her in his bed. Now he noticed it with desire.

She was virgin and innocent and totally inexperienced. He had known that from the start. She had not even known how to kiss sexually. And now she lay still and passive, obviously not knowing either what to do or what exactly was about to happen to her. But there was a willingness and a longing in her stillness, even an eagerness. He could tell that. She wanted what was to happen. With him. Because she loved him.

He was fiercely glad that it was not the other John loving her tonight. Only he could give her everything there was to give. Only he could give her the whole of himself.

He found her inexperience wholly endearing and not a little exciting. She had thought he had a fever. . . . And then her embarrassment at realizing the truth had been almost palpable.

He undid the buttons that held her nightdress closed to the throat and opened back the edges. He touched her breasts one at a time, stroking them lightly, cupping them, rubbing his thumb very gently across the nipples, pulsing lightly against them. And while he did so, he leaned his head back from hers so that he could watch her face in the faint light from the window. She looked back until her eyelids fluttered closed and she made soft sounds of pleasure.

She was exquisitely feminine. He had to close his own eyes for a few moments in order to bring his desire under control. He did not intend to do anything with her tonight that might shock her too deeply. He intended only basic foreplay and a more lengthy union of their bodies. But he certainly did not want to rush anything. He wanted to give her pleasure, and more than pleasure. He wanted her to feel herself loved and cherished and worshiped and—married.

He kissed her mouth, her cheeks, her temples, her eyes, her ears. He closed his teeth over one earlobe and felt her

shiver. He lowered his mouth to her breasts, drawing the
nipples one at a time into his mouth and sucking as he
wanted his child to do in nine months or so. And he took
her nightgown with both hands and moved it down and off
her arms and down her body until he could toss it to one
side. He pulled off his own nightshirt and sent it to join
her nightdress.

"Don't be embarrassed," he said, drawing her back into
his arms. "You are so very beautiful, Adèle, and I did
promise at our wedding to worship you with my body, did
I not?"

"I am not embarrassed," she said. "I want you to see
me, John. I want you to touch me. I want you to know me.
I want to feel you i-inside me. That *is* what happens, is it
not?"

He had to draw a slow, steadying breath before answering. "Deep inside," he murmured against her ear. "Where
we will share bodies and beget children. Where we will be
husband and wife together."

He moved his hand over her as he spoke, feeling the
small waist, the feminine curve of her hip, the firm, shapely
buttock. He slipped his hand into the warmth between her
legs, parting the folds with gentle fingers—stroking, probing slowly, giving her time to master the shock that had
been indicated by a sharply indrawn breath, and to relax
again.

"Mm," he said, his mouth against hers. "Wonderful.
You are warm and wet. No, don't tense. It is as you should
be. Your body has readied itself so that we can unite without discomfort."

But he knew there would be pain for her. He had no
experience with virgins. He hoped he could be careful
enough. It would not be easy. He was on fire for her.

She did not help him. She looked up at him as he turned her onto her back and lifted himself over her. But she did not hinder him either. She let him push her legs wide astride his and she slid her feet up the bed when he whispered the suggestion to her. She watched him steadily as he positioned himself and mounted her very slowly.

The passage was small and tight. He could feel his heart beating in his throat and in his ears. He ignored two warring urges—one to withdraw lest he hurt her, the other to thrust mindlessly inward for release—and opened her as gently as he could. He felt the barrier and saw the pain of it in her face as she closed her eyes and bit her lower lip. But then it was gone and he moved inward to his full length.

He had never really thought before of sex as a uniting of bodies. He thought of it now. It was as if he had fitted himself to the missing part of himself. It was a magnificent, heady feeling, despite the fact that he was still fully aroused and pulsing with the need to thrust himself to climax.

Her eyes had opened again. He kept most of his weight on his forearms.

"Am I hurting you?" he whispered.

"There could be no happier moment than this," she said. "If only I could keep you here forever and ever."

He smiled at her. And he held still in her, allowing her body to accustom itself to the stretching and the invasion, allowing her mind to adjust to this new status of her being. Then he withdrew slowly.

Her hands pressed against his waist. "Oh, not yet," she said. "Must it end so soon?"

He lowered his head and kissed her softly. "It is beginning," he said to her. "I am going to love you, Adèle. Relax and enjoy it. Or if you want to move, if there is anything you wish to do for your pleasure, do it. We are together—not master and servant, but man and wife. We are both lover and we are both beloved.''

"Oh," she said, "I am so ignorant. There was no one to tell me . . . I did not expect . . . Oh!''

He had pushed firmly back into her.

He had always been an energetic lover and he had always had experienced, uninhibited women. That was true of both his persons. He had always been able to take his own pleasure in the confident knowledge that his woman would take her equal share. It had always been two separate people taking pleasure from each other. Even with Allison.

Having to think of someone else, having to remember that this was all new to her, having to hold back his own pleasure so that she would remember her first experience with joy—it was all paradoxically erotic. He had never desired as much as he did now; he had never enjoyed as much as he did now. And he had never before now, he realized, made love. He had had sex—marvelously satisfying sex in many cases, but never more than that.

He made love to Adèle.

He moved slowly at first so that her body could learn the beauty of rhythm. When the insides of her thighs pressed more firmly against his and her pelvis tilted to allow him greater depth, he moved faster, pumping deeply into warm, moist depths, almost delirious with his knowledge of her— biblical knowledge. He had never before thought of the term while having sex.

Despite the weakness of his body, he used a strength and a control he had not thought himself capable of, working steadily in her until her hands spread over his buttocks and her legs twined about his and she closed her inner muscles about him. She was making soft guttural noises.

Then he slowed, deepened even further, coaxed her to

the orgasm he could feel coming, held firm in her while it came and blossomed about his hardness—and while she shuddered into quiet fulfillment. He reached his own climax swiftly, urgently, blessedly, and let his seed gush deep inside her. His body had become one pulse, it seemed. He relaxed down onto her.

She was crying helplessly, with deep, painful sobs, a minute or two later. He drew free of her body, rolled to her side, gathered her to him, and pulled the blankets over their sweat-dampened bodies. He smoothed one hand through her hair, kissed her tears, made soothing, shushing noises.

She was his wife. They had been one as he had never imagined two people could be one. He knew why she was crying. He was not alarmed.

"One body," he said to her. "We know what that means now, do we not?"

"John." His name was almost an agony on her lips. "What have I ever done that God has been so good to me?"

"At the risk of being sacrilegious," he said, kissing her nose, "I do not believe God had much to do with that."

"Oh, but He did," she said earnestly. "John. Do you *know* just how ill you were? Do you know that just a few weeks ago I thought the pinnacle of human happiness would be to have your name? That I wished for nothing else—nothing!—except the privilege of holding you in my arms until you d—" She choked on the word. "I would have thought myself well-blessed. I *did* think it when you agreed to marry me—I never expected that you would. Our wedding day was the happiest day of my life. I never expected—oh, I never expected *marriage*."

"It is what you have, nevertheless," he said, finding her

46

mouth with his. "And what you will have for years and years to come, God willing. You had better get used to it. Once or twice a night for the next fifty years or so, not to mention the days—do you like the sound of it? Or will it become one of those wifely chores that women have to endure in exchange for the respectability of marriage?"

She giggled—he loved the way Adèle could giggle without sounding in any way childish but only gloriously joyful. "*Only* for fifty years?" she asked. "But twice, John? Is it possible?"

"Perhaps not for another week or two," he admitted, grinning. "I must confess to feeling close to exhaustion. But after another week or two . . . You had better prepare yourself."

Being Adèle, she had caught only one thing he had said. She moved closer, getting slightly above his level as she did so. She drew his arm away from her neck and put her own arm beneath his instead. She drew down his head to pillow it on her breast while her free hand smoothed gently through his hair.

"Sleep, my dearest love," she said. "No more talking. You are exhausted."

"Yes, ma'am," he said, feeling deliciously warm and comfortable and sleepy. "But it was in a very good cause, you know."

"Sh," she said, "and don't be foolish."

He was smiling as he slid into sleep.

She had always wanted to be John's wife. Certainly she had always known that she would never be any man's wife if she could not be his. But there had been a few years— perhaps about five after the age of fifteen, when she had actively dreamed of what marriage with him would be like. It had always been dream rather than hope. By that time he had been away from home a great deal and had treated her only with a careless sort of affection when he was home—except perhaps for that kiss on her seventeenth birthday.

And by the time she was fifteen she had understood the difference in their stations. He was the heir to a viscount's title and properties and fortune—he inherited when she was eighteen on the death of his father. She was the eighth and youngest child of a gentleman of no particular fortune or importance. When she was nineteen a great-aunt had taken her to town for a month of the Season. She had hated it. She had felt out of her depth surrounded by such wealthy and important people. And she had seen that John was a great favorite—and that he had something of a reputation as a rake.

The year after that he was ill.

Dreams—which she had never expected to become reality—had given way to despair. She would not be able to bear a world without John in it.

And then the dream had become a different one. One that had come achingly true just a few weeks ago. It had been such a narrow dream. She had not asked for much. She had been more grateful than she had ever been able to put into words for what she had been given. She had not been greedy.

Now the dream had expanded again like a glorious explosion of light, and she was happy beyond thought. And afraid.

The disease had gone. There seemed no doubt about it now. Although he had not seen a physician and she did not suggest it to him, she knew that he was getting better. She knew it no longer just with faith but with certainty. Every day he was stronger. Although he was still very thin, he was noticeably putting on weight and acquiring a healthy color. There were no more fevers and no more coughed blood. His eyes no longer looked on death but on life.

They walked now every day on the beach, sometimes almost briskly. They climbed the hills, pausing for breath as much for her sake as for his. They talked and read and wrote letters to their numerous brothers and sisters and to her mama and papa. They even argued—usually about the wisdom and comfort of leaving windows open. Those arguments always ended the same way. If she was chilly, he always said, grabbing her, she would just have to submit to being warmed—but not by closing the windows.

They made love so often—by night and by day—that sometimes her cheeks could become flushed just thinking about it and wondering if it was normal and proper. She decided that if it was not, she did not care for normality or propriety. On the few occasions when she hinted that he should not exhaust himself, he would laugh and tell her that she could cuddle him afterward as she had done that first time.

Making love, she had discovered, was a process that was taking a very long time to learn. Every time there was something new and something different. He was surely the best teacher in the world, though he claimed sometimes— she did not know how it could be—that he was also a pupil, that she was teaching him dimensions of the art he had never dreamed of before.

Making love, she had decided, was the most wonderful bonding experience imaginable. She could not understand how any two people could do those things when they were not married or even particularly devoted to each other. She could not imagine the pleasure being divorced from the love and the commitment and the union of hearts and souls.

As she had expected after their walk to Awelfa, they soon had company. People for miles around with any claim to gentility left their cards and returned for tea and conversation. The calls had to be returned. They issued a few invitations to dinner and cards. They accepted a few similar invitations. The dance at the assembly rooms above the tavern in the village was approaching and John seemed determined that they would go—and dance.

Adèle was more happy than she had known it was possible to be. She had had a month of married life when she had expected a few days, a week or two at most, of nursing a dying man.

But reaction was beginning to set in. Happiness had always been something to dream of, not something to be lived. She began to be afraid of happiness. What if, after all, he was merely going through a respite in his illness? What if there should be a sudden relapse and death? Could she bear it now that she had let down her defenses, now that she had tasted what life with him could be?

It was a fear she tried to ignore. If it was to be so, there was nothing she could do to prevent it merely by worrying about it. And surely if she did not live to the fullest now, she would forever regret it should she be left alone and grieving for the rest of her life.

Other fears were more nebulous, but they nibbled away at the edges of her happiness with equal relentlessness. He would tire of Cartref soon despite what he had said when he first began to recover. The house was small by the standards of his main home. There were not many families of his own social standing in the area. They were far from any social center. They had been in Wales for a month. He was going to be bored soon and restless. John had always been restless. And now, day by day, his energy was returning.

She feared that when they returned to England she would lose him. She had nothing with which to hold him except her love and her devotion to him. They had never been quite enough. She knew that in the normal course of events, if he had not been ill, he never would have thought of her in terms of marriage. He would tire of her. She had no doubt that he would always be kind to her, that he would always feel an affection for her, that he would always guard her from hurt. But she could picture how their life would develop. She would live in the country. He would join her there for a few weeks several times a year. For the rest of the time he would live in London or some other fashionable center. He would have mistresses, whom she would know about, though no one would ever tell her and he would protect her carefully from ever finding out.

They would tell each other and themselves that the arrangement suited them both.

She did not believe she would be able to accept such a life after this month of living and of loving. But she would have to accept it. She would have no choice.

She dressed for the assembly with a mingling of excitement and wariness. She had always loved dances, except perhaps the few *ton* balls she had attended in London with her great-aunt. And yet she feared that John would find this one unsatisfying and would begin to have a hankering to return to his old life.

She was wearing her wedding dress of silver gauze over white satin, with the pearls John had given her as a wedding present. She fingered them dreamily as her maid put the finishing touches to her hair. She remembered how she had felt when he had given them to her—the one and only gift she would ever receive from him. She had realized how she would prize them for the rest of her life.

There was a tap on her dressing room door and he stepped inside and held the door open to allow her maid to leave.

"Ah," he said, his eyes wandering over her after he had closed the door again. "Your wedding clothes, Adèle." He frowned for a moment. "Was I really that sick? It is almost hard to remember already. I thought you must be a harbinger of the angels who I hoped would soon be meeting me on the other side."

She bit her lip and felt the tears spring to her eyes.

"The pearls look good on you," he said. "Your 'something new' for your wedding." He smiled and stepped close enough to lift her left hand. He looked down at her rings. "And your something old and something blue." He frowned again, then, and paused for a while, thinking. "I have said that before—just recently."

"You said it the day before our wedding, when you put it on my finger," she said.

He continued to frown for a moment longer and then shook his head and smiled. "Yes, of course," he said. "And it was the something borrowed, too—yours for life and then to return to the family treasures."

He raised her hand and kissed the ring, and then turned her hand over to kiss her palm and her wrist.

"Did I tell you on our wedding day how beautiful you were?" he asked.

The tears were back again. "You were very ill," she said, "and using all your energy to try not to look it."

"I shall tell you now, then," he said, setting his fingertips against her cheek and bending to touch his lips to hers. "You are the most beautiful woman in the world, Adèle—in your wedding gown and without it." He grinned at her, looking quite like the old handsome John. "Especially without it."

She blushed. It seemed rather foolish to her that she could still blush at such words after two weeks of continual and quite uninhibited intimacies.

"I like making you do that," he said. "Are you planning to get up from that stool tonight, or shall I have the horses and the carriage returned to the stables? Horses and carriage—a slow and quaint method of travel, but very romantic."

She stood and picked up her shawl and fan. "That was a strange thing to say," she said. "Quaint?"

"Yes, it was strange, was it not?" he said, rubbing two fingers from the bridge of his nose to his hairline and back, and frowning once more. "I have been having strange dreams. I do not know what I was thinking. Are you ready?"

"Yes." She smiled at him. He was dressed in blue and silver and white. He had not yet, of course, regained his former splendid physique. Perhaps it would be months before that happened. But even so he looked splendidly handsome to her. "John, you look—gorgeous."

"Thank you, ma'am." He chuckled and made her an elegant bow as he offered his arm. "A gorgeous cadaver, perhaps. But gaining flesh at a steady rate. My valet has hopes of having to squeeze me into my clothes rather as into a second skin before too many months have passed. He despises being able to slide me into them with such ease."

She laughed and took his arm. She was going to put fear behind her, she decided. For now at least there were health and happiness to be celebrated. And an assembly to be enjoyed. And it seemed—it *was*—so ungrateful to be afraid.

He was going to waltz with her. She had never waltzed before, though she had learned the dance and had watched it being performed. And she had dreamed. . . .

Tonight he was going to waltz with her.

He thought of Allison during the carriage journey to Awelfa. While he did so, he held Adèle's hand in both of his and played with her ring, twisting it with a forefinger and thumb.

How could he have forgotten even for a moment when it was he had spoken those words last? He had spoken them to Allison as he put the ring on her finger. He could remember it clearly now—though he could also remember saying the same words to Adèle the day before their wedding—God, he had been feeling ill.

He had to concentrate very hard to remember Allison's face. He knew she was tall and slender and elegant and blond. But he could not quite bring her face into focus. He thought of his car as the carriage lurched rather uncomfortably over the far from smooth track—calling it a romantic mode of travel had not been altogether accurate. All he could remember for the moment was that his car was red. He could not for the life of him remember what make or model it was. Allison had once accused him, half seriously, of loving his car more than he loved her. Yet he could not recall even the make of the car? Or her face?

He looked at Adèle, quiet and apparently relaxed beside him, though he knew that she was bubbling with suppressed excitement at the prospect of the assembly. He thought back on her as a child and as a girl and found the memories clear and detailed and filled with emotion. He had always adored her. He had not even realized that fully until now. His father had warned him against falling in love with her. His father had been more ambitious for his eldest son. And it was true that he had had wild oats to sow and had sown them with great energy and enthusiasm. But surely he had always known that there was only Adèle.

Or perhaps it was only his near-death experience that had shown him how precious love is, how unimportant in this life are anything and everything else but love.

Only Adèle mattered.

He raised her hand to his lips and kissed it. "A penny for them," he said.

She looked up with luminous eyes, which she was trying to keep quiet and dignified. He knew her so well. He knew her thoughts. Adèle had always been a part of himself, the uncompleted part of himself until he had married her and united his body and his heart with hers.

"I have never waltzed," she said. "Perhaps I will disgrace you."

He smiled slowly at her. "You dance beautifully," he said.

"You have never seen me dance," she said. "We have never danced together."

"We have," he said quietly. He wished the carriage were not dark inside. He wanted to see her blush. "We move together perfectly. We always share the same perfect rhythm."

She looked at him blankly for a moment. And then he saw comprehension light her eyes. "John," she whispered. "Oh, for shame."

He lowered his head and kissed her. "As I thought," he said. "I cannot *see* the blushes. But your cheeks feel fiery hot."

"For shame," she said again. "Where are your manners, sir?"

But he knew she was pleased. She always called him "sir" when she was pleased.

He wondered suddenly how it was he had recovered from his consumption. He did not know of anyone else who had done so. For what sort of miracle had he been singled out? And why? It must have been done as a reward for Adèle's goodness. Certainly there was nothing he had done in his life to deserve such a reprieve. And then he felt dizzy—and remembered exactly what the miracle had been. Except that it seemed too fantastic and too bizarre to be believed. Had it really happened?

Their arrival at the assembly rooms was greeted with avid curiosity and great enthusiasm. The assemblies were open to everyone, he and Adèle had been told, there not being enough people of the upper classes to make them worth holding. There was a certain charm, he thought, about mingling with people of all classes, about watching groups of farm laborers performing an energetic and intricate Welsh folk dance, and about hearing the Welsh and English languages mingling in the conversations about them.

Not many of those present knew the steps of the waltz. Only two other couples apart from him and Adèle took the floor when the dance was announced. Everyone else gathered about to watch the new dance, which was reputed to be somewhat scandalous. Adèle looked rather alarmed.

There had been a time, he thought as the music started, when he had waltzed as an excuse to get a female body against his own—a body that he hoped to put beneath his own on the bed at his flat after the dance was over. He could not for the moment remember when that time could have been. But now he danced the waltz as it was meant to be danced, keeping Adèle at arm's length from his body, twirling her to the steps of the dance about the perimeter of the ballroom.

There were murmurs of appreciation from the nondancers, a smattering of applause. There was the exhilaration of moving to music and no thought for the moment of his weakness. And there was the beauty and grace of his partner. She soon forgot her alarm at having to waltz for the first time before an audience. She kept her eyes on his and followed his lead as if she were a part of him.

He forgot the audience. He forgot their surroundings. He forgot they were waltzing. They danced together as they made love—in perfect rhythm, in perfect harmony, a world and a universe unto themselves.

He loved her. He had always loved her—from the beginning of time, it seemed. She was part of him, more a part of him than his own heart. Closer than that. She was all that was good in him, all that was loving.

It was over too soon. He was dazed when the music stopped and he realized that he had been merely waltzing with her in the assembly rooms at Awelfa. She was flushed and bright-eyed and so beautiful that he found himself looking around jealously at all the other men present.

*She is mine*, he foolishly wanted to warn them all.

"John." She stepped a little closer to him as a crescendo of applause and laughter greeted their efforts and those of the other two couples. "You are tired. Sit down for a while."

"Yes, little guardian angel," he said, grinning at her. But she was quite right, of course. His energy was not yet boundless.

He spent an interesting hour sitting and talking with a group of men on a variety of topics, including the state of farming in West Wales and the dangers of the coast for navigation. There was great need for lighthouses and other warning devices in the area, it seemed. Adèle—he scarcely took his eyes off her all the time—talked and laughed with other women and danced one quadrille with a portly tenant farmer who had two left feet and no musical sense at all. Yet she smiled at him throughout the set with sweet charm.

She was at home in this sort of place with this sort of people, he thought. As was he. The thought surprised him. He had always loved the country, but he had always been restless and eager to get back to the bustle and the sophistication of town life. He felt no such eagerness now. He still felt, as he had felt a few weeks ago, that he could stay here forever. Provided Adèle was here, his whole world was here. And perhaps there would be children. Now where had he heard recently that there would indeed be children? Who had predicted something so unpredictable?

But of course he knew it himself. He knew it from his own studies of family history. He found himself frowning. How could he have studied the *future*? But then it was not the future he had studied. It was the past. He was from the second half of the twentieth century. How could such a momentous fact keep slipping away from him?

It was long past midnight when he and Adèle finally rode home. She curled up against him on the carriage seat when he set an arm about her shoulders, and yawned.

"Sleepy?" he asked, rubbing his cheek against her hair.

"Mm," she said. And then she sat up hastily. "But you are the one who must be tired, John."

He chuckled and brought her head back where it belonged. "Did you enjoy the evening?" he asked.

"Yes," she said. "Everyone was kind and very friendly. Mrs. Beynon was trying to teach me some Welsh. But everyone went off into peals of merriment at something I repeated after her. I dared not ask what it was I had actually said.'' She giggled.

He yawned.

''John,'' she said, spreading a hand on his chest. ''It must have seemed quite pathetic in comparison with *ton* balls. Did you find it very—provincial?''

He understood her insecurities far better than she realized. He had taken Adèle and her constant, unconditional love so much for granted in the past. He had given her no such constancy in return.

''I have never enjoyed a ball as much as tonight's,'' he said, shrugging his shoulder so that he could touch her lips with his own. ''Because you were there with me, Adèle. Because all evening long I could feast my eyes on you and tell myself that you were mine.''

''Oh.'' Her lips formed the shape of the word against his. He felt the warm exhalation of her breath.

He kissed her.

Sometimes, he thought, he could almost persuade himself that he had died and gone to heaven after all—only to find her there before him, waiting for him so that she could love him for all eternity.

And so that he could love her for an equal length of time.

He was going to bathe in the ocean. It was a dreadful thing to do, because the ocean water was always cold and there were always waves and breakers to take one unawares. He was just asking to catch a chill. He was so very much better—full of new strength and vigor, slender still but no longer painfully thin. But there was no point in tempting fate.

She told him all that and more until she was afraid of sounding like a nagging wife and he grabbed her and kissed her soundly and told her that was the only treatment a scold deserved. And he laughed at her—he dared to do that—his eyes sparkling with merriment and affection.

He took three large towels with him. She went, too, but she made it perfectly clear that he was to get no fancy ideas. Why did he need *three* towels? He bent his head and kissed her when they were still well within sight of the house and any servants who happened to be looking after them.

"Because I did not think I would need five," he said.

Sometimes he talked such nonsense. "Thank you, sir," she said. "I should have thought of that for myself."

They were going to walk along the beach and around the headland so that they would be out of sight of prying eyes. The tide was out again and it was possible to walk past the headland.

"It is the best place to go, then," she told him. "Only I will see your foolishness."

He laughed at her again. And then he grew serious. She could feel his eyes on her. "Adèle," he said, "I am going to tell you something. A story. A true story. It is the strangest, most bizarre thing you will have ever heard and you may well have me carted off to Bedlam when you have heard it. But I have decided that you should know—that everything I know you should know too."

He was going to make a confession. He was going to tell her about all the whores and mistresses he had ever had. So that he could clear his conscience and lay the burden of knowledge on her shoulders. She did not want to hear it.

"No," he said gently, squeezing her hand. "It is not that kind of story, love. It is the explanation of how this miracle happened. I know, you see. I know the how. I do not know the why. I think you have something to do with that. Your unfailing love, your devotion, your willingness to accept uncomplainingly whatever of life was offered you. But you can be the judge of that.''

He knew how the miracle had happened? Had he been taking some strange new medicine that she had not seen and knew nothing of? She looked at him with eager inquiry. ''Tell me,'' she said.

''After the swim,'' he said. ''We will lie quietly on the beach and I will tell you.''

She hated having her curiosity piqued and not satisfied. But it was something important. He wanted the moment to be right.

Finally they reached a point on the beach at which they could not be seen either from the house or from the road. He dropped the towels and began to undress, looking out with narrowed eyes to the water. It was a hot day. Even the breeze off the ocean was warm. She watched him strip down to his long drawers. Lean. That was how he looked now. Lean and healthy and handsome.

''You like looking at me?'' he asked.

Despite herself she blushed. But she looked steadily back into his eyes. ''Yes,'' she said. ''Very much.''

''I like looking at you too,'' he said.

The look in his eyes alerted her and she took a hasty step back. ''No ideas, I said,'' she told him, holding out one staying hand.

But he was laughing and stepped easily past her defenses. Her bonnet went first and her hairpins, then her dress, and then her slippers and stockings. She was standing on the open beach in just her shift.

''John,'' she said, shocked.

''Much better,'' he said, looking at her.

''I shall sit here and watch you,'' she said hastily, trying to suit action to words. ''I shall wrap—''

But she had suddenly lost contact with the warm sand of the beach. He had swung her up into his arms and was grinning at her like—oh, like a foolish, immature school-boy.

"John," she scolded as he turned and set off for the water, "put me down. You are not strong enough. Oh, you will not be content until you have done yourself an injury, will you?"

His feet were splashing in water. She felt one stray drop on her bare leg. It felt like a droplet of ice.

"John." She clung more tightly. "Don't. It is like ice. This is most indecent. You talked of forfeits once. Let me pay a forfeit. What would you like? A kiss?" She was desperate for him to take her seriously, though the effect of her plea was marred somewhat, she had to admit, by the fact that she was giggling helplessly.

"I would not let you fall in the water, my love," he said when he was waist-deep and had to hold her higher. "Trust me." He grinned into her face. "Kiss me."

She did so.

"Of course," he said, "you have been right all along. I do not have nearly as much strength as I thought I had."

Concern was just beginning to register on her face and on her mind when he dropped her. He was laughing like an imbecile when she came up gasping and sputtering and coughing. She found her footing with difficulty and went straight to the attack. The first great spray of water took him full in the face. She would have laughed with glee if she had finished mastering the shock of the cold. Instead she threw herself backward on the water and swam away from him.

And then he was beside her, matching her stroke for stroke, examining the blue sky above them and the few fluffy clouds, as she was doing. She remembered his teaching her to swim when she was five years old and terrified of water. He had taught her how to put her head under and how to open her eyes—and then he had taught her all the rest. He had been nine years old—totally dependable, totally adult.

"You wretch," she said when they were standing again in water that reached almost to her shoulders. "John, that was a dreadful thing to do." But she was putting her arms up about his shoulders and leaning her body against his and lifting her face for his kiss.

"John, you wretch," she whispered again, shocked, after a minute or so when she felt his hands hoisting her shift to her waist. He lifted her in the water, parting her legs to wrap about him. He was inside her with one firm thrust.

It took very little time. The mix of buoyancy and cool water and heat at their core was delirious. It seemed that the lessons would never end. There was always something new.

He floated onto his back when they were finished, and she swam beside him in a lazy crawl.

"You are going to be tired," she could not resist saying.

"No future tense about it," he admitted, smiling lazily at her. "Shall we go back to the towels?"

"Yes," she said. "We can lie there drying off in the sun and you can tell me your story."

They walked hand in hand up the beach. She knew he was tired. But it was the tiredness of healthy exertion. After he had told his story, she would let him sleep and she would stay awake to make sure that they did not bake too much in the sun.

\* \* \*

He had decided to tell her his story. There should be no secrets in marriage, he thought, except perhaps details of one's past that could only hurt. She should know that the John who had recovered from consumption and consummated their marriage and lived with her ever since was not quite the same John she had loved all her life and married.

Perhaps she would not believe him. But he thought she probably would. She loved him and trusted him enough to know when he spoke truth to her.

Their flesh had chilled in the walk up the beach. They toweled off briskly and then he spread the dry towel on the sand so that they could lie down and relax after their swim and their lovemaking and be warmed by the sun. He held her hand in his, turning her ring between his thumb and forefinger. Life was very good, he thought, and had been very kind to them.

"John," she said, "don't fall asleep yet. You have a story to tell me."

"And so I do." He turned his head to smile at her.

"Well?" she said after he had been silent for a few moments.

He had had a story to tell her. Something important. Something he had felt she had a right to know. He frowned. His mind was a blank. "I cannot remember," he said.

"Don't tease." She shook his hand. "Tell me. It had something to do with the miracle that has happened to you."

"Oh, yes, of course," he said. Yes. It explained the how, he had told her earlier, but not the why. He knew the why. But what on earth was the how? "I—It has gone. It could not have been very important if it has gone, could it?"

She was gazing at him, her head turned to one side. "How did it happen, John?" she said. "You had *con-*

*sumption*. In its final stages. You were coughing blood. It *was* a miracle. Nothing else could have saved you. How did it happen?''

How? He knew how it had happened. He concentrated hard and had fleeting images of her ring in a velvet pouch and of his being afraid to touch it; of a red horseless carriage; of a blond woman. Disjointed, meaningless images that would not form themselves into any graspable thought. And then he knew again. Of course. He looked at her in some relief.

''I have remembered now,'' he said. ''It is this place, Adèle. When you were kind enough to marry me, to saddle yourself with a dying man, I had just one thought in my mind. I had to come here with you. It was madness. I had no strength left. I had only a few weeks left at most. But I knew that I had to come here. That if I brought you here the miracle would happen. I knew it. I had to come here with you as my wife and you had to be wearing the family betrothal ring. I swear I knew it. It is this place, you see.''

Her eyes had filled with tears. Two of them spilled over and ran diagonally across her cheeks as he watched. ''I knew it too,'' she whispered. ''I thought you would die on the journey, John. You were so very weak, so very ill. But I knew that if I could only get you here to Cartref all would be well.''

''The world would think us mad if we offered this as an explanation,'' he said.

''The world may think what it will,'' she said.

''Adèle.'' He lifted her hand to his lips and kissed the ring. ''I know that for many years I was too busy to love you as you deserved to be loved. I had to be near death to understand how far more precious than anyone or anything else in my life you are. Will you stay here with me for the rest of our lives? Will you work with me here in this neighborhood? There is much we can do. There is a lighthouse to build, for one. Will you have our children here and bring them up with me here?''

Her eyes were soft and huge with wistfulness and love. "You will miss England," she said. "And London. You were always restless.''

"No longer," he said. "I am where I belong and where I want to be—for the rest of my life. Why leave heaven merely to go back to earth?''

He saw final surrender in her eyes then to faith and trust and love. She finally believed in him. It was the greatest gift she could have given him. Though he almost changed his mind a few moments later.

"John," she said softly. "About those children. I think—I am not quite sure, but I think I am with child.''

For all the heat of the sun beating down on their bodies then, he took her into his arms and held her close. He kept his eyes tight shut. He did not know how the miracle had happened or why. But it had happened. He had been given the gift of a new life and he was going to give back the gift of love for the rest of his life. Every day of it.

"My love," he whispered to her before drifting toward sleep. "Ah, my love.''


"Some grand engagement day this is turning out to be," she said as he was waking up. "You fell *asleep*, John. How totally humiliating to have had that effect on a man." But there was laughter in her voice to temper the words.

Yes, he had been fast asleep. The first thing that struck him as he came floating up to the surface again was that he felt different. Totally different. Unaware of his body, unaware of his breathing, unaware of his weakness, almost as if he were healthy again. Or as if—as if he had died and was waking up to a new world.

He *was* healthy. There was sudden conviction in the thought and his eyes shot open.

He found himself gazing into Allison's accusing—and amused—eyes.

He knew her name. He knew her. He reached back cautiously and a little fearfully into memory and found that he had a memory that was not quite his own.

"Heavenly days," she said, "you must have been very fast asleep. Where were you? A million miles away?"

A million miles? Two hundred years, actually. He had fallen asleep in Adèle's arms. He had been very close to death. He had known that. He had wished he had the energy to tell her how much he appreciated what she had done for him, marrying him, surrounding him with her love so that he might die in peace. And yet, honest within himself, he had known that his own love, though real, was no match for hers. He had always loved her tenderly but without passion. Dear, gentle Adèle.

"Something like that," he said, turning onto his side, turning onto the tall, slender body of Allison—*who was his fiancée*. "Actually I was building energy. And don't try contempt on me again. You were sleeping too. It was a long journey." He was able to remember the journey and at the same time think of it in amazement. A red sports car—no horses. London to Cardiganshire in one day. Wow! What had the world come to?

"Energy." She set her arms about him and wriggled her legs out from under him, one on either side of his. She pulsed suggestively beneath him and smiled at him from half-closed eyes. "Interesting. Proof necessary. Lawyers are always armed with proof."

Energy. He felt his strength and vitality with something bordering awe. It had seemed an eternity since he had been able to do anything—even lifting an arm—without having to gather every last ounce of energy for the effort. And it had been an eternity—or two hundred years anyway.

They dispensed with clothes in a frenzied, undignified rush and made love on a gust of energetic and impassioned lust. He had never enjoyed making love more.

But then, he realized while they lay together afterward, panting and relaxing and smiling at each other, and while he found her hand and played with her ring with one thumb and forefinger, he had never loved anyone as he loved Allison. She was the perfect mate for him—as energetic and as restless and as ambitious as he. And as much in need as he of the anchor of love—married love.

"John," she whispered to him. "Without meaning to be in any way critical of past performances, I would have to say that that was by far the greatest. There were fireworks. And symphonies—with loads of percussion."

"I shall try an encore later," he said. "After dinner. Are you hungry?"

"Ravenous," she said.

He had eaten nothing but gruels and liquids for longer than he could remember, though he was also able to recall the vegetable curry he had eaten on the road from London earlier in the day.

"For food?" he asked her, leering at her. "Or for—"

She punched him none too gently in the stomach. "For food," she said. "But then later—dessert, please, sir."

Adèle called him "sir" when she was feeling light-hearted and pleased with him. It had not happened a great deal lately. Poor Adèle. Had he really died and been reincarnated? Was she grieving for him? He knew that Adèle would grieve in her own quiet, accepting way for the rest of her life. But that had been two hundred years ago.

And then, as he was tidying himself, ready to go down for dinner at the Cartref Hotel, he remembered something—with the memory of the twentieth-century John Chandler. The Regency Viscount Cordell and his wife had lived a long life here at Cartref. They had had children. He must have recovered from his consumption, then. He felt dizzy for a moment. Was he going to go back? Soon? He felt guilty, hoping not.

He was very deeply in love with Allison, he realized. He felt as if he always had been—or with the idea of her before he actually met her two months ago.

All that had been a week ago. They had spent their week in Cardiganshire on a sort of trial honeymoon, as they frequently told each other, laughing. But they had not spent all of it wandering the beaches and hills as he had intended when they came. They had zoomed all about West Wales in his car, seeing the countryside and the places worth seeing, like St. David's Cathedral and Pembroke Castle, sampling the quaint restaurants and pubs they passed on country lanes.

They had done one thing they had planned to do when they came, though—many things, actually. They had made love enough to exhaust them both for a year, they had agreed on one occasion before going at it again. He was going to have to make an honest woman of her soon, they had both agreed, too.

In fact, all week they had seemed to be in total agreement over everything. In total harmony with each other.

He was afraid at first that he was going to have to go back. He was afraid every time he woke up that he would find himself desperately ill again with Adèle nursing him with her selfless love.

He knew why he was healthy, of course. This John Chandler was strong and healthy and resistant to tuberculosis. And he knew what must have happened—what he hoped had happened. John Chandler—the twentieth-century one—had taken his place, taking his virtual immunity to the disease with him. He had recovered and lived with Adèle for many years.

Had he felt trapped in the past? Had he been bitter about the separation from Allison? About having to give up all the conveniences of late-twentieth-century living? Or had he found happiness with Adèle? Looking back into the memory of his new persona, John discovered that the other man had been having some niggling doubts about his commitment to Allison. It seemed that he had been unsure about his lifestyle being quite compatible with hers.

They were leaving at the end of the week. They were taking one last stroll on the beach before starting back. It was early. The air was cool, with the promise of heat later.

"Now the weather turns perfect," he said. "When it is time to go home." He stopped walking, her hand in his, and gazed out at the old lighthouse. It was still used, they had learned in the course of the week, though everything was automated by now, of course.

She set her head against his shoulder. "But you are not sorry to be going back?" she asked rather wistfully.

"Sorry?" He rested his cheek against her hair. "No, of course not, love. It was great to come here. We both needed the break. But I can hardly wait to be back at work. I left some cases that I want to conclude myself. I hate leaving loose ends for someone else to tie up. And I can't wait to start looking for a flat so we can move in together—and plan the wedding."

"Ah." It was a sigh of relief. "I thought when we came here that you would want to stay. I thought you were getting tired of London and were about to suggest opening a country practice or something horrific like that."

Yes, he had felt a bit that way when they had come. He smiled now at the memory. It seemed rather incredible.

"I think I was meant to come here," he said, "just to discover what it is I really do want of life. A week has been quite long enough."

"And you want London?" she said. "You are quite sure, John? It is not just because of me?"

"I made another discovery too," he said, turning to take her into his arms. "I want you more than anyone else or anything else in this life. I love you, Allie. Why do those words always sound so inadequate?"

"They sound quite adequate enough to me," she said, sounding almost shaken. "John. Oh, John, I have felt all week that it is true. It has been the most wonderful week of my life. But when we came here I was afraid. I don't know of what, exactly. We came here to get engaged. I just felt—well, as if you were not quite sure."

"We were meant to come here," he said, tightening his arms.

He was going to tell her then. All week he had been debating with himself whether he should. It was surely too incredible to be believed. But all week it had been becoming incredible even to him. Sometimes he had thought he must have imagined it all, become too involved in his own research into family history.

But he should tell her anyway. Perhaps she would believe that the John Chandler who held her now and loved her totally was not quite the John Chandler who had come here from London with her a week ago.

The trouble was that when he tried to form the words in his mind with which to tell the story, he could not for the life of him remember what story it was he had been going to tell.

He drew back his head and kissed her instead.

If it was important, it would come back to him, whatever it was. It could not be very important or he would have remembered.

# A Dream Across Time

## Constance O'Banyon

*I love thee with the breath,*
*smile, tears of all my life!*
*and, if God chose, I shall but*
*love thee better after death.*

—Elizabeth Barrett Browning

## *Prologue*

### *New Orleans, 1813*

NOT A BREATH of air stirred the gray Spanish moss that hung from the gnarled old oak trees as Jade St. Clair rode heedlessly through their spidery net on her way to the cathedral of St. Louis.

Frantically, she urged her gelding into a thundering gallop down Chartres Street, afraid that she would be too late. Raige Belmanoir, the man she loved and was to marry, had challenged Tyrone Dunois to a duel, and she had to stop it!

Raige was too proud to ever forgive a misdeed, but she had to make him understand that Tyrone was innocent of any wrongdoing—that she was innocent, that no matter what he thought he had seen in the garden last night, she had not betrayed their love.

A crowd had gathered at St. Louis Cathedral to watch the predawn encounter, and as Jade approached, the people scattered to keep from being trampled by the flying hooves of her great black horse.

Not waiting for her mount to come to a halt, Jade leaped

to the ground in a flurry of petticoats and ran to the garden behind the cathedral. But when she heard the sound of clashing steel, she knew that she was too late!

For a fleeting moment her eyes rested on Raige, who stood, rapier poised, ready to strike a haggard and weary Tyrone. Raige looked forbidding—white-lipped, unforgiving, his features savage in anger. He was the better swordsman, so it was just a matter of time before he killed Tyrone.

Jade watched in horror as Raige's sword flashed in the sunlight, his movements like quicksilver as he relentlessly drove Tyrone against the garden wall. He slashed through the air with practiced skill, merely toying with his foe, and soon Tyrone's white-ruffled shirt was bloodstained in several places.

"Stop this at once!" Jade cried, heedlessly trampling delicate flowers beneath her riding boots as she raced toward the two duelists. She reached Raige, and in desperation grasped his arm. "Please do not do this," she pleaded. "You have already drawn blood; will that not suffice to appease your pride?"

Raige gave her a long, level stare. Where once his tawny eyes had been warm and loving, they now appeared cold and implacable. Roughly, he shoved Jade aside, then turned his attention once more to his opponent. "Would you hide behind a woman's petticoat, Tyrone?" he asked contemptuously.

Tyrone raised his blade. "Keep Jade out of this," he replied angrily. "What transpires here concerns only you and me."

"Ah," Raige said, his words mocking, "so noble of you to defend the lady's name against me, who was to be her husband."

Where once there had been friendship between the two

men, there was now only hatred. Neither heeded Jade's pleas as they became locked in a fierce contest, each intent on the death of the other.

Jade cried out as Raige's blade slashed across Tyrone's face, leaving a deep gash. Poor Tyrone, noble fool that he was, would die—and for what? Honor? Pride? What good would they do him if he were dead?

Without considering the consequences, Jade moved toward the two men, dread engulfing her like a shroud.

Pierre Monier, the gentleman who was acting as Raige's second, caught her arm and shook his head. "It's gone too far, Mademoiselle St. Clair. No one can stop them now."

She thrust Pierre's hands away, and in a last desperate attempt, ran to Tyrone, who had fallen to his knees and was struggling to rise.

"Non, please, Raige, no more," she implored. "Do not do this to Tyrone."

Raige paused for a moment, his eyes driving into hers. "You have the face of an angel, my lovely. Pity that I did not see your true character until it was too late. There is no more fool than I."

For a fleeting moment Jade saw what looked like a flash of pain in Raige's opaque eyes, and then he turned away.

"Stand aside," he ordered. "I will finish what I have begun."

Unmindful of the peril to herself, Jade threw her body in front of Tyrone, trying to shield him from the oncoming thrust of Raige's sword. There was a look of surprise on her face as she felt a sharp, stinging pain in her chest, and it took a moment for her to realize that the blow Raige had intended for Tyrone had struck her instead.

She saw the look of disbelief on Raige's face as he threw down his sword and grabbed her in his arms.

"My God, Jade, what have I done?" he cried in a strangled voice. He could tell by the position of the bloodstain on the front of her dress that the wound was fatal!

Jade reached her hand up to her chest and felt a wet stickiness. Strange, she thought, there was hardly any pain.

"It wasn't your fault, Raige," one of the observers said, as the crowd gathered about them. "We'll all bear witness that she just ran in front of your sword."

Raige's hand trembled as he gently touched Jade's face. "Did you love Tyrone so much that you were willing to die in his stead?" There was pain in his voice, but accusation as well, the accusation of a man who thought he had been betrayed by the two people he trusted most in the world.

Jade licked her dry lips. "I . . . love . . ." She was screaming on the inside, but she could not give voice to the words that would make him understand. She wanted so desperately for Raige to hold her and keep back the darkness that hovered over her.

In that moment, Jade knew she was dying, and she saw that Raige knew it as well. She wanted to comfort him and tell him not to grieve—not to blame himself—but she was too weak.

She closed her eyes for a moment and whispered a prayer that God would be merciful and give her another chance—if only she could turn back time and relive last night, this would not have happened.

Jade focused her eyes on Raige, wanting his face to be the last thing she saw before she died. She loved him with her whole being, but he would never believe it now.

Raige had dropped to his knees and was cradling her head on his lap. Jade, his only love, her delicate face now so pale, her glorious green eyes dull with pain. He was tormented and would gladly give his own life to save hers if he could.

"Why, Jade—why?" His voice was choked, his eyes were bewildered and swimming with tears. "We were to be married in two days. Why did you betray me?"

She tried once more to speak, but could not—her throat was too dry and the darkness was winning over the light.

Helplessly, Raige watched as she struggled to breathe. Then he felt the life leave her body as she went limp in his arms.

A large crowd had gathered and pressed forward to witness the aftermath of the tragedy. A doctor appeared, but sadly shook his head, turning away from Jade to treat the wounded Tyrone.

Raige lifted Jade in his arms, refusing all those who offered to help. He raised his head to the heavens as an agonizing sound issued from his lips.

"Dear God, non—I killed that which I loved most in life!"

## Chapter One

SEATED IN THE window seat of the 747, Olivia Heartford unconsciously uncapped her ballpoint and began to trace an outline of a face in her open notebook. The pen seemed to move of its own volition, tracing the manly beauty of a godlike person.

There was arrogance in the lofty tilt to his chin, and although she had never met him, she knew that his eyes were golden brown. She had imagined this face many times, but never before had she drawn him. In fact, Olivia had not even known she could draw.

The man was not real, but a vision she had conjured up out of her loneliness, a face that came to her almost nightly in her dreams. Her pen dipped down to trace the sensitive mouth and its mocking twist. A strange yearning mixed with sadness came over her as it always did when she thought of him.

At times Olivia was afraid that she was losing her mind—she must be, to chase a dream all the way from Boston to New Orleans.

The roar of the giant aircraft was deafening as it dropped its landing gear and tilted to the right on its final approach to New Orleans International Airport. Olivia pressed her forehead against the oval window for her first view of New Orleans—lush and green, with fingers of waterways weaving their way through the land like a colorful tapestry.

"Quite breathtaking, isn't it," Ada Harmon, the grandmotherly woman seated next to Olivia, observed. "You are going to love it here—everyone does. New Orleans is like no other city in the world."

Ada was returning from visiting her daughter in Boston, and she and Olivia had become acquainted on the long flight. Olivia had found her to be a fountain of information, and Ada could not have found a more attentive listener, because Olivia was fascinated with everything that concerned old New Orleans.

"I must say," the older woman observed, glancing over her bifocals at Olivia, "for one who was born and raised in the East, you are very knowledgeable about our history. One would almost think you were a native."

"I have been interested in your history as long as I can remember. As a child, I read every book I could find on it." Olivia smiled shyly. She had never revealed so much of herself to a stranger. "As I told you, I'm a librarian and have access to many books."

Stuffing her knitting gingerly into a canvas bag, Ada eyed her young companion critically. Olivia seemed nice enough, but she was not a woman who would stand out in a crowd. There was nothing remarkable about her face, and she wore such thick glasses that it was difficult to tell if her eyes were blue or gray. Her hair was a nondescript brown, and although she was young, she wore it pulled away from her face in a tight little bun.

Ada somehow found herself pitying her companion, who could certainly use some advice on how to dress. The pale yellow suit she wore made her skin look washed out and sallow, and the skirt was much too long to be in style.

With interest, Ada noticed the drawing on Olivia's lap. "You are quite good. Did you have art lessons?"

"N-no," Olivia admitted. "Until this moment, I had no idea I could draw."

Ada looked doubtful, but then she smiled in her friendly Southern manner. "Where will you be staying in New Orleans, dear?"

Olivia's face became flushed with excitement. "At a bed-and-breakfast called the Bridal Veil Inn. Have you heard of it?"

Ada looked dismayed. "Yes, I have, but it is so far from the city and it's desolate and run-down—hardly anyone stays there." Not wanting to criticize Olivia's choice, she selected her words carefully. "Bridal Veil was once a great plantation, until the daughter of the house met a tragic end. They say the inn is haunted."

Olivia nodded. "I know. I have read the legend of how Jade St. Clair was accidentally slain by her intended husband."

Ada shrugged. "There are those who say it was no accident." She saw Olivia tense, so she tried to reassure her. "But, there now, you have come to enjoy yourself and don't want to hear old ghost stories."

Olivia could have told Ada that every choice she had made in her life had brought her to this moment. She could have told the kindhearted woman that Olivia Heartford was not her real name, but a name the Catholic sisters had given her at the orphanage where she had grown up, because no one knew who her parents were. She had never told anyone about the vivid dreams she'd had since childhood, dreams that were so real they were more like visions, and the people in those dreams were more real to her than the people she knew in everyday life. The odd thing about her dreams was that they were from a bygone era, which her research had indicated was the early 1800s.

Olivia would never forget that day two years ago when she had been thumbing through a travel magazine and came across an article featuring the Bridal Veil Inn. Her throat had tightened and she had felt frightened, for she knew that house well. Although the years had changed the facade and grounds, it was the house in her dreams. That very day she had started planning this trip, not knowing what she would find at the Bridal Veil Inn, but knowing she had to go.

The plane landed with a soft thud and taxied down the runway toward the terminal. Soon everyone was pushing and shoving in the aisles, and Olivia said a hasty good-bye to Ada Harmon.

A short time later, with her luggage in tow, Olivia stepped out into the humid afternoon air. There was no way to describe the feeling she experienced, the tightening in her chest, the hammering of her pulse—it was almost as if she had been on a long journey and had come home at last!

She was soon seated in a taxi, and the driver spoke to her in a thick Cajun accent. "Where to, ma'am?"

"To the Bridal Veil Inn," she answered, anxious to reach her destination. "Do you know where it is?"

Through the rearview mirror, he gave her a measured glance. "I know about it, lady."

With a honk of his horn, he pulled into the traffic and they left the airport behind and merged onto the freeway. Olivia soon became so absorbed by the scenery that she hardly noticed when they left the city behind and turned onto River Road.

Excitement throbbed through her when she first saw the Mississippi snaking its way through the lush countryside. Before long, she had her first view of a swamp, and though it was merely a narrow inlet with ghostly moss hanging from strangely shaped cypress trees, she found it fascinating.

"Is it much farther?" she asked when they turned down what appeared to be a country lane. Ada Harmon had been right—it was desolate here.

"Just up the road," the man muttered. "Looks like fog's settling in," he observed in irritation. "It'll take me an hour to get back to town now."

Olivia felt that he was asking her to apologize, although she could have pointed out to him that nature, and not she, controlled the elements.

She turned her attention to the long, oak-lined drive, which was eerily enveloped in a swirl of mist. But neither fog nor ghost stories dampened her enthusiasm, because even though she could not see the landscape very well, she already knew what it looked like.

Until that moment, she had been lonely and incomplete. Now she knew that whatever her destiny was, she would find it at Bridal Veil Inn.

The sensation that she had been there before intensified as they stopped in front of the great house that rose from the mist. Olivia paused with her hand on the door handle, knowing that when she stepped out of the taxi, her life would change forever.

It suddenly had turned cold and a shiver went down her spine. Olivia had the curious feeling that she had just stepped back in time.

Just then, Betty Allendale, the owner of the Bridal Veil Inn, threw open the door and descended the steps. Her blonde hair was flawlessly styled, and she wore a green print dress and a white organdy apron. Her smile was genuine as she greeted Olivia.

"Miss Heartford, at last we meet—welcome, welcome! Come inside; Harrison will see to the driver and place your luggage in your room."

"Betty, please call me Olivia. After all, we have been corresponding for two years."

"Very well," her hostess said. "I do feel that we know each other well."

At that moment, Olivia could not have spoken if her life depended on it. Suddenly, she could hardly breathe because there was a heavy sadness in her heart. Betty did not seem to notice anything unusual in Olivia's manner and chatted endlessly as she accompanied her guest inside.

Olivia was confused by the change in the entryway. The floor was polished wood with a red Turkish runner, and she was quite certain that it had once been black marble.

Betty Allendale led her into the front parlor, where a blazing fire was a welcoming sight. Hungry flames licked at the applewood log, filling the room with a sweet scent.

"Where are the other guests?" Olivia inquired.

Betty looked apologetic. "I hope you won't mind being my only guest. It seems that most people today want all the conveniences of the big chain hotels, and we are a bit far from town."

Mind! Olivia was elated, because she didn't want to share her time at Bridal Veil with other people. "No, I prefer it this way, Betty."

"Through our correspondence," Betty said, "you learned quite a lot about Bridal Veil Inn—still, I will give you the same speech I give all my guests.'' After a small pause, her voice took on the tone of a tour guide. ''This was once the main house of Meadow Brook Plantation, owned by the St. Clair family. It passed through six owners before my husband and I bought it. Since John died seven years ago, I have sold off most of the property and opened the inn. Besides myself, I have a maid, a cook, and Harrison, who acts as gardener and handyman.''

Betty added a log to the fire before she continued. ''When we first purchased the house twenty years ago, it had not been occupied for over fifty years. Although we did extensive renovations, we chose to add few modern conveniences. You will find the plumbing is quite modern, but everything else is as near to the original house plans as our limited knowledge would allow.''

''You did an exceptional job,'' Olivia said, turning around in the room that felt so familiar. ''Was this not once the master's study?''

''Why, yes, although not many people know that. I'm sure I never wrote you about that—did I?''

''No. It just seems obvious.''

''Yes, I suppose so. Logically it would be advantageous to the master's needs,'' Betty admitted. ''As you know,'' she continued, ''tragedy befell the daughter of the man who built this house. Although it was hushed up at the time, it is reputed that young, beautiful Jade St. Clair was tragically slain by the man she was to marry. Not many details have come down to us, although we know that soon after Jade's death, her fiancé, Raige Belmanoir, disappeared. Some say he went into the swamps and never came out because he couldn't live with what he had done.''

Olivia felt as if a hand had just clutched her heart. ''It

was not his fault. Jade St. Clair stepped in front of his sword.''

"So you wrote in your letters," Betty said dismissively. "Everyone who comes here has a theory on just how Jade St. Clair died. While some try to glamorize her demise, the probable truth is she was slain by the man she loved while he was in a jealous rage. Some overimaginative guests have sworn they saw Jade's ghost roaming the halls in her wedding gown and veil, and I must say that at times even I have seen things out of the ordinary. I know it adds to the romance of the inn to have a legendary ghost, but I hope Jade St. Clair has found peace."

"Do you have a portrait of her, or any other possessions besides the wedding veil you named the inn after?"

Betty shook her head. "No, nothing else of hers has survived. But come with me—you will not be disappointed."

Olivia followed Betty Allendale up the wide stairs to the second-floor landing. There, on a rosewood table, covered with a tall glass dome, was Jade St. Clair's faded lace wedding veil.

"It's so delicate, so beautiful," Olivia said in a trembling voice, reaching out toward the glass enclosure and then allowing her hand to drop away. "The pearls are from the Orient, and the lace was made in Brussels."

"You have done your research," Betty said, becoming disturbed by Olivia's obsessive interest in Jade St. Clair. This had been apparent in her letters; it was even more apparent in person. Betty thought there was something very sad about the lonely young woman.

"May I . . . would it be possible to try on the . . . veil?" Olivia asked hesitantly.

Betty looked horrified at the thought. "I never take it out of the protective case. It is fragile and very valuable."

There was pleading in Olivia's eyes. "I will be careful with it if you will only allow me to touch it."

Betty felt a rush of pity for the plain young woman who was so entranced by the legend of this house that she had saved her meager salary for almost two years so she could make the trip. "I suppose it will do no harm," she said, at last capitulating. She lifted the glass and laid it aside. "You can see that it really is quite delicate."

With trembling hands, Olivia reached for the veil, almost touching it and then drawing back, only to reach out again. At last her fingers brushed softly against the lace and she felt as if a shock of electricity had gone through her body. She had touched this veil before; she knew she had. It had once sat atop her own head.

Seeing the longing in Olivia's eyes, Betty Allendale made a quick decision. "If you will never tell a living soul, I'll allow you to put the veil on. But just for a brief moment, and just this once."

Olivia stood statue-still as her hostess gently lifted the lace veil from the wooden form. When the material floated across Olivia's head and brushed her cheeks, Betty Allendale faded from view and another woman stood in her place, a woman dressed in a floor-length gown—a woman that Olivia knew was Jade's mother, Emmaline St. Clair.

"Jade, dearest, you will make a lovely bride. Wait until Raige sees you!" her mother exclaimed.

Olivia felt paralyzed and she wanted to cry out. She was so frightened that she wanted to rip the veil from her head, but then the ghostly face of Emmaline St. Clair faded and Betty Allendale once more stood in her place.

Olivia carefully removed the fragile lace veil that had given her a glimpse into the past and handed it to Betty, who did not seem aware of what had occurred.

Betty smiled as she took the veil and replaced it under the glass dome. "Now," she said, turning to Olivia, "I'm sure you are tired after your long flight. I'll show you to your room."

As they walked down the long hallway, Olivia only half listened to Betty's chatter. She was trying to close her mind to frightening sensations—the feeling of familiarity, the knowledge that she had walked these halls before.

"Dinner is at seven; we are rather informal. Breakfast is served in your room unless you are an early riser and wish to dine on the veranda."

"I'm an early riser. I was always the first one to arrive at the library."

Betty didn't doubt it. She opened the door and the strong scent of roses permeated the air, a smell so nostalgic that Olivia leaned against the wall, trying to stop her body from quaking.

"Are you ill?" Betty asked in concern, noticing how pale her guest was.

"No. I'm just tired. You must have other things to do— I can get settled in myself."

Betty looked concerned. "If you are sure. Perhaps I should send Rosalie to help you unpack."

"Thank you, but that won't be necessary. I like to do my own unpacking."

Betty smiled. "If there is anything you need, just let me know."

Olivia watched Betty Allendale move down the hallway with a gracefulness known to a bygone time, or perhaps it was a gracefulness inherent in Southern women. Then Olivia entered the bedroom and closed the door behind her. For a long moment, she kept her eyes cast downward, almost afraid of what she might find. She had requested Jade

St. Clair's bedroom, and she already knew what it looked like.

Slowly she raised her eyes—yes, the double doors that led to a balcony, the fireplace carved with cherubs, the poster bed, they were all the same. Here, as downstairs, there were changes, but subtle ones. Olivia hoped that the rose arbor she had so often dreamed about would still be in the garden.

Stiffly, almost reluctantly, she moved across the room, holding her breath. Taking her courage in hand, she stood on the balcony, her hands gripping the cast-iron railing. Yes, there it was, the white arbor covered with climbing roses. It hadn't changed at all!

"I'm home," she said to no one in particular, wondering how she could explain her knowledge of a house she had never been in before.

The last crimson rays of the sun lingered against the horizon as Olivia descended the stairs to the dining room. Soft candlelight mellowed the rooms she passed through and she felt more alive than she had ever felt before. She dined on baked chicken served in wine sauce. Afterwards she went into the parlor and curled up on the overstuffed sofa while Betty Allendale played the piano and the maid served fruit punch and coffee.

At last, feeling contented and at peace, Olivia wished her hostess good night and made her way up the stairs. For so long she had imagined herself here at Bridal Veil, and she was not disappointed by what she had found. Boston seemed so far away, another world, another time—this was where she belonged; she knew that now.

When Olivia reached her bedroom, she undressed and slipped into her nightgown. She turned off the lamp and the room was illuminated by the soft moonlight that spilled through the open door that led to the balcony.

Climbing into the soft featherbed, she sank into comfort of the mind and body, feeling warm and protected. Lying where Jade St. Clair had once lain, she could feel the young girl's thoughts, experience her emotions and her loves.

Olivia was no longer frightened, for there had been love in this house. She could feel it. Jade had known the love of her mother and father and a much younger sister. She'd had a friend named Charlene, with whom she'd shared her deepest secrets.

While Olivia knew well the faces of Jade's family members, and even the face of the man Jade had loved, she had never seen an image of Jade herself. With new understanding, Olivia realized that was because she had been seeing life through Jade's eyes.

She knew that with sleep would come the dreams, and she welcomed them. She had come here for a purpose, although she had not known it until now. She was here to help the tormented ghost that walked the halls of Bridal Veil Inn.

"I don't know exactly why, Jade St. Clair, but I am here," she whispered.

Was it her imagination, or had she heard a sigh from somewhere in the darkened corners of the room?

# *Chapter Two*

I N THE FALLEN dusk, Olivia's steps were guided by the light from the Chinese lanterns that danced against stone walls. With one purpose in mind, she moved down the path at the back of the house in the direction of the rose arbor, knowing that something out of the ordinary was about to happen. She could hear music and laughter in the background, and was puzzled. Betty must be entertaining.

When she reached the arbor, Olivia went inside and sat on a cushioned bench. She was feeling sad and could not have said why.

Hearing the sound of footsteps, Olivia pressed herself back against the bench, not wanting to see anyone just now. A form in the shape of a man detached itself from the shadows, and she knew at once that it was Raige Belmanoir!

His voice was deep and laced with humor. "I know you are here, Jade, so do not try to hide from me."

Olivia realized she must be dreaming again, only she was

not seeing the dream as a third person, an onlooker—she was Jade St. Clair!

She watched as Raige's bold stare turned into a flashing smile. Her eyes fixed anxiously on his while he appraised her. She had first become aware that she loved Raige when she was only twelve years old. Tonight she was celebrating her seventeenth birthday, and he had not paid the slightest attention to her until this moment.

"I just came out for a breath of air," she said, fanning herself with an ivory fan, knowing her cheeks were flushed, but not from the heat. "It was stifling in the ballroom."

Raige moved closer to her and took the fan, her birthday gift from Tyrone, carelessly tossing it onto the cushion. "It is little wonder you escaped. Every gentleman in the room, be he old or young, wanted to dance with you."

"Not every gentleman, Raige. You did not ask me to dance," she said flirtatiously.

"Don't do that, Jade."

Her lashes swept over her eyes, a tactic that had worked magic on countless admirers. "Do what?" she asked, feigning innocence.

"Never treat me like those simpletons who are satisfied with just a smile. It's more than flirting I want from you, Jade."

Excitement throbbed through her body like a raging tide. "I was not flirting with you. I don't know what you mean."

His voice was deep. "Do you not? Let's just say that I have an aversion to being just one of the adoring crowd."

She looked at him, admiring the cut of his green tailcoat. The matching trousers hugged his lean body, and an elaborately tied cravat circled his throat. He was tall and lithe, slender of waist and wide of shoulder, quite the handsomest man in three parishes. She raised her eyes to his, suddenly feeling shy.

He smiled as if he knew what she was thinking and feeling. Then he took her hand and studied the tapered fingers. "How could you not know that I am jealous of every man that looks at you?"

Jerking free, she clasped her hands behind her, still feeling the warmth of his touch. Jade felt as if butterflies were fluttering in her stomach. Of course Raige did not mean what he was saying; he had always teased her.

"You have been in Europe for almost a year, Raige; I believe you never gave me a thought in all that time."

"You are wrong—I thought of you. And now I have returned to find you have grown into a young lady." His voice deepened and she thought she might faint when he sat down beside her. He was so near that she could feel his breath warm against her cheek.

"I have been waiting for you to grow up, Jade, and now you have."

She could imagine him saying this same thing to other females and it hurt so badly. Raige could have any woman he wanted. She had seen how silly girls simpered and giggled when he walked by. She had heard them sigh and make remarks about his manliness. She did not want him to think that she was like them.

"Please don't tease me anymore, Raige."

Standing, he pulled Jade up beside him, his eyes sweeping over her golden hair and dipping down to assess her beautiful face. "And why is that?"

The night was like black velvet, without benefit of moon or stars. His eyes were probing, seeking, entering her mind and making her ache and tremble. Her tongue flicked out to moisten her dry lips, a move that was not lost to him. It was difficult for her to concentrate with him standing so near, touching her.

"As . . . as you said, I have grown up."

He touched her hair, his hand drifting down the silken curls, causing her to shiver with longing.

"It was your eyes that haunted me while I was away. Did you know I have never seen a woman with green eyes like yours?" Gently his hand went to her waist and he pulled her to him. She did not resist.

He took a guarded breath. "I have wondered what I would do when this moment came, Jade. Have you any notion how a man can ache for a woman? While I was gone, I could imagine the numerous admirers who might come to your door beseeching you to marry them."

There was fever in her blood and longing in her breast. He was only toying with her, but what did it matter—at last she was in his arms. "You have quite an imagination," she said, trying to show that she was immune to his charm.

"You missed me, Jade," he said with bold determination. "You cannot deny it."

At that moment Jade knew that she could not bear to be just another of Raige's many conquests. She was determined to shake his cool confidence as he had shaken hers. "You hardly crossed my mind at all," she said, turning her back to him so he would not read the truth in her eyes. "And, yes, there have been many gentlemen who have asked me to be their wife, while you do no more than torment me, trying to make me think you really care."

He turned her around to face him and laughed triumphantly at the uncertainty he saw in her eyes. "What is it you think I want from you?"

She was very near tears. "To mock me, as always."

He placed his hands on either side of her face, forcing

her to look at him. "Jade, I would sooner rip out my own heart than to hurt you. Do you not know that?"

"I . . ."

He dipped his dark head, his lips lightly touching hers. She could neither breathe nor move as she clung to him.

When he raised his head, he gave her a devastating smile. "You see how it is with me?"

The chaste kiss he had given her so carelessly left her heart hungering for more. "N-no."

He moved away from her, as if he feared he would take her in his arms again if he did not put some distance between them. "How could you not know how I feel about you? Everyone else does."

She dared not hope he was being serious. "How can that be, when you have never paid the slightest bit of attention to me? Even tonight, when I had not seen you in over a year, you ignored me—and do not try to deny it."

He moved back to her, lightly touching her cheek. "My eyes followed you around the room all night. And when you danced with Tyrone, even though he is my friend, I wanted to rip you out of his arms. I have always felt that you belonged to me."

His words sent her heart soaring. The love she felt for him flowered until the pain was almost more than she could endure.

"What do you want from me, Raige?"

Gently his arms circled her and he cradled her against his chest so she could hear his heart thundering.

"Jade, my dearest love, I want the right to go to your father and ask for your hand in marriage. Will you grant me that right?"

As his words penetrated her thoughts, she stepped away from him. "You . . . want to marry me?"

He reached over her head and broke off a rose, handing it to her. She clutched the token to her. "There has never been a time when I considered anyone but you as mistress of Tanglewood."

Suddenly a swirling mist engulfed them both and she reached out to him, pricking her finger on the rose and dropping it to the floor of the arbor. He was gone, and she felt empty inside.

"Raige," she cried, "don't leave me—I cannot find you in the dark."

Olivia awoke, sitting upright in bed. She was wringing wet with perspiration, and her heart was drumming in her ears. The dream had been more real than any she had ever had. For a short time, she had been allowed to dwell in Jade's body, to feel what Jade had felt and to know a love so strong that it could not die.

She lay back against her pillow as tears filled her eyes. What fate had drawn her into the tangled lives of the star-crossed lovers? She was in love with a man who had been dead for well over a hundred years, and there would be no escape until she lived the dream to its heartbreaking conclusion.

There was a light tap on the door and Olivia reached for her robe.

"Morning, Miss Heartford," Rosalie said cheerfully as she swept into the room. "I'm to ask if you want breakfast on the veranda."

"Yes, I believe so." Olivia smiled at the maid, who was tall and slender and looked to be about thirty. Then she turned to the balcony door and saw bright sunlight filtering into the room. "Luckily that thick fog that hit last night is gone."

Rosalie looked puzzled. "There was fog yesterday afternoon when you arrived, but a northerly wind blew it away. Last night was a full moon, and bright as daylight.''

"But, I—'' Olivia turned pale as she remembered the heavy mist. Was nothing at Bridal Veil what it seemed?

"I ran your bath for you across the hall, and while you bathe, I'll straighten your room," Rosalie offered.

Olivia agreed with a nod and moved out of the room, carrying her clothes and toiletries. After a refreshing bath in an old-fashioned bathtub with claw feet, she dressed in a pair of jeans and an oversized T-shirt. In slight irritation, she wiped the steam from the small mirror that hung above the sink. Was she mistaken or was her hair lighter in color? And why was it curling about her shoulders—her hair was straight. She shrugged; perhaps it was from the humidity. She reached for her glasses and realized that she'd left them in the bedroom.

The mirror had steamed up again, and in exasperation, Olivia applied a thin sheen of pale pink lipstick. She would leave her hair down today—no reason to pin it back.

When Olivia came downstairs, she was thinking about her dream the night before and did not see anyone until Betty stepped out of the dining room, carrying a pitcher of orange juice.

"Good morning," Betty said, indicating that Olivia was to precede her to the veranda.

"It's a glorious morning," Olivia replied, sitting at the table, which was covered with a white damask tablecloth and set with antique china and silver. She took a napkin and spread it across her lap while Betty poured her a cup of coffee.

"Betty, was there a heavy fog last night?"

"I don't believe so. The fog that hit at your arrival dissipated before sundown. As I recall, there was a bright moon last night. Why do you ask?''

Olivia shrugged and changed the subject. "I thought I heard music—did you have guests arrive after I went to bed?''

Betty looked perplexed. "No. There was no one here and there was no music.''

Olivia picked up a blueberry muffin and spread it with butter, trying to calm herself. Betty must think her a complete fool, and she didn't blame her.

"Olivia, I must say that I like your hair worn loose. It's quite lovely.'' With a bemused look on her face, she watched Olivia for a moment. "You know, I could have sworn that your hair was darker. Perhaps it just looks that way when you wear it up.''

Olivia could only stare at her hostess. "But I do have dark hair.''

"Oh, I see—you colored it. Well, it looks very natural.''

Olivia tilted the silver coffee server until she could see her reflection. Her hands were trembling as she reached up and touched the golden curls that spiraled about her face. What was happening to her?

There was something else that could not be explained, Olivia thought in a panic as she pushed aside the coffee server. She had forgotten her glasses, yet her vision was perfect. How could that be when she had worn thick bifocals since childhood?

Could this be a gift from Jade?

She stood up, placing her napkin beside her plate. "I find that I am not hungry. I believe I'll go for a walk before it gets too hot.''

Betty was busy watering the flower boxes on the veranda, so she was unaware of Olivia's distress. "Yes, do that. Be sure to walk by the rose arbor; it's quite lovely there. If you keep to the path, it will eventually take you to the river.''

Olivia moved quickly down the path, the same path she had walked last night. Of course there was no sign of the Chinese lanterns because they had not really been there—she had only dreamed them.

When she reached the rose arbor, she sat down on the cushioned bench. Last night had seemed so real. She glanced at her finger where she had pricked herself with a thorn and found a small wound. Her eyes dropped to the floor of the arbor, and there, crushed beneath her feet, was a single rose.

Olivia was suddenly terrified. With no aim in mind, she moved out of the arbor and ran down the path as if she could escape what was happening to her. She ran until she came to the spot where the path met the river. She had the strongest urge to leave this place and never come back. If she had Betty drive her to New Orleans this morning, she could spend the night in a hotel and catch a flight to Boston tomorrow.

She turned to glance back at the plantation house, with its mellow red bricks shining in the sunlight, beckoning to her like a ghost from the past. No, she could not leave. Not until this drama came to an end.

Perhaps the dreams would not come again, but that thought brought her no comfort. She ached to see Raige, to have him hold her in his arms. Last night he had asked her to be his bride—he must love her.

"No, fool," she told herself. "He did not ask you to marry him—he asked Jade St. Clair to be his bride. It was Jade he loved, not me."

# Chapter Three

OLIVIA WAS TORN between not wanting to dream of Raige Belmanoir and fearing that she might not. She tossed and turned, thinking she would never sleep. At last a cool breeze came through the balcony doors, and she drifted off to sleep.

Until now, all her dreams had taken place at night. But the part of her that was Jade was growing stronger, and she made her first appearance in daylight.

As Jade stepped out the front door of the plantation house, she flipped open her green parasol and positioned it between herself and the sun.

"I have grown accustomed to these annual outings at Fairmont," Emmaline St. Clair remarked. "I do think it is lovely there this time of year."

"But you are not fond of Felicity Dunois," Jade's sister, Lizette, said with the honest observation of a young girl.

Jade's father arched his brow at his wife, but made no comment.

"I have no antipathy toward Felicity . . . exactly," her

mother answered carefully. "I am just not one of her close confidantes."

"I know a secret," Lizette said, beaming at her sister. "Would you like to hear it?"

Jade smiled at the young minx. At eleven, she was forever being scolded by their mother for not acting in a ladylike manner.

"Oui, please do tell us your secret, Lizette," Jade cajoled dramatically. "I am waiting with bated breath—on tenterhooks—with wild anticipation."

"You would not jest if you knew what I had overheard Madame Dunois say to her husband after Mass on Sunday. They did not know I was within hearing."

"It is not polite to repeat gossip," her mother admonished her. "You will say no more on the subject."

In her eagerness, Lizette continued as if her mother had not spoken. "Madame Dunois told her husband that she wanted Jade to marry Tyrone so she could get her hands on Meadow Brook."

"She did not say such a thing!" their mother exclaimed in disbelief and indignation. "The boldness of that woman is not to be endured!"

"She said it. I heard her as clearly as I hear you," Lizette stated emphatically.

Jade only smiled. "I adore Tyrone, but he is like a brother to me. And, chatterbox," she said, tugging on one of her sister's curls affectionately, "Tyrone only thinks of me as a sister."

"Little you know," Lizette said with a toss of her head. "You have been mooning after Raige for so long that you never can see what's before your own nose. I've watched you standing at the mirror, primping and daydreaming, ever since Raige came home."

"Lizette, we'll have no more of your mischief," her father said sternly. "Is that understood?"

Jade looked at her father, wondering if Raige had approached him with an offer of marriage. Obviously he had not, or her father would have told her. Raige had not meant anything he'd said that night in the rose arbor. Well, if he came to the outing today, she would just ignore him and let him see that she had not gone into decline because of him.

Jade glanced down at her new white silk dress, which was embroidered with pink rosebuds. The Grecian style, with the high bodice and puffed sleeves, was flattering to her and did little to hide her womanly body. Would Raige like the dress on her? she wondered, then chided herself for being a fool. What did she care if Raige noticed her? There were many other gentlemen who would.

By now they had reached the Dunois house, a great white pillared mansion. Monsieur and Madame Dunois came down the steps to greet them, and Jade noticed her mother's forced smile. But her mother was a lady born and bred, and she would never be discourteous when she was someone's guest.

Jade smiled as Tyrone rushed down the steps to her. He was about the same height and build as Raige, but there the similarity ended. Tyrone, tall and fair, was popular with everyone, while Raige was often dark and brooding and intimidated most people. Despite their differences, the two men had been friends since childhood.

Tyrone helped Jade out of the carriage and she linked her arm through his.

"Please rescue me," he said, laughing down at her. "The gentlemen have gathered in the library and talk of nothing but the American upstarts who will surely be the ruination of us all, by making us a star on their flag—and how France has sold us out for thirty pieces of silver. And I'll rescue you from the women, who will talk of nothing but the latest fashions from France.''

Jade wrinkled her nose. ''You are right, of course—that is exactly what they always do, and it would be a bore.''

''You are the most beautiful girl here today,'' he said earnestly. But then Tyrone had always told her she was pretty; she'd come to expect it of him.

''And you, monsieur, are surely the most gallant gentleman here.''

They walked along the path that led to the back of the house, where other young people had gathered.

''I do not see Raige anywhere,'' Jade said, glancing through the crowd.

''I invited him, but I doubt he'll come. You know how he detests parties.'' Then Tyrone grinned down at her. ''Should I worry that he will take my place with you now that he has returned?''

She looked at him carefully, remembering what Lizette had said. ''No one could take your place. You are the brother I never had.''

Was that anger she saw in his eyes? When he laughed, she was sure that she had been mistaken.

''I must be the envy of every gentleman from Baton Rouge to New Orleans since you favor me with your . . . friendship. Will you eat your picnic lunch with me?''

She felt that someone was watching her and turned back to see Tyrone's mother staring at her. There was definite dislike in the older woman's eyes, though Jade could not have said why.

''Of course I'll eat with you,'' she said, turning back to Tyrone. ''That is, if you are not carried off by all the females who will want to scratch my eyes out.''

Jade expected him to laugh, but he looked preoccupied, as if he had something on his mind.

"Jade," he said at last, "don't . . . allow Raige to treat you in the manner he does other women."

She raised her eyes to him, pretending a disinterest she was far from feeling. "Whatever do you mean?"

A shadow fell across Jade's face and she stared into the mocking eyes of Raige himself. "He means, Jade, that he feels honor bound to protect you from me—do you need protection from me?"

She raised her chin defiantly and tightened her grip on Tyrone's arm. "I can take care of myself."

"I have little doubt of that, Jade St. Clair. You see, Tyrone, my friend, it is I who am in danger from our charmer—who will save me from her?"

Jade spoke haughtily. "You are in no danger from me, Raige. I have no designs on you."

After a long, poignant silence where Jade and Raige stared into each other's eyes, he offered her his arm. "Will you picnic with me?"

"No" she said almost too quickly. "I promised Tyrone I would lunch with him."

Raige's eyes moved to his friend. "You will excuse her from her promise, won't you?"

Jade held her breath, unsure if she wanted Tyrone to relent or not.

"I would be a fool to forfeit her company," Tyrone said, his hand going to Jade's arm possessively.

Raige bowed to Jade and then placed a hand on Tyrone's shoulder. "The day will come when you will have to give her up, my friend—and soon." His eyes moved to Jade. "I grow impatient to claim what has always been mine."

\* \* \*

A rooster crowing in the new day brought Olivia back to the present.

"No," she moaned in distress. Why did she always have to be pulled back to the present? Why couldn't she remain in the past? It was where she wanted to be—it was where she belonged.

For a long moment she lay there, listening to the sounds of the house coming to life. With a resigned sigh, she slid out of bed. How much longer could she stand being pulled from one world to another? Surely she would soon be a raving lunatic!

It was a dull, gray day. The sky was overcast, and it would surely rain before noon. But that did not keep Olivia from going horseback riding. Bridal Veil boasted a fine stable of horses, and while she was not an experienced equestrienne, she did like to ride.

It was midmorning before Olivia, dressed in jeans and sneakers, rode down the worn path that led away from the river. She was assured that the mare she rode was gentle and would give her no cause for alarm. She bounced along jauntily, feeling the wind in her hair and thinking about nothing in particular.

Suddenly, without warning, her mount reared on its hind legs and bolted across the meadow. Olivia clung to the animal with every ounce of strength she possessed, fearing she would be thrown. Her heart was pounding with fear when the supposedly gentle mare became uncontrollable.

Jade was an excellent horsewoman and she allowed her gelding a free rein. They raced across the meadow, past the ripening corn and into the valley beyond. The sun felt good against her face and the wind had torn the ribbon from her hair, allowing it to blow free.

Her gelding picked its way down the incline to the stream, where she allowed it to drink from the clear water.

Jade could not have said at what moment she realized that she was no longer alone. It was not a sound that alerted her, but more a feeling of being watched. Slowly, she turned, her stomach knotted like a tight fist.

Tall and erect, Raige stood poised against the trunk of an oak tree. The sunlight shimmering through the branches glistened on his thick black hair, and his golden eyes flamed with the fire of life. He was magnificent.

Raige casually propped a booted foot against a wide tree root while his horse grazed nearby.

"You seem surprised to see me, Jade."

She quivered as his dark eyes raked hers.

"How long have you been here?" she demanded.

"For over an hour. But I know your habits and I knew you would come if I waited long enough."

"You shouldn't have troubled yourself."

He grinned. "It was no trouble, I assure you."

Jade held herself stiffly as he walked toward her with lithe movements.

"I was in New Orleans this morning and met your mother and father at the Exchange," Raige told her. "They said they wouldn't be home until tomorrow. Do you know what that means?"

She pushed her tumbled hair away from her face, wishing she hadn't lost the ribbon. "Non, I don't."

He drew in a tolerant breath. "It means, Jade, that we can spend the day together."

"I was on my way to visit a friend." She wasn't, but

she was afraid that if she remained, he would surely discover that she loved him.

His strong hands circled her waist, and before she could protest, Raige lifted her from the saddle. Instead of setting her on her feet, he held her close.

"Do not play coy with me, Jade. You know how I feel about you." She saw his nostrils flare and wanted to run away, but he still held her close.

At last he set her on her feet, and she had to crane her neck to look up at him.

"You don't really have anywhere to go, do you, Jade?"

"I . . . I do later in the afternoon."

Without a word, he swept her into his arms, and his lips descended to kiss her mouth.

It was torture, it was bliss, as her hair entwined around his fingers. He pressed her tightly against him and she could feel the bulging outline of his manly body. Wave after wave of emotions tangled her mind, and she pressed tighter against him, needing to feel his very essence.

Suddenly, in a moment of sanity, she tore her mouth from his and took several retreating steps.

Raige merely smiled and held his hand out to her. "Come here, Jade."

She hesitated, trembling with emotions she did not understand. "Non. This is not right."

He took two long strides that brought him to her. "There is nothing more right in this world than you in my arms. We were created to be together. You belong to me; do you not know that by now, Jade?"

Her eyes searched his, and in that moment, he saw agony.

"But you went away and left me." It was a cry from her heart.

"I had to."

"Why?"

"To allow you time to grow up."

She looked puzzled. "That is no reason. I would have grown up even had you stayed. Do not say things to me that you don't mean, Raige."

"I will never lie to you, Jade. I want us to have a marriage based on complete honesty. That's why I want you to tell me this moment that you love me."

Her admission came out in a rush that surprised her. "I thought I would die when you left. I counted the days until you would return." She had to look away from the brilliance in his eyes. "And then you came back, and you seemed to ignore me."

Gathering her close, he kissed her earlobe and nuzzled her neck. "There was not one day in that long year that I did not think of you. But, you see, I am a patient man, Jade. I always knew you would one day belong to me. I told you this that night in the rose arbor. Did you doubt me?"

She looked into his eyes. "I thought you were just . . . there have been women—"

His grip tightened on her shoulders. "Let there be no misunderstandings between us, Jade. I have been with other women, but I have never spoken to them of love. Whether you allow it or not, I will love you until the day I die."

Such a beautiful declaration melted her heart, but caution made her afraid to believe him. He could have any woman—why her? "Are you sure you love me?"

His laughter was warm and his eyes held a light of triumph—he was a man who had just won the woman he loved.

"Shall I tell you the first day I knew I loved you?" he

asked, trying not to think of the soft young body that enticed him.

Jade looked at him eagerly. "Oui, please, tell me."

Olivia felt rain on her face and sat up in a daze. The sun was gone, and Raige was gone. She looked about in bewilderment. The horse had thrown her. Slowly coming to her feet, she tested her legs and arms to see if they were broken—they weren't, but she was going to ache for several days.

Looking about her, she took in the stream and the oak tree where Raige had been waiting for her. Everything was the same as she had envisioned it. Raige had been about to tell her when he had first realized he loved her. Why, oh why, did she keep getting pulled away from him?

The mare was grazing along the riverbank and did not move as she approached. Carefully Olivia mounted and turned in the direction of the house. She had ridden up the hill before she realized she was riding like one born to the saddle.

This, like her newfound ability to draw and her changed eyesight, was another gift from Jade.

# *Chapter Four*

O LIVIA WAS DELIGHTED when Betty suggested that she accompany her into New Orleans for a day of shopping. They climbed into the late-model van, and on the long drive, the two of them talked about their favorite subject— the legend of Bridal Veil.

"Is there nothing more you can tell me about the friendship between Jade and Tyrone Dunois?" Olivia asked.

"Not too much. However, Jade's friend Charlene, who eventually married Tyrone, kept a written account of her own life. According to her, Tyrone's mother pushed him forward and made him believe he could win Jade. He wasn't a bad sort, but his one weakness was his love for Jade. In the end, it destroyed three lives, four if you count Charlene."

"There is such a quagmire surrounding the truth. I wonder why," Olivia speculated. Many things were becoming clear to her, as she became more entangled in Jade's life. Of course, she knew details she could share with no one, not even Betty.

"After Jade's death," Betty continued, "Tyrone quarreled bitterly with his mother. Until the day he died, he never spoke to her again. In later years, he was so eaten up with hate and bitterness that he became something of a recluse."

Olivia thought of the boyish Tyrone she had met through Jade. It was hard to imagine him an embittered old man. "I wonder what really happened to cause the rift between Tyrone and Raige?"

Betty shrugged. "We will never know for certain. But I believe that Jade truly loved Raige, and I don't think she betrayed him with Tyrone, as many others do."

"What more can you tell me about Tyrone's mother?"

"There again, because of Charlene we know quite a lot about Felicity Dunois. She was an outsider, not a drop of French blood, which was unacceptable in the aristocratic Creole circles. William Dunois brought her here as a bride. She was from Philadelphia, and not from a wealthy family, but she certainly married well. The strange part is that she was no beauty and she was ten years older than her husband. Still, she bore him a son and a daughter, and by all accounts, William was a contented man."

By now they had reached New Orleans, which was teeming with life. While Betty did her shopping, Olivia strolled down the narrow streets of the French Quarter as any tourist might. For some reason, she avoided St. Louis Cathedral, not wanting to visit the site where Jade had died. She wandered through quaint shops and walked through the colorful open-air markets, where vendors still displayed their wares much as they had in Jade's time.

After exploring a stall where there were dried spices and herbs, she left the market and climbed the wooden steps that led to the top of the levee so she could see the Mississippi in all its glory.

Colorful paddle boats seemed to skim the murky water, their huge wheels making a melodic sound. It took Olivia several moments to realize that something was wrong.

Paddle boats? she thought with trepidation, counting three, four, five, six! There might be one or two of the graceful old relics that ferried tourists up and down the Mississippi, but not half a dozen.

She glanced down and saw that she was wearing a long gray silk dress with an empire waist and puffed sleeves. Dear God, she was Jade, but with the consciousness of her own mind! This had never happened before. Somehow she and Jade were beginning to merge into one being, and Jade was growing stronger every day, while she was becoming weaker. How much longer could she hold on to her identity—did she even want to?

One thing she was certain of was that Jade was not aware of her existence.

Behind her, Olivia could hear the sounds of horse-drawn buggies clattering down the street. She felt herself getting dizzy and she seemed to be falling into a dark crevice, into the very arms of oblivion.

Betty Allendale elbowed her way through the crowd to Olivia's side. The girl was pale and shaken and was being assisted by a policeman.

"Olivia!" Betty cried with concern. "What has happened to you?"

"She just collapsed," the policeman stated, putting away his notebook. "I offered to take her to the emergency room, but she says she's fine. Are you a friend of hers?"

Betty took Olivia by the arm. "Yes, I am, Officer, and I'll take care of her."

Olivia pushed a damp curl from her forehead and smiled with embarrassment. "There is nothing to be concerned about. This has happened before. Could we return to Bridal Veil now?"

Betty looked doubtful. "Yes, of course, if you are sure you're all right. Lean on me and I'll help you to the van."

Once they were speeding along River Road, Olivia closed her eyes and tried to comprehend what was happening to her. She felt like she was suffocating, so she adjusted the air conditioner vents to direct cool air on her face. Her nerves were raw and her mind was being tugged in two different directions.

The transitions were happening more frequently and they could happen at any time. How much longer could she dwell in this twilight of unreality?

"Betty," she asked, turning to her companion, "have you ever had an out-of-body experience?"

Betty turned to her, her brow furrowed in thoughtfulness. "I'm not sure I know what you mean."

"I can't explain it. But something is happening to me. I don't expect you to believe me, but I have walked in Jade St. Clair's shoes, felt what she felt, and for reasons I cannot explain, I often occupy her body."

Betty had growing concerns about Olivia's fixation with Jade. She was getting worse, as if she were truly obsessed. "I have watched you change your appearance to what you think Jade might have looked like. You lightened your hair, and I assume you've changed the color of your eyes by wearing green-tinted contacts. What you're doing is unhealthy, Olivia."

"Betty, you don't understand." Olivia knew that she sounded demented, but she had to tell someone what was happening to her. "The changes you see in me are not of my doing—you must believe me! I did not color my hair and I am not wearing contacts. Explain how this has happened to me.''

Olivia seemed so sincere. That was the pity of it, Betty thought. She actually believed that she was becoming Jade. ''Perhaps all you need is a good night's sleep.''

''Betty, have you noticed—have . . . have I been absent from Bridal Veil for long periods of time?''

''Not that I am aware of.''

Olivia buried her face in her trembling hands. ''More and more I am becoming Jade St. Clair. I believe Olivia Heartford will soon cease to exist.''

''And *I* believe we should turn around right now and take you to a doctor. You're scaring me.''

''And tell the doctor what—that I am losing my mind? I think not. Besides, a doctor wouldn't be able to help me.''

''What can I do to help you, Olivia?''

''Nothing. But thank you for not calling me a lunatic.''

''I admit,'' Betty said, gripping the steering wheel until her knuckles whitened, ''that ever since your arrival I have felt something was wrong. Although I can't explain what it is, I do know it's unnatural.''

''Sometimes I'm frightened, and other times I feel more alive than I've ever felt in my life,'' Olivia said softly.

''Perhaps you should return to Boston,'' Betty suggested, thinking that everything might return to normal when Olivia left.

''Whether I go or stay won't make any difference—I know that now because I have no control over what's happening to me.''

Betty pulled into the driveway and switched off the ignition. Then she turned to Olivia, her eyes filled with sympathy. "You must be careful. Remember that Jade St. Clair died tragically."

That night, dark nightmares stalked Olivia. All through the early hours of a restless night, vague sketches of memory were beating against her mind like flashes of lightning, striking and then disappearing. Her mind was a vast wasteland—no memory, no thoughts, no love or hate—nothing.

Cold, clammy hands reached out to her and baleful eyes burned into hers.

"Jade, my dear, I have been wanting to speak to you for some time. I am glad you accepted my invitation for tea."

The young girl blinked her green eyes. After a moment, she looked into Felicity Dunois's pale gray eyes, which seemed like those of a statue—blank, cold, dead of feeling. Madame Dunois was a thin woman, almost too thin. Her cheeks were sunken, her small, pinched mouth was held in a spiteful pose, and her breath was sour, causing Jade to move back in her chair.

"You said you had a reason for asking me here. I cannot remain long, because I am on my way to Charlene Brevelle's."

Harsh laughter grated on Jade's ears. "You are just like your mother, cutting right to the point. But, very well, I shan't waste your time or mine. How would you like to marry my son, Tyrone?"

Jade had just taken a sip of tea and choked. It took her a moment to catch her breath. Felicity Dunois's audacity angered her.

"Madame, Tyrone is a dear friend to me and I hold him in high regard. However, I shall never marry him, nor would he ask me. His feelings for me are not what a man should have for the woman he would marry."

The air was suddenly thick with evil; Jade could feel the malice, and it was directed at her.

"You are mistaken. Tyrone loves you a great deal and he would make an admirable husband." Felicity measured her words. "I know you think Raige Belmanoir will ask you to marry him, but he will take what he wants from you and then replace you with another."

Jade was too shocked and angry to reply to the woman's vicious assessment of Raige's character.

"Well," Felicity said at last, taking Jade's silence for consideration of her proposal, "do you make my son a happy man or condemn him to a life of loneliness?"

Jade came to her feet, her anger overcoming the good manners her mother had instilled in her. "Tyrone cannot know that you have asked me here to propose marriage for him. He would certainly disapprove of your boldness, as will my mother and father." She reached down for her riding gloves, which had fallen to the floor, and clutched them tightly in her hands. "I will wish you a good day, madame."

Felicity laughed, undaunted by Jade's resistance. "The young are often so foolish. You will soon see that I am right."

Jade hurried out of the room and through the front door. A swirling mist blocked out the sun just as she was assisted into her saddle by the Dunois's groom. She urged her horse forward, knowing she had to get away.

Jade had not realized where she was going until she found herself by the stream that ran through Meadow Brook. Sliding to the ground, she leaned her head against the oak tree, wishing she could stop shaking.

At that moment, she felt comforting arms go about her and she was held in a strong embrace.

"I have been waiting for you," Raige whispered against her cheek. "Time has no meaning when you are not with me. I need you, Jade. Say you will be mine." His passionate glance burned through her body. "To love a woman as I love you is like a fever in the blood. There is but one cure."

She tried not to think about the conversation she'd just had with Tyrone's mother, but it hung over her like a dark pall. She was in the arms of the man she loved, and nothing else should matter.

Raige gripped her shoulders and held her away from him, studying her intently. In his eyes a sharpness, an intelligence, told her that he was not a man to be easily duped. He knew that something was wrong.

"What has happened to upset you, Jade?"

"It's nothing. Anyway, I don't want to think about it."

"If you are troubled, I want to help you—do you not know that by now?"

She softly touched his face and he closed his eyes. "I don't want anything unpleasant to spoil our time together."

Raige smiled, pressing his lips against a golden curl. "You are becoming a bold little baggage. But I'm glad you came."

"I hoped you would be here," she said, touched by the love shining in his eyes. Madame Dunois was wrong about Raige. Jade knew in her heart that he meant to marry her.

"This morning you were going to tell me the first time you fell in love with me," she said, smiling up at him. "Will you tell me now?"

Amusement danced in his dark eyes. "It happened the year you were thirteen and I was nineteen. Your mother was having a lawn party, and you were playing with several other children, tossing a ball. Someone threw the ball over

your head and you ran backward, determined to catch it—
you tripped and fell into the fountain.''

"I remember that day," she said with irony. "But I can
see nothing to love in the half-drowned girl who had to
face a crowd of scandalized onlookers.''

He tilted her chin upward. "You were like a shimmering
mermaid rising to the surface. I tried not to notice how your
wet gown clung to your young curves, but discreetly concentrated on your eyes. You stood there haughtily, your hair
streaming down your face, your satin slippers ruined and
your expression daring anyone to laugh. With your head
held high, and your eyes sparkling, you announced to
everyone that you had caught the ball. Little did you know
that you took my heart with you that day, and you have
had it ever since.''

How wonderful it was to be loved by the man she had
loved for so long. "I can only remember being humiliated
because you witnessed my shame.''

As he encircled her narrow waist, his touch moved
through her body like a sword of flames. His lips were soft
as they settled on hers, and she could feel herself going
downward with him, soon to lie on the soft grass, while his
kisses intensified and her body shook with new, raw emotions.

"What I feel for you is love in its purest form, Jade.''
His voice deepened with emotion. "I want you in every
way a man can want a woman." He laced his fingers
through her hair and gazed into her green eyes. "I must
not forget how innocent you are. If I wanted to, I could
take that innocence—your eyes tell me that. But I honor
you too much to take advantage of you." His voice deepened and he laid his cheek against hers. "I shall wait until
our wedding night, making the pleasure all the sweeter.''

Jade didn't want to wait, she wanted the joy his hard body promised her virginal one. She moved toward him, her lips parted for his kiss.

With a smothered oath, Raige grabbed her to him, his lips hard and plundering, his tongue stabbing into her mouth, making her quake with yearning.

He pulled away, shaking his head. "I will not do this, Jade. You do not know the consequences of your actions."

"Do you not want me?" she asked, touching his face.

He took her hand and kissed the palm. "At this moment, it takes all my willpower to keep from giving you what you ask. For me, it would be to fulfill my most coveted dream—for you it would be dishonor. If you knew anything about a man's needs, you would require no more proof of my love for you."

Suddenly Jade was frightened and she did not know why. "I thank you for your nobility, but I . . . am afraid if . . . that tonight is . . . our last . . ."

With a muttered cry, Raige crushed her to him once more. His hands were rough as they moved over her curves, and his lips moved across her mouth, drawing a moan from her.

"I must not do this," he whispered in her ear. "Sweet, sweet, Jade, I do not know if I can stop now."

She took his hand and placed it at the laces on her riding habit. With a questioning glance, he unlaced the bodice and exposed her breasts. It seemed to take him an eternity to lower his head. When his mouth moved over her skin, she cried his name and shivered with the delight he brought her.

Raige pushed her skirt up, his hand inching toward the core of her body. She buried her face against his shoulder while his fingers worked their magic. He stroked, kissed, and caressed her until she was mindless.

When at last she thought she would die with longing, his sensuous movements became more intense and she had a new awareness of her own body. Raige knew where to touch her to fulfill her needs. She clung to him while he kissed her lips.

Suddenly he raised his head, his voice deep with passion, for while he had satisfied her, his desire was raging out of control. With superhuman strength, he withdrew his hand, pulled her skirt down, and then fastened her bodice.

Jade did not understand when he stood and walked to the stream, then bent to splash water on his face.

When he returned, he took her in his arms, cradling her head against him. "I did not intend to awaken your passion, but you did sorely tempt me. You will never know what it cost me to stop when I did."

"I—"

He saw her blush and lower her head, and he cupped her chin, making her meet his eyes. "Never feel shy with me, Jade. What happened between us was nothing to be ashamed of, because we belong to each other. There will be many other pleasures I will show you on the night you come to me as my bride."

She laid her head against his chest, trying to imagine how it would be when their bodies finally joined and they became one.

Jade pulled back to look at him. "I must go now—it's late."

"Remember your mother and father are in New Orleans."

"Oui, and everyone thinks I am with Charlene."

He smiled. "Are you telling me that no one will miss you?"

"No one. I was to stay the night with Charlene."

"Stay with me, Jade."

She came back into his arms, giving her silent consent. "Raige, when will you speak to my father about our marriage?"

"Soon. I find I am impatient to have all of you. I will not want a long engagement."

"Nor do I."

There on the sweet-smelling grass, no nightmares chased Jade's dreams that night, for she lay in Raige's loving, protective arms. When she fell asleep, it was with his warm kiss on her mouth. He pressed her to him and she nestled against his hard body.

Once during the night she awoke, fearing Raige would not be there, but he was.

"Have you not slept?" she asked sleepily.

"I have been watching you sleep," he said. "For some reason, I also fear what the future might bring. You are my heart and soul, and I will never give you up."

They came together in a burning kiss that left them both breathless.

The silver hours of dawn found Jade still curled up in Raige's arms.

## Chapter Five

IT WAS A cloudless day and a slight haze covered the land. Olivia had taken a walk to clear her head. The shadowy world that was on the edge of her mind was so absorbing that it was becoming difficult to concentrate, and at times the past and present seemed to merge into one.

She had to force herself to remember who she was, especially after the night she had spent cradled in Raige's arms.

Olivia knew that Jade was definitely growing stronger and would soon take over completely, until there was nothing left of Olivia Heartford.

Sadly, Olivia had come to love Raige with her whole being, and when she was not the embodiment of Jade, she still longed to see him.

She pondered her situation. She had never really had a life, not a happy one anyway. She had belonged to no one, and no one belonged to her. Oh, she'd had men friends, but none of them had left a lasting impression on her. There was little to go back to in Boston.

On the other hand, as Jade, she had a family and she was going to marry the man she loved—or would she? She thought of the tragic way Jade had died and realized that it would probably happen again. And then where would she be?

Olivia feared there was no way to change history—or so the experts said. Popular belief was that if one could travel back in time, and if so much as a tiny grain of sand was disturbed, it would have a domino effect on the future and bode disaster.

There had to be a way she could change the past without disturbing the future; otherwise, why was she here?

Olivia had come to believe that God had given Jade a second chance, and she was to make certain that Jade did not make the same mistakes again.

Lizette ran to the garden, with petticoats flying and her cheeks flushed with excitement. She threw her arms about Jade, hugging her tightly. ''Something wonderful yet quite disturbing is happening!''

''What are you talking about?'' Jade asked, planting a kiss on the young girl's cheek. ''Tell me quickly, before you burst.''

''It's just that I am going to miss you much more than I realized. I always knew this would happen, but not just yet.''

''What are you talking about? I'm not going anywhere.''

''Oui, you will be. I heard Papa and Mama talking to Raige, and they gave their consent for you to marry him.''

Jade clasped her hands, her face flushed with joy. ''So, he has asked them at last. I feared this day would never come.''

''I listened outside the door,'' Lizette boasted. ''Raige

told Mama that he loved you—did you know about that?''

Jade laughed down into the precocious little face. ''I did, you imp.''

''All the men love you, Jade, but I'm glad you chose Raige. I like him better than most.''

Jade clasped her sister's hand and they walked down the path. ''So do I.''

As the two girls entered the house, Gideon, the butler, approached them. ''Your papa wanted me to send you to the library the minute you came in, Miss Jade.'' He beamed, apparently aware that Raige had offered for her hand.

Jade quickly patted her hair into place and winked at her sister before she walked purposefully to the study door and knocked softly. On entering the room, she saw that her father was deep in conversation with Raige, and her mother had a pleased expression on her face.

''Jade, my dear,'' her father said in a jovial voice, ''we have something to discuss with you—come in, come in.''

''Oui, Papa,'' she said demurely, trying not to look at Raige.

''Greet our guest, daughter, and then be seated beside your mother.''

Shyly Jade raised her head to look at the man she loved, but she could not bring herself to look at his face, focusing instead on the whiteness of the cravat that lay in neat layers beneath his strong chin.

''Good morning, Raige. It's always nice to see you.''

''And it always brings me pleasure to see you, Jade,'' he said, as circumspect as she.

She slipped onto the sofa beside her mother and received a reassuring pat on the hand.

''Jade,'' her father began, ''Raige was just reminding me

that his mother has been dead these last five years, rest her soul, and Tanglewood Plantation has had no mistress in all that time. And since his father died some time back, that leaves Raige with something of a dilemma.''

Jade raised her face to her father. ''What kind of dilemma, Papa?''

''He has been telling your mother and me how difficult it is without a woman to manage the household.''

Now she glanced at Raige. He stood near the window, looking magnificent with the sunlight shimmering off his ebony windswept hair. He wore tight leggings and Hessian boots and a pleated white shirt and short-waisted tailcoat.

''I can see where that might be difficult,'' she said at last, feeling foolish because she could think of nothing clever to reply.

''Jade,'' her father continued, ''your mother and I have always agreed that you and your sister would not be married against your wishes. Raige has asked for your hand in marriage. Is this agreeable to you?''

Again she looked at Raige, and he smiled slightly.

''Oui, Papa, I find it agreeable.''

Her father looked pleased and her mother clasped Jade's hands joyfully, then hugged her. ''I can think of no more suitable match. What a happy day this is for us all,'' Emmaline said.

Jade's father took her hands and pulled her to her feet, hugging her tightly. ''Know this, Raige: When you take our Jade, you take one of our most precious jewels. We will expect you to treat her as such.''

''Have no concern on that score, Monsieur St. Clair. She will be my greatest treasure.''

Jade's father nodded in satisfaction. ''That is how it should be. Now, I believe it would be within reason for the two of you to take a stroll in the garden. There must be many things you will want to discuss.''

''Thank you, monsieur,'' Raige said, holding his hand out to Jade. His clasp was warm and stilled her trembling hand.

As they moved out the door, Emmaline St. Clair looked at her husband with an expression of elation. ''Imagine our daughter as mistress of Tanglewood!'' Her happiness suddenly turned to concern. ''He will be good to her, will he not?''

''Have no worry on that, my dear,'' her husband assured her. ''I have always said that you can tell a lot about a man's character by the way he treats his animals. No one keeps a tidier kennel for his hunting hounds than Raige. And he is against using a whip on his horses, nor does he allow anyone else to. Our daughter should be fine in his care.''

She laughed at her husband's analogy. ''Have you no shame that you would compare our daughter to a horse or hound?''

He was quiet for a moment, and then he spoke with feeling. ''I have lately been concerned that Jade might one day marry Tyrone Dunois. His hounds are underfed, their ribs showing through, and I have seen him whip a horse until it bled.''

Emmaline shivered. ''I have seen this too, and it has been a concern of mine as well.''

When they reached the garden, Raige took Jade's hand, turned it over, and planted a warm kiss on the palm. His eyes were so intense, she had to lower hers.

''You have made me a very happy man today, Jade.''

She smiled at him, thrilled by his admission. ''When you were acting so distant in front of my parents, I realized,

Raige, that although I have known you all my life, I do not really know you."

"I thought that during the night by the stream when we shared such intimacy we became quite well acquainted."

She could feel her face burn and he laughed softly.

"What do you want to know about me, Jade?"

"Everything."

His eyes swept over her beautiful upturned face, and a feeling of ownership took possession of him. "I'd say, my dearest love, that will take just about a lifetime to tell—and a lifetime is what we will have together."


Jade greeted Tyrone as he stood at the front door, hat in hand. "Have you heard the wonderful news?" she said, placing her hand on his arm.

"If you mean have I heard about your impending marriage to a man I once called my best friend—Oui, I heard," he said stonily. "Bad news travels fast, as they say."

Jade looked into his eyes, trying to discern his meaning. "I thought you would be happy for me. Let us go into the garden where we can talk undisturbed, Tyrone."

With great long strides, he moved ahead of her and waited for her to join him.

"Why have you done this, Jade?" he asked coldly.

She was puzzled at his anger. "Are you speaking of my betrothal to Raige?"

His one hand twirled and untwirled a gold watch chain in agitation. "You said nothing of this to me—neither did Raige. I had to hear it from my mother."

Jade gave him a questioning stare, and said in surprise, "And you are not happy for us?"

He regarded her with caution, then said with frosty politeness, "You know how I feel about you, you've always known. You played me for the fool, Jade.''

Even though the day was warm, she shivered, feeling winter form in her heart. ''I did no such thing, Tyrone. I will ask you to explain what you mean by that.''

He stood ramrod straight, his eyes boring into hers. ''I always thought, given time, you would come to love me.''

Her anger melted, and she was anguished that she had hurt him. If only she had known how he felt about her. ''Your mother told me as much, but I did not believe her. I promise you, Tyrone, I would never purposely hurt you.''

He looked stupefied. ''My mother spoke of my feelings for you?''

''Oui.''

He ran one hand nervously through his hair. ''Forgive me. It's just that this has all been a shock.'' He smiled tightly. ''I only need time to grow accustomed to the idea.''

She brushed her cheek against his. ''There is nothing to forgive among friends. We will pretend this never happened.''

''You won't tell Raige that I was such a fool?''

''It will be our secret.''

He tenderly touched her face. ''I do want your happiness above everything else; I had only hoped it would be with me.'' Without another word, Tyrone turned and walked away.

Thick fog suddenly blanketed the land, and Jade walked numbly into the darkness. The black mist of dread engulfed her and she gripped the railing of the garden gate, which was cold beneath her hands.

She shivered as a raw wind hit her in the face with the force of a blow.

\*     \*     \*

Jade was so busy with the many social gatherings held in her honor that there was little time to think of anything else. Then there was her trousseau to be fitted, and, of course, her wedding gown.

To her disappointment, she had not seen much of Raige. But it was planting season, and as master of a large plantation, he was needed at Tanglewood.

Jade stood perfectly straight as she was laced into the creamy white silk wedding gown made of brocade with sprays of cream flowers. A long train trailed behind her, and she could imagine how it would look as she walked down the aisle to join her love in marriage.

The dressmaker stood back with a look of satisfaction. "A perfect fit, mademoiselle."

"Jade, dearest, you will make a lovely bride. Wait until Raige sees you!" her mother exclaimed.

The gossamer lace veil was placed on Jade's head. It drifted softly across her face. She caught her breath as a feeling of foreboding swirled around in her mind. The wind sounded mournful as it rustled the leaves on the magnolia tree, and it seemed to whisper, "You will never be a bride."

Jade yanked the veil from her head and tossed it on the bed, covering her ears with her hands to block out the sound. "I am weary. I will try on no more gowns today."

Emmaline nodded for the dressmaker to leave, then she hugged Jade to her. "You are just tired, dear. Why don't you rest a bit."

Jade wanted to tell her mother about the feeling of deep foreboding that would give her no peace, but Emmaline would only worry.

She closed her eyes and thought of Raige, and was caught by a longing so sharp it was almost painful. She wanted desperately to make him a good wife. She would give him sons with his same dark eyes and sense of honor, and daughters with his wonderful humor.

Again she heard the voice, this time in the deep recesses of her mind.

"You will never be mistress of Tanglewood Plantation!"

# Chapter Six

B ETTY ALLENDALE CHATTED as she moved about the already immaculate living room, straightening a picture, centering a vase on a table, picking an imaginary speck of dust from the arm of the sofa.

"Tonight will be the masked ball I wrote you about. It's quite fun, really," she said, thinking it might be good to distract Olivia. "If you didn't bring a costume, we'll find you something suitable."

"Oh, I brought a costume. I had it made by a seamstress in Boston. It's a lovely creation. I'm going as Juliet." She did not tell Betty that she had once seen the gown in a dream, when Jade had worn it to a masquerade party.

"Good. The ball will last into the wee hours of the morning, so you had better rest this afternoon."

Olivia could not keep the excitement out of her voice. "Will there be a lot of people there?"

"But of course. We inhabitants of New Orleans never miss an opportunity to have a party, and a masquerade is always the most fun."

"Where will the ball be held?" Olivia asked with interest.

"This year it will be at another inn. It was once Brevelle Plantation."

"That was the home of Jade's friend Charlene before she married Tyrone," Olivia said, going over in her mind what she knew about the woman.

"Yes, it was. Sadly, Tyrone and Charlene never had children, so the plantation fell into ruin, and much of the rich bottom land was reclaimed by the swamp."

"Pity," Olivia said, her mind focused on the red gown and mask she would wear tonight. If only she could meet her Romeo, someone to love her, then perhaps she would not be so caught up in the life of a girl who had lived so long ago.

Dawn burst upon the land with the luster of bright sunlight. Jade yawned, stretching her arms over her head, watching the maid move about the chamber, tidying as she went. Remembering that today was the beginning of the carnival season, she threw aside the coverlet and slipped out of bed. Tonight she would be a guest at the most exciting party of the year, a private costume ball that was attended by all the elite families of New Orleans.

Jade had been looking forward to the masquerade for months, hoping Raige would be her escort, but she had neither seen nor heard from him in over three weeks. It was with profound disappointment that she realized she would be escorted to the ball by her mother and father. Why was Raige ignoring her when their wedding was only three days hence?

Jade was filled with doubts. Did he regret asking her to marry him? What would she do if he didn't really love her?

\*    \*    \*

As far as Jade was concerned, the fun of the ball was trying to see how long she could keep her identity a secret. So she insisted on entering the ballroom alone, because everyone would recognize her mother and father, who once again wore their Caesar and Cleopatra costumes, the same ones they wore every year.

The room seemed to explode with shimmering lights, and Jade was equally shimmering in her red gossamer gown and matching red mask. Atop her head she wore a veil that concealed the color of her hair and atop the veil she wore a beaded cap.

Jade had taken great pains to keep her costume a secret, and she was irritated when she advanced into the room and several people greeted her by name.

The ball was not as much fun as it had been in previous years. Jade had hoped that she could spend some time with Raige, but as the evening progressed, it was apparent that he would not be attending.

Charlene appeared at Jade's side and whispered in her ear, "What a calamity. Everyone knows you are Juliet and I am Queen Elizabeth. Would it not be a lark if we exchanged costumes? I could be you for the evening and you could be me. Of course, we would have to speak as little as possible so no one would recognize our voices."

Jade was intrigued by the idea. "Oui, let's do it! I'm certain that we could fool everyone, because they would not be expecting it."

A short time later Jade emerged from Charlene's bedroom, where a maid had helped her dress in the dark green Elizabethan gown with lace ruff and red wig. Charlene was still in her room, being laced into Jade's costume.

Jade moved through the crowd of merrymakers until

someone grabbed her about the waist and whirled her around the parquet floor.

"Charlene," he said laughingly, "you fooled no one with your disguise. We all knew you the minute we arrived."

Jade smiled, making no reply. The ball was becoming more amusing because of Charlene's plan.

It was later in the evening when the man dressed as a knight approached Jade and Charlene. He bowed before Charlene and spoke in a disguised voice, but they both knew it was Tyrone all the same.

"Fairest of the fair, my Juliet, you have won the heart of this knight," he said, unaware of the laughing glances the girls exchanged.

Delightedly, Jade watched her friend being led outside by Tyrone. Jade knew that Charlene desperately loved Tyrone, and she was certain that they would make an admirable couple, if only Tyrone would realize it for himself. Perhaps tonight Charlene would get her fondest wish.

Jade spent the rest of the evening dancing and posing as Charlene. The crowning moment came when Madame Brevelle mistook Jade for her daughter. But Jade soon became weary and made no objection when her father suggested they leave.

Once they were home, Jade went directly to her room. She undressed, carefully placing Charlene's costume across a chair so it would not be wrinkled—she would have someone return it tomorrow.

She climbed into bed and snuggled into the soft, downy mattress. As she lay there, she had the strongest feeling that something terrible was about to happen.

Her door opened slowly, and Lizette entered on tiptoes, placing a finger at her lips.

"Why are you up so late, little sister? You know Mama would scold you if she knew," Jade reprimanded mildly.

The precocious child plopped onto the foot of Jade's bed and propped her head on her hand. "Tell me all about the ball—was it glorious?"

"It's late, Lizette," she groaned. "I'll tell you every detail tomorrow."

Undaunted, Lizette swept a stray curl out of her face, looking smug. "Raige recognized you right away, didn't he?"

"Non he did not, little Miss Inquisitive. Raige did not even attend tonight."

Her sister looked perplexed. "Then why did he trick me into telling him you would be dressed as Juliet?"

"He did what! When?"

"Last week, when Mama and I were in New Orleans. I saw him at the bank and we talked while Mama was speaking to Mr. Franchette. Before I realized what he was about, he had tricked me into revealing your costume." She raised up on her knees. "I didn't mean to tell him, but he is very clever."

Jade smiled at her sister. "It is of no consequence since he did not go to the ball. Now off to bed with you—I am weary."

Her sister moved off the bed and walked to the door. "You promise to tell me about the ball in the morning?"

"I promise."

Lizette nodded and left, closing the door behind her.

Forgetting about her earlier premonition of disaster, Jade fell into a peaceful sleep, not knowing that at that moment, events were taking place that would bring the world crashing down on her!

\* \* \*

Wearing black and disguised as Romeo, Raige moved about the ballroom, searching for Jade. When he did not see her, he moved out the door and into the garden.

The night was aglow with millions of stars and he quelled his impatience to be with his love. She must be wondering why he had not come to see her for several weeks. Tonight he would explain to her that he had been overseeing the redecoration of Tanglewood because he wanted it to be perfect when he brought her home as his bride.

Hearing voices on the other side of the box hedge, Raige rounded the corner and stopped in his tracks, feeling as if his heart had just been ripped from his body. For there, with the moonlight illuminating her distinctive red gown, was Jade in another man's arms.

Charlene knew it was wrong to keep up the pretense, but it was wonderful to be alone with Tyrone and have him make love to her, even if he thought she was Jade.

"You can't marry Raige," Tyrone said, pulling her into his arms. "You love me."

Charlene said nothing, but nestled against him. Neither knew that they were being observed by jealous eyes, golden eyes that closed for a moment, feeling the agony of betrayal.

"You do love me; you know you do," Tyrone stated with assurance.

Trembling, Charlene could only nod. Oui, she loved him and she would steal this moment of happiness for herself. Surely it would do no harm. Tyrone's warm mouth bruised her tender lips in a kiss that made her giddy with delight.

"I knew it!" Tyrone exclaimed, tearing his mouth from hers. "Mother assured me that you cared for me, and if I placed my heart at your feet, you would not turn me away."

His companion did not answer.

"Jade, my dearest love, you cannot marry Raige. Not after the way you just returned my kiss."

"He's right," a deep voice spoke up from the shadows. Raige moved into the light, his face a mask of fury. "I can see how it is, Jade." His eyes moved to the woman behind the red mask, the woman he had trusted with his love, the woman who had just admitted she loved Tyrone.

Tyrone stepped back, his arm going protectively around his Juliet. "I did not intend for this to happen, Raige, but I love Jade and she loves me."

Charlene knew that she should tell Raige that she was not Jade, but it would be too humiliating. Tyrone would hate her for pretending to be Jade.

Raige moved closer, his heated gaze on Tyrone. "You know what this means?"

"I do," Tyrone said with a sneer.

Raige worked his fingers out of his glove and slapped Tyrone across the face, leaving red welts. "Tomorrow in the gardens behind St. Louis Cathedral."

"I'll be there. My second will call on you early."

In a moment of wild panic, Charlene ran down the path, seeking the sanctuary of her room. She had to get away, to hide. Oh, God, what had she done!

Olivia awakened early and went for a long walk, trying to clear her mind. She was like a sleepwalker, because the dream she'd had last night had drained her of life and substance. She now knew what had caused the duel between Raige and Tyrone, and she had to find a way to stop it—but how?

As she approached the garden, she spied Betty Allendale picking fresh flowers.

"Good afternoon," Olivia said, stopping to admire the crimson-colored tulips and dipping her head to smell their light, delicate scent.

"Good afternoon," Betty replied stiffly, looking at the pale woman rather strangely. "Can I help you with something, miss?"

"No, I was just out for a morning stroll. It's so peaceful and beautiful at this time of day."

Betty gathered her bounty of flowers and smiled tightly, her eyes frosty. "You are welcome to walk on my grounds if you keep to the path. This is private property, and I do not encourage trespassers."

Olivia was suddenly shaken by a cold dread that seemed to surround her heart. There was no recognition in Betty's eyes—she did not seem to know her. "Surely you are joking, Betty. I'm your houseguest."

"No, you're not, and I don't appreciate your trying that subterfuge." Her hostess's eyes flashed and she shook her head, her usual serene expression replaced with one of distrust. "I do not welcome strangers to my grounds, because this is not only an inn, it is my home as well."

Olivia was frantic, her eyes unseeing, her mind unfeeling as she tried to hold on to her identity. "Betty," she whispered through trembling lips, "you have to know who I am!"

Now there was fear in Betty's eyes. She took several quick steps backward, her eyes darting toward the house, planning her escape from this crazed woman. "If you don't leave now, I shall be forced to call for help."

The now familiar swirling mist descended, consuming Olivia within its murky depths. Reaching out her arms, she cried out to Betty, knowing that the woman was not even aware what was happening just a few feet away from her.

She also knew in that moment that she had ceased to exist as Olivia. She had no more substance than the mist that consumed her.

There would be no one who would mourn Olivia Heartford, if indeed she had ever really existed. There was no sadness in her heart as she became completely absorbed by Jade's world. But she must fight to retain some of what was Olivia if she was going to prevent the tragedy that would take place on a spring morning in 1813.

"Please, God," she prayed, "show me a way to help Jade St. Clair!"

# Chapter Seven

IT WAS STILL dark when Charlene dashed up the stairs, not even stopping to catch her breath; nor did she bother to knock on Jade's bedroom door, but threw it open and hurried to Jade's sleeping form.

"Wake up!" she cried, jerking on Jade's arm. "You have to help me; I've done something dreadful!"

Jade blinked her eyes, trying to focus on what Charlene was saying. Her friend had always overdramatized everything. "Tell me what has happened," she said, yawning.

Charlene tearfully explained what had occurred after Jade had left the ball the night before. "How could I know my deception would lead to a duel?" she sobbed. "It will be my fault if anyone is killed!"

Jade's mind was racing ahead as she stripped off her nightgown and took her riding habit from the wardrobe. "How could you have been so foolish, Charlene? You allowed Tyrone to believe he was making love to me, and you did not explain to Raige when he came to the same conclusion."

"I know what I did was wrong. I lay awake for hours, trying to decide what to do. Someone has to stop them before Raige kills Tyrone."

Jade turned so Charlene could fasten her blouse in the back. "Where is the duel to be fought?"

"In the city, behind the cathedral."

Jade nodded. "While I finish dressing, go to the stables and have someone saddle my horse and have a boat made ready to take me to New Orleans. And hurry, Charlene! Even now it may be too late."

As Charlene rushed out of the room, Jade pulled on her riding boots, her hands shaking so badly she could not control them. In the back of her mind, it seemed she had lived this day before. It was a vague feeling, a dream—she wasn't sure what.

Jade moved quickly toward the door and paused. Turning back, she saw the Elizabethan costume where she had placed it the night before. Grabbing it up, she ran out of the room and down the stairs.

She was the only one who could stop this madness.

After leading her horse off the boat, Jade frantically urged the animal into a thundering gallop as she raced toward the cathedral. When she neared her destination, she could hear the sound of rapiers echoing off the stone walls of the garden.

Not waiting for her mount to come to a halt, Jade leaped to the ground and hurried in the direction of the duelists.

For a moment, her eyes rested on Raige, who was poised with his rapier ready to strike. He was white-lipped, unforgiving, his features savage, intent on nothing but killing Tyrone.

She watched as Raige's sword flashed with lightning, his

moves like quicksilver, driving poor Tyrone backward.

She cried out when she saw that Tyrone had already been wounded and his shirtfront was bloody.

"Stop this at once!" Jade cried, clutching the beaded costume and racing toward the two men.

In desperation, she reached Raige, taking his arm. "Please allow me to explain."

He gave her a long, level stare. Where once his tawny eyes had been warm and loving, they now appeared dispassionate and unforgiving. Roughly, he shoved her aside, turning once more to his opponent, his voice laced with sarcasm. "Would you hide behind a woman's petticoat, Tyrone?"

Tyrone raised his blade. "Keep Jade's name out of this," he replied with the same anger. "This is between you and me."

"Ah," Raige replied sarcastically, "so noble of you to defend the lady's name, when it was you who tarnished it."

"My name needs no defense from either of you," Jade said angrily.

Neither man seemed to hear her as they once again became locked in their deadly contest.

Jade watched in horror as Raige's rapier slashed Tyrone's face, drawing blood. Tyrone fell to his knees, too weak to stand.

Jade still clutched the costume she had brought to show them, but the combat had gone too far for either of them to listen to reason.

In that moment, she saw scenes of her own death, and a small voice inside her head directed her next actions.

Tossing the costume at Raige's feet, Jade hurried to Tyrone and ripped his rapier from his numb fingers. With the sun reflecting off the blade, she turned to Raige.

"If you want to avenge yourself on someone, try me. I am as blameless as Tyrone."

Raige looked at her as if she'd lost her mind. Then his eyes became incredibly sad. "You have the face of a seductress, my lovely, but I saw only the innocence of an angel. There is no more fool than I to have placed my heart with you."

In frustration, Jade slashed the sword through the air. "Do we fight or talk?" she asked heatedly.

Raige could only stare at her. She was glorious with her hair flying in the wind and her eyes sparkling with anger, a goddess ready to do battle regardless of the fact that she had never before held a rapier.

"Well, which is it to be?" she demanded.

Raige's hand trembled as he reached out to touch her face. "Do you love Tyrone so much that you are willing to die in his stead?" There was sadness in his voice, but accusation as well, the accusation of a man who thought he'd been betrayed by two people he trusted.

Jade licked her dry lips. "You fool—I love you—I always have. But if you keep on with this madness, I may reconsider."

Raige lowered his blade, looking at her mistrustfully. "How do you explain my finding you in Tyrone's arms last night?"

Jade speared the costume she'd dropped earlier and extended it to Raige on the end of Tyrone's sword. "That, my husband-to-be, is the gown *I* wore last night. Charlene and I exchanged costumes early in the evening because everyone recognized us."

She turned her attention to Tyrone. "It was Charlene you were kissing last night, not me."

Tyrone struggled forward. "You need not lie. We both know it was you."

Jade's eyes blazed like green fire. "How dare you! I have told you on more than one occasion that I love Raige—is that not so? What made you think I had changed my mind?"

Tyrone met her eyes and realized his mistake. "But last night I thought—"

"Well, you thought wrong. You can ask my mother and father if you don't believe me. They took me home an hour before Raige arrived at the ball. I was asleep while you played out your little scene in the garden."

"How did you know about it?" Raige asked, not ready to believe her, even though he wanted to.

"Charlene came charging into my bedroom this morning, babbling about how she was the cause of the duel. I should have left the two of you on your own. I don't know why I bothered to come here."

By now, Charlene had arrived, frantically looking for Tyrone. Seeing him bloody, she ran to him. "What has Raige done to you?" she cried, dabbing her handkerchief at the wound on his face.

Tyrone looked confused. "Was it you I kissed last night, Charlene?"

Charlene looked at Jade pleadingly, but Jade had had enough.

"Tell them the truth," she demanded.

Charlene blushed and lowered her head. "I . . . oui, it was me."

Raige looked at her cynically. "You would lie for Jade."

Jade tossed the sword down and looked at him in disgust. "Do you think so little of me that you believe I would betray the vows I made to you? I do not want to marry a man who doubts my word or my virtue. What kind of marriage would we have, Raige?''

The three young people watched Jade as she walked away from them.

''You'd better go after her,'' Tyrone said at last. ''I have a feeling that if you don't, you'll lose her. And you two belong together.''

A slow smile lit Raige's face. ''You are right.'' Forcefully, he threw his rapier upward, where it wedged in an overhanging branch of an oak tree. Without pausing, he ran after Jade, calling her name.

Jade had reached her horse, and since there was no one to help her, she was having difficulty mounting the sidesaddle. When she saw Raige approaching, she glared at him.

''Go back and finish what you started. And I am glad I know you for the kind of man you are. Are you going to challenge every man who looks at me to a duel?''

Laughingly, he came to her and turned her resisting face up to his. ''I can't promise not to. You see, I'm hopelessly in love with you.''

She lowered her eyes, studying the scuffed toe of her riding boot. ''I don't . . . love you anymore.''

He tilted her chin upward. ''Oui, you do. Your lips might deny it, but your eyes say otherwise.'' There was contrition in the depths of his golden eyes, and something more. ''Can you ever forgive me for being such a fool?''

In that moment, Jade heard a voice in her head, a faint voice. She knew not where it came from, but it urged her to take the happiness Raige offered.

''Oui,'' she said at last. ''I forgive you, and I did not mean it when I said I no longer loved you.''

There was triumph in Raige's eyes as he pulled her to

him. "For now and forever, and even beyond, Jade, I will love you."

It was a day like no other. The sun was shining and the birds were singing a melodious song that sweetened the air.

Jade hurried down the aisle, her lace veil trailing behind her, her gaze on the man who stood at the altar.

As Raige waited, his dark eyes locked with hers, and in that moment, Jade knew such intense happiness that she thought her heart would burst.

She took his hand, and there before God, friends, and family, she pledged him her life and love for all eternity.

## Epilogue

BETTY ALLENDALE GREETED the three young couples who had just arrived from New Orleans. The Bridal Veil Inn was prosperous, often booked a year in advance, and most often by honeymooners who found the isolation and the history of the old plantation house romantic.

Betty smiled as she recited the same historical facts she had told for years.

"The inn, of course, draws its name from Jade St. Clair's wedding veil. Jade lived in the early 1800s and was as spunky as she was beautiful. She once challenged the man she loved to a duel. She married that same man, and she and Raige Belmanoir lived happily until the end of their days. They had five children and nineteen grandchildren, and twentieth-century descendants include a senator, three doctors, two of whom are women, five lawyers, and me, your hostess."

She paused, gazing upon the faces of her guests, who were hanging on her every word.

"On behalf of us all, I bid you welcome to Bridal Veil Inn."

# Man of Her Dreams

### Virginia Brown

# Chapter One

*Holly Springs, Mississippi, 1994*

"YOU DON'T THINK they'll actually tear down the old house, do you? I'd forgotten it's so beautiful." Amanda Brandon Cresswell paused, gazing around the shadowed entrance hall. Though it had been more than two years since she'd come back to her childhood home for a visit, the house seemed to envelop her in a silent, dusty welcome. "I don't want them to destroy it."

Jessica Griffith stepped inside with a rattle of keys and a muffled exclamation. "But they probably will, Manda. And it's about time. This monstrosity looks as if it should be condemned. Why, the acreage the house sits on is worth more than the house itself."

Amanda stifled a sharp defense, saying instead, "It's been in my family since it was built in 1852. It has historical value, I would think."

"It might have at one time. Now it's too run-down." Tilting her head just as she had when they were both little girls playing dress-up in the third-story attic, Jessica gave her a sympathetic smile. "Look at it this way—it's for the best. With your great-aunt Hannah in the nursing home these past two years before she died, the trust fund ran so low it couldn't take care of her as well as this ol' house.''

Amanda sighed. "Poor Aunt Hannah. She never expected to outlive my daddy. When he died, I think she just ignored the fact. I wish someone had told me about the will not being changed. Now it's too late. According to my attorney, there's nothing I can do to keep the house and property from being sold.''

"It's your mean cousin Ronald's fault, but I guess that doesn't help any.''

"No.'' Amanda drew in a deep breath. "It doesn't help at all. I wish his granddaddy had gone to California with the rest of the Scotts. Then this wouldn't be happening.''

Jessica was silent, not pointing out the obvious truth that if Amanda's grandfather had properly provided for such a contingency in his will, the house would still belong just to the Brandons. But somehow Ronald Scott had found the old deeds and discovered that the limitations had run out. He'd immediately filed a claim. The judgment had been levied at a time when Amanda had been caught up in her own affairs in Memphis and Great-aunt Hannah was already in a Holly Springs nursing home. Without Hannah having appointed a proxy, Scott had been successful in his suit to have the property sold and the proceeds divided between all the remaining heirs on both sides of the family.

"Too bad your cousin wouldn't agree to try to get the house listed on the National Register of Historic Homes,'' Jessica said after a long moment of silence. "But maybe it's best this way. After all, you'll get a lot of money.''

"I'd prefer keeping the house in the family. I even made the Scotts an offer to share ownership of the house as well as the surrounding acreage if they would agree not to sell to developers. They refused.''

Amanda's throat tightened. Coming on the heels of other tragedies in her life, this was almost overwhelming. To keep back her tears, she focused on the delicately carved plaster frieze above the parlor door. Figures of knights errant and beautiful heroines had infused her imagination as a child. Now they left her with poignant memories as blurred with time as the plaster figures. Yet the two-story red brick antebellum home held more than just childhood memories of happier times; it was her only legacy.

Jessica turned to look at her, her head tilted to one side and a faint smile on her lips. ''You know, you should be living in this house. It fits you better than anyone I can imagine. You were just born in the wrong time.''

''What do you mean by that, Jess?''

''Oh, you know—wearing long skirts, little white lace gloves, a big hat and ribbon sash under your chin—like we used to play dress-up when we were little girls, remember?''

She laughed. ''I remember. You always wanted to be Rhett Butler.''

Jessica grinned. ''Why, with your wicked green eyes and blonde hair, you'd have given Scarlett O'Hara a run for her money with Rhett. You even remind me of your aunt Hannah a little bit.''

''An eccentric old maid?''

''Oh, you're not an old maid. You've been married. No, I meant . . . romantic. That's it. You're the romantic type, all dreamy eyes, soft smiles, and long blonde hair. You were just born a hundred years too late. I always thought you fit in here.'' Jessica shrugged. ''I never have understood about that ridiculous family feud between the Scotts and the Brandons,'' she said frankly. ''Not that it matters.

Nothing can save the house now. Unless you can change history.''

"I only wish I could," Amanda murmured. "But I know that's impossible."

Wandering into the parlor, Jessica wiped a hand over the elegantly carved edge of the heartpine mantel gracing the fireplace, then grimaced at the dust on her fingers. "It's probably just as well. Heartpine is worth a fortune nowadays. Can hardly find it anywhere, and collectors and builders pay a pretty price for it. This house will be worth much more piece by piece."

Amanda winced, and glancing up, Jessica added hurriedly, "You did everything you could, Manda. But once Hannah died and the ghouls demanded their portion of the inheritance in cash, there was nothing you could do but sell."

"I know." Amanda wandered restlessly from the front parlor to the curved staircase leading to the second-floor bedrooms. The handrail was worn smooth and satiny by generations of Brandon hands sliding along its elegant length. Golden wood had darkened with time and use. "You'd think," she murmured, caressing the smooth finish, "that the Scotts would want to keep it intact. After all, it's their inheritance as well as mine."

"Obviously they don't. I hear developers plan to put a mall here." Jessica's keys clattered like a metallic rattlesnake as she lifted her hand to pat a stray strand of hair back into place. "You know how large corporations pay top dollar for prime locations, so I imagine the lure of money would fast overcome any kind of sentiment they might feel. And it's not as if any of them even care about the old house. At least you came back here as often as you could for a while."

Amanda shrugged. "After all, I did spend most of my

childhood here before my parents were killed. Lord, what was I—fifteen?—when I went to Memphis to live with Grandma Weaver? I would have been a junior in high school the next year. Everything happened so fast, it seemed; my world turned upside down in the blink of an eye . . . I could hardly bear to think about this house for a long time. It held so many memories for me, and I was too young to be able to separate the good from the bad. Poor Aunt Hannah. I know she wondered why I didn't come visit her for so long.''

''Somehow,'' Jessica murmured, ''I think she understood. She always spoke of you when we chanced to meet, and always said how you would be back soon.''

''It was five years before I could make myself return, though, and that wasn't until Aunt Hannah got sick the first time.'' Amanda sighed. ''She was so glad to see me that I felt guilty it had taken me so long. But she just gave me a pat on the cheek and told me that she understood, and it was as if I'd never left. Then I met and married Alan—and things got so bad so quick, it seemed.''

Jessica shifted uneasily. ''I really was sorry to hear about Alan, Manda. This has been a rough few years for you, hasn't it?''

''Pretty rough. Grandma Weaver died, then Alan's cancer, and now Aunt Hannah's gone—for the first time in eleven years, I'm completely alone. I've no family left.''

''Except the Scotts, and all of Holly Springs knows they haven't spoken to the Brandons in years.'' Jessica reached out and put a hand on Amanda's arm. ''Hey, I'm always here for you. Just like when we were little. Remember our secret place?''

Amanda laughed. ''Not as secret as we thought—a tree

house only twenty yards from the house had to be as obvious as you can get.''

"But we thought it was well hidden, and that's what really mattered then. Maybe our tree house is gone, but the tree's still there. And there's always my kitchen. You can always come back to Holly Springs to live, you know.''

Shrugging, Amanda said vaguely, "I've still got a job in Memphis, and an apartment in a nice area, and—''

"And ghosts. Alan's dead, Manda. There's nothing in Memphis to keep you anymore. He was sick for so long, and you plumb wore yourself out taking care of him. It's over. You can go anywhere.''

Amanda managed to shake her head. "I can't even think of anything like that right now, Jess. Everything's so overwhelming that I just feel tired.''

"I understand. Well, I should go. I'll be back in the morning to help you itemize everything for the auction. Sure you'll be all right here by yourself?''

Amanda forced a confident smile. "I'll be fine. You did stock the pantry with a few necessities for me, didn't you?''

"Of course. Tea and sandwich fixin's.'' Jessica leaned toward her and kissed the air by Amanda's cheek. "See you early, sugar. Get a good night's rest.''

Following her as far as the wide front porch, Amanda gazed across the front lawn which was dotted with red and white clover. She drew in a deep breath, relishing the fragrances of honeysuckle and the lemony-sweet tang of magnolia blossoms. Only three of the once numerous magnolia trees were left, the others having fallen to time and weather over the years since they'd first been planted. Somewhere there were old family photographs of smiling people in front of the house in its early days, when the towering oaks that now lined the long driveway were still saplings.

Shadows stretched across the lawn; lightning bugs blinking in the waxy green leaves of the magnolias reminded her of earlier, happier times at Oakleigh. Sitting on the top porch step, Amanda keenly felt the losses in her life: her parents, grandparents, husband, and most recently her last close relative, Great-aunt Hannah. All gone. And now even Oakleigh would be taken from her.

As dusk faded into the deep shrouds of night, Amanda rose from the porch and went into the large, empty house. It seemed to close around her, enfold her with memories and wishes.

# Chapter Two

MORNING BROUGHT HUMID temperatures along with bright, hazy sunlight. Dressed in shorts and a T-shirt, Amanda went downstairs to eat breakfast. Jessica arrived a short time later, letting herself in the front door with the key in the mailbox. Even from the kitchen at the back of the house, Amanda could hear the muted echoes of the front door closing behind Jess.

"Mercy," Jessica complained as she came through the pantry into the kitchen, "it's as hot as blazes out there already, and it's only June." She slung her purse and keys to the kitchen table. Wearing a thin organdy blouse and white linen shorts, she looked more like a model than a woman about to help sort through the accumulated dust and belongings of generations. She eyed Amanda with a lifted brow. "Aren't you hot, sugar?"

"Yes. I don't know why they never wired this house for air conditioning." Chair legs scraped loudly against the linoleum floor as Amanda got up from the table and put her empty cereal bowl in the huge white porcelain kitchen sink.

She said over her shoulder, "Let's start at the top of the house while it's still fairly cool. We're liable to be baked if we don't."

"A great idea. I'll bring a fan up to the attic. Far as I know, no one's even opened that door for years, so it's bound to be pretty stuffy."

Amanda climbed the steep back stairs to the attic, tucking her hair up into a knot atop her head as she went. It took several moments of fumbling with the glass knob of the attic door before she successfully wrenched it open. The door creaked loudly and a rush of hot, stale air filled the narrow staircase. It smelled like musty old papers and years of dust, and she blinked as she felt for the light switch. A single bare bulb swayed overhead, casting patches of light and shadow over furniture, stacks of crates, and old trunks.

Electricity had been added to the house only about forty years before, and wires could be seen dangling from old eaves and tracing down the outside of walls. Trapped heat made it difficult to breathe.

Stepping gingerly around a precariously leaning stack of wooden crates, Amanda made her way across the crowded floor to the small window that looked out over the front lawn. It took several moments of trying and a broken fingernail to pry the window open. Finally, it slid upward with a screech and rattle of the wooden frame. A breeze filtered into the attic, smelling of fresh-cut grass and honeysuckle.

Amanda leaned her palms on the wide wooden sill and gazed at the magnolia trees. Heavy branches rose above the rooftop of the house and all but obscured a view of the driveway. Memories of happier times returned in a rush. God, she would miss this old house. . . .

"Manda?"

She turned to see Jessica in the doorway, blinking in the

dim light and gingerly holding an ancient fan. Once it was plugged into the single outlet in the attic, the old black wire fan stirred the stuffy air and dust, its blades whirring loudly. Amanda sneezed several times.

"I think it was better without it," she muttered as she readjusted the fan to blow in another direction.

"Probably." Jessica stood in the center of the attic, hands on her hips as she gazed at the clutter. "It will take a week to go through all this. You should have hired a professional."

"I can't imagine allowing a stranger to go through these mementos and decide what's valuable and what's not," Amanda murmured as she peered into a wooden crate. "Oh, look—an old album." She blew a layer of dust from the leather cover before opening it. Several metal squares tumbled from between the thick pages, and she barely caught them. "I remember seeing this," she exclaimed. "Aunt Hannah used to show me this album when I was a child. See this man?" She held up one of the tintypes as Jessica peered over her shoulder. "I used to dream about him."

"Which one?" Jessica asked as she lightly brushed away a film of dust from the metal photograph.

"The tall, dark-haired man in the background. I'm not certain why, but he caught my imagination when I was a child. I guess because no one in the family knew who he was, or could remember why he was in a family portrait." Gazing at the lean man with the crooked smile, Amanda felt as if she were seeing the face of an old friend again. There was character in the firm set of his jaw and in his clear gaze, implied strength in his wide shoulders. She wished she had a name to apply to the image, something besides forgotten dreams.

Tapping a finger on another old tin photograph, Jessica said, "Who is that?"

"Let me see...." Amanda peered closely at the photograph, but it wasn't until she turned it over that she saw someone had written on the paper back. The ink was faded, but she could make out the name. "James Brandon—oh, yes. This is my great-great-grandfather. The feud started with him, I think."

"The feud between the Scotts and Brandons?"

Amanda nodded. "I think so. Lord, I was told all this so long ago, and it's hard to remember all the details. I do remember that it was back during the Civil War—or as Aunt Hannah used to say, 'The War of Northern Aggression.' James Brandon's half brother—they had the same mother—married a woman who had been promised to James. Apparently this caused a big uproar, but it wasn't the final cause of the feud, according to Aunt Hannah."

"Sounds like a good enough reason to me," Jessica muttered with a lifted brow.

"To me, too. Michael Scott and Grandfather James lived here in the house together for a while after the wedding. The feud started later, if I remember correctly. If you ask me, I'd guess that it had its roots in the fact that Michael wed the woman his brother wanted. Aunt Hannah never did give the real reason. Said it was over and done, and the family scattered to the four winds. Half of them ran off to South America."

"South America? What on earth for?"

"After the war, a lot of the men in our family who'd fought for the Confederacy migrated farther south to escape Reconstruction. I imagine that the dark-haired man I used to dream about was one of them."

Jessica tapped the metal square thoughtfully. "He's quite

handsome, isn't he? I suppose that's why he caught your imagination. I wonder who he was?''

Laughing, Amanda teased, ''The man of my dreams, of course.'' She tucked the loose tintypes into the album, then closed it and placed it gently on the floor. ''This pile will be the keeper pile. Things to be sold will go on the other side.''

''Sounds like a good plan to me.'' Jessica reached for the notebook and pen she'd brought with her. ''Now, what we need to do is start listing things to be auctioned. What's first?''

Amanda held up a crimping iron. ''Shall we start with this?''

Scribbling on a clean page, Jessica muttered, ''That ought to bring fifty cents.''

Three hours later, the stack of items to be auctioned had filled five pages and one side of the attic. Leather-bound trunks, dishes, framed portraits, old furniture, and even mule harnesses cluttered the floor. A cheval mirror tarnished with age and sagging in its frame leaned against one wall.

Jessica raked a hand through her frosted hair, leaving a smudge of dust on her forehead. ''Dealing with all this junk is exhausting. And it's unbearably hot up here. Let's stop for a while.''

Pulling forward a heavy, dust-covered trunk, Amanda said, ''One more thing. I found this trunk behind some loose boards in that alcove. Someone obviously hid it there, and I'm dying to see what's inside.''

''Lordy, it's hot enough to fry eggs up here, Manda.''

''What if it's hidden treasure?'' Amanda coaxed. ''I might find enough to save the house. Come on, Jess. Help

me. Then we'll go down for lunch and cooler air, I promise.''

"All right. But I'm more than ready for some iced tea.''

It took a moment to open the trunk's latch, but finally
they managed it. The smell of moth crystals stung Amanda's nose as she lifted the top. Frothy layers of tissue paper
crackled when she pushed them aside.

"Old clothing,'' she murmured, carefully lifting the gar-
ment beneath the tissue paper. Satin folds slid over her arms
in a rustling fall. Then her breath caught. "Oh, my—it's
the most beautiful thing. . . .''

"What is?'' Jessica peered over her shoulder. Her nose
wrinkled at the smell of moth crystals. "Ugh. Those things
still stink after all these years. Why, Manda—I've seen that
dress before.''

"You have?'' Amanda gently shook it free, and tiny
glimmers of pearls glinted in the musty light. "It's not one
we ever used to play dress-up. I'd remember this dress. Are
you sure?''

"Yes. Earlier today, I saw that dress in one of the old
portraits we found stacked against a wall . . . let me find
it.''

While Jessica rummaged through the framed portraits
they had leaned up against the wall for later inspection,
Amanda unfolded the gown as carefully as possible. A few
of the pearls fell to the floor with tiny *ping*s, scattering.
Even though time had yellowed the satin, she could see
that it had once been ivory. Delicate lace edged the high
neck and sleeves, and had been stitched down the bodice
in a ruffle that must have once been full. Now it was flat-
tened and limp.

"It looks like a wedding dress,'' she murmured as she
held up the gown.

"Here it is," Jessica called, and Amanda draped the gown over the trunk and joined her. They angled a heavy gilded frame against the wall and stood back to gaze at the painting. "This portrait used to be up here in the attic when we were little girls," Jessica said after a moment. "Don't you remember?"

"Hey—I do remember. Only because Aunt Hannah once told me that this was a portrait of a ghost. She said it was whispered that she'd died unhappy, and her poor spirit still haunted Oakleigh years after her death. It scared me out of my wits as a child, but I never saw or heard any signs of a ghost, so I just forgot about it in time."

"Who was she?"

Frowning, Amanda said, "Aunt Hannah called her Deborah. I can't remember if she was close family, or a distant relative. I'm not certain why we have this portrait of her, except maybe because she's supposed to have haunted the house for a while. Oh, look—this was painted in front of the house. The porch looks almost the same. Look at the trees, how small they were then. . . ."

A shaft of hazy light from the window fell across the portrait of a youthful woman garbed in the gown and seated on a bench in front of the house. A thick line of young magnolia trees provided the background; pale, creamy blossoms framed the woman's rather sad face.

"If this is a wedding portrait," Jessica said, "it must not have been a love match. She looks much too unhappy."

"Not according to family legend. Deborah went ahead with the sitting for this portrait even though her husband had just been killed in some war—Spanish-American, maybe? Anyway, she was pregnant, which made the tale more tragic. She said her husband had wanted the painting done, so now it would be a memorial to him and their love.

According to Great-aunt Hannah, she never remarried.''

"Just haunted the place. Great.'' Jessica replaced the portrait against the wall and covered it again. "No wonder this dress has been packed away and lost all these years. It's unlucky. Well,'' she said, dusting her palms briskly, "shall we have lunch now?''

Afternoon brought heat with it, and the attic was left to be finished the next morning. By dusk, Amanda and Jessica had managed to clear out most of the second-floor bedrooms, itemizing the scanty contents quickly and efficiently.

"My back is aching,'' Jessica complained as they sat on the front porch sipping iced tea and watching evening shadows creep over the lawn. "All that junk—it's amazing what can be accumulated in so many years.''

Amanda sipped her tea, thinking of those who had once lived in this house. Old memories had been sparked with every find, whether a crystal perfume bottle from the twenties or an 1890s' volume of poetry with spidery writing inscribed to a sweetheart on the front page. Bittersweet memories of forgotten times . . . Her chair creaked loudly as she rocked forward. Crickets hummed in the still, sultry air.

"I wonder,'' Jessica mused, "what would have happened to this house if not for that feud.''

"I imagine it would remain in the family. I wish I knew the real reason for the feud.''

"Well, you'll probably never find out. That information is lost to history.'' Jessica rose, pressing a hand to the small of her back and groaning. "I'm going home to my husband. I'll be back in the morning to help you finish up the attic.''

"I appreciate your help,'' Amanda said softly. "You're a good friend.''

Jessica grinned. "Well, somebody has to be nice to you big-city girls who run off and leave us small-town hicks behind. Who would we have to envy if not for you?"

But once Jessica left and the house seemed to enfold her in its embrace again, Amanda felt as if she had come home. Losing this house was painful. But she had the next few days here, and she was determined to wrest all the comfort and memories she could from them. Tomorrow would come soon enough. It always did.

## Chapter Three

I<small>T WAS A</small> hot night. Stuffy. Amanda sighed irritably and tried once more to get comfortable. The second-story bedroom windows were open, the black wire fan was on the dresser, and she was wearing only a thin-strapped nightie of ivory silk that reached midthigh, but she was still uncomfortably warm. Maybe she should read. There was a stack of books in the attic, along with decades of old magazines that might prove boring enough to put her to sleep. And if nothing else, it would at least make her insomnia informative. Sighing, she swung her legs over the edge of the bed and fumbled for a robe.

The wood floor was surprisingly cool on the bare soles of her feet as she went down the hallway to the back stairs leading to the attic. The bottom step creaked loudly beneath her weight. It was dark on the stairs, and Amanda muttered to herself as she felt her way along.

Perseverance got her up the dark stairs to the attic door. The door was ajar, propped open with a heavy flatiron she'd found in one of the wooden crates. The irons made great doorstops, and she'd wanted the attic to air out before the next morning. She opened the door wider and stepped inside.

Dim patches of moonlight dappled the floor, filtered by the heavy magnolia trees that shaded the house. Fumbling for the switch, she turned on the light. The single bare bulb swung back and forth in a breeze from the open window, casting patches of light and shadow. Amanda scanned the attic floor for the stacks of books she'd placed aside. One of them caught her eye, a leather-bound journal tied with faded ribbon.

Lifting it curiously, she untied the ribbon and flipped open the leather cover. Neatly scrawled on the fly page was the name *Deborah Jordan Scott* and the date *January 1864*. She mulled over the name for several minutes, then caught her breath with excitement.

Could this be the same Deborah in the portrait? If so, the unnamed husband was probably Michael Scott—her distant uncle and great-great-grandfather's half-brother. This journal might possibly hold the key to the family feud, she thought as she turned the pages. But to her intense disappointment, moths and rain had apparently destroyed all of the journal entries. Only scattered words were still legible, and those were blurred.

Regretfully, she closed the journal and retied the ribbon. No help there. When she glanced up, she saw the dress she was certain had belonged to Deborah Jordan Scott. It was still where she'd left it, draped gracefully over the open trunk.

Moving around a stack of books, Amanda reached for the dress. The fabric felt cool and satiny, the folds of material rustling slightly in the silence. She held it up to herself and stepped to the old cheval mirror propped against a wall. As a child playing dress-up, long skirts had trailed the floor and tripped her many times. But what would it be like to really wear the gowns of the antebellum period? Scarlett O'Hara had made it look so glamorous, when the reality was probably uncomfortable, inconvenient—and hopelessly romantic.

Amanda yielded to impulse and slipped out of her robe and unfastened the pearl buttons on the dress. She stepped into it rather awkwardly, slid her arms into the sleeves, and pulled it up. Her silk nightgown wadded up around her waist. It took her a moment to wriggle it down before she could adjust the satin folds of the wedding gown. Drat. It would be almost impossible to fasten all the buttons. Women back then must have been very agile. Or employed a maid to help them dress.

When she had most of them done, she turned to peer into the mottled glass of the old mirror. Even in the dim light, she could see that the gown had lost none of its beauty over the years. It fell in simple lines that draped elegantly over her hips down to her ankles. Masses of petticoats would have once swelled the long skirts into a swaying bell shape. Tiny pearls sewn into the material caught the light from the single bulb and shimmered in a misty glow. Intricate bead-work must have once adorned the gown, though now a lot of it was missing. Probably at the bottom of the trunk, along with other long-lost treasures.

Amanda stepped to the trunk and moved aside the tissue that had cradled the gown. Some of the pearls should surely be here, perhaps still nestled in the crinkly folds of tissue paper. She unfolded some of it and heard a faint rattle as if pearls were falling into the bottom of the trunk. Digging deeper, Amanda found several folded sheets of yellowed newsprint below the tissue paper. She pulled it out carefully, in case some of the pearls were caught in the folds.

A pen-and-ink drawing of a man with a small beard and plumed hat caught her immediate attention as she unfolded an old copy of the *Memphis Appeal.* The date of the paper was June 19, 1864.

BATTLE AT BRICE'S CROSS ROADS RESULTS IN FORREST VICTORY, read the caption above the ink drawing. Intrigued, she read the long article relating the details of Confederate General N. B. Forrest's lengthy fight and ultimate victory over Federal forces at Brice's Cross Roads in northern Mississippi. Why had someone saved this particular article? she wondered.

Then she glanced toward the bottom of the page as bold print seemed to jump out at her: HOLLY SPRINGS MAN KILLED SIX MONTHS AFTER WEDDING, it read. Curious, she scanned the article beneath. "Tragedy strikes former Memphian in the wake of General Forrest's great victory over Union forces. After vanquishing the Federals on the Guntown Road between Holly Springs and Ripley on June 10, the chase continued into the small hours of the next morning. On June 16, in the effort to roust the enemy from northern Mississippi, a former Memphian's husband of only six months was slain. To add insult to this grave injury, Yankee soldiers—who were cowering in the Coldwater swamps in their cowardly flight toward Memphis—then had the effrontery to claim the young man had been slain by his own half brother. Lieutenant James Brandon stoutly denies such grievous charges against him. . . ."

Amanda took a deep breath. The name of the dead man was listed as Lieutenant Michael Scott—leaving behind his widow, Deborah Jordan Scott. So here it was—the real reason behind the feud that still dogged her family. It was enough to divide a family, the suspicion that one brother had killed another, like Cain and Abel. She read further, and learned that the two had been scouts for General Forrest. How tragic. What had really happened? *Had* her great-great-grandfather killed his own brother?

Carefully folding the paper, she laid it atop the crate and sighed. After all this time, knowing the reason would hardly make any difference now. Things would still be the same, and the family estrangement just as strong.

"Too bad," she murmured as she straightened up, "that I can't change history." The wedding gown rustled softly as she moved to stand in front of the mirror again. Her image was reflected in a rosy halo of light and shadows. The gown hung loosely. On a whim, she reached behind herself to fasten the last three buttons, then turned back to look into the mirror.

Her reflection shimmered, and it seemed that it grew brighter and brighter, the satin folds of the gown taking on a luminous sheen. A sudden gust of wind through the open attic window made the light bulb swing wildly. It dimmed, then burned out, leaving the room in darkness. Amanda suddenly felt weak and dizzy, and reached out blindly to catch herself. There was nothing but empty air, and she sank slowly to the floor, arms flung out in front of her as she dropped to her knees.

Panting, fighting nausea, Amanda's head began to whirl. All her senses grew so muddled she couldn't form a coherent thought. It seemed like forever before her head stopped whirling. Her senses slowly returned to normal, though there was a ringing in her ears that seemed loud enough to be heard fifty miles away in Memphis.

Amanda sat back, groping for support. This was vaguely frightening, for she had never fainted before in her life. It was probably the heat. After all, she was accustomed to air conditioning, not this humid stuffiness.

Getting slowly to her feet, Amanda stood still for a moment to regain her balance and bearings. As her eyes grew used to the dimness, she was able to perceive squares of silvery light coming through the open attic window. It was bright, brighter than she remembered it being earlier. Was there a full moon? She couldn't remember. Everything was still so fuzzy, her mind unable to properly focus. Nothing seemed right. She felt out of place, oddly unsettled. Stifled, as if there weren't enough air.

Still slightly dizzy, Amanda made her way toward the window for some fresh air. She curved her palms over the window sill and leaned out, breathing deeply. The smell of honeysuckle was strong, mixed with the sweet fragrance of clover. It wafted in on a breeze that blew the hair back from her face. The night was cool now, and very dark. No sign of distant lights marked the highway, which was blocked out, she supposed, by the tall trees.

She frowned. There was something different—out of place. Trees . . . the huge, gnarled magnolia trees in front of the house didn't seem as tall now. And there were so many of them—not just the three, but a half-dozen or more. Instead of soaring higher than the house, they barely reached the top of the porch roof below. She blinked and rubbed her eyes. How very odd. It must be her perception. It was off, askew somehow, and distorted by her fainting spell.

Amanda took a deep breath and briefly closed her eyes. Then she heard a strange rumbling noise that sounded vaguely familiar even while recognition eluded her. Opening her eyes, she leaned out the window again. Flickers of motion could be seen between the tall, slender trunks of the oaks lining the driveway. Odd, but the oak trees looked so much smaller in the moonlight, shorter and not as spreading. The indistinct rumbling evolved into the definite sound of hoof-beats. Horses? To her shock, a band of mounted men thundered up the driveway. What on earth—?

Her fingers dug into the wooden frame as she stared down. Details leaped out at her in the bright moonlight. The gravel driveway was now rutted and muddy. The horsemen wore gray uniforms spattered with mud, and carried rifles and swords. They looked like—soldiers. One of them wore a plumed hat, and he swept it off as he reined in his horse in front of the house. Another horseman dismounted and leaped up onto the steps, moving out of Amanda's view. She heard him pound on the door and call out.

Confused, and assaulted by so many alien images that her mind could not assimilate them all, Amanda froze. Had she locked the front door? She tried to remember. Locking doors was habit in Memphis, but this was a small town with little need for locked doors. When the pounding grew louder, Amanda moved toward the attic door.

Tripping over the dragging hem of the dress, she realized that she could hardly go downstairs wearing a hundred-and-thirty-year-old gown. Quickly, she unbuttoned it, accidentally tearing loose one of the tiny pearl buttons. It fell to the floor and rolled away as she hastily draped the gown over a trunk.

Where was her robe? Hadn't she worn a robe? Where was the open trunk? The attic looked strangely empty, though there were stacks of boxes against one wall, and an old cradle next to two trunks. Her robe must have fallen behind something, and she spent several moments searching for it before deciding to look in one of the trunks. More pounding from below made her hurry, and she grabbed up a white cotton robe from the trunk and threw it around herself, fumbling with the lacy ribbons that tied it together across the front.

This was ridiculous. Why couldn't she find her robe? And who in heaven's name were those uniformed men down there? The National Guard? Were there flash floods? Tornado warnings? Something must be wrong for them to arrive so late at night. And why on horseback?

Amanda found her way down the back stairs in the dark, feeling her way along the wall until she reached the bottom step. The borrowed robe flapped around her ankles as she crossed the dark hall between the stairs and the kitchen. A flickering light glowed in the front parlor and entrance hall. She frowned. Hadn't she turned out all the lights downstairs?

Then she heard a murmur of voices that were muffled and hushed. Apprehension made her voice shaky when she called out, "Who's there? Jess? Is that you?"

No one answered, and she drew in a deep breath as she stepped into the entrance hall. The front door was open. A tall figure in the doorway blocked her view of the porch, and it took a moment to register that it could not be Jessica. As she drew near, she heard a man say that he'd just left Rucker's regiment.

Amanda jerked to a sudden halt, fear making her voice sharp as she demanded, "Who are you?"

As the figure turned, he held up a lantern, and the light revealed strong male features. Amanda choked back a startled cry. It must be the hazy light. Her recent fainting spell had obviously caused a marked visual problem. Or even brain damage.

"Who are *you*?" the man asked bluntly. His eyes narrowed at her, then widened slightly.

Amanda couldn't utter a sound for what seemed an eternity. It was him—the man of her dreams, the man from the old family photograph that had haunted her childhood fantasies. She couldn't be mistaken. This face had remained embedded in her dreams for too many years for her not to recognize it now.

Only this man was no dream—he was real. Very real. And very close. He was close enough that she could touch him, and she was startled by the impulse to do so. It was obvious he'd been awakened, for his dark hair was rumpled and his shirt was unbuttoned. A large expanse of bare chest gleamed beneath the open edges of his white shirt. With an effort, she dragged her gaze up to his face again.

He was staring at her from beneath the thick bristle of his lashes, a faint smile curving his mouth. Her heart did another flip, and she took a deep breath to clear her head.

## Chapter Four

Flushing when the man's gaze drifted down her body to her bare feet, Amanda managed to say, "I asked you first—who are you and what are you doing here?"

He made an impatient motion with his free hand, then turned his back on her and spoke to the man just outside the door. "I just got here. Tell the general he's welcome to come inside, and I'll make my report to—"

"Excuse me," Amanda interrupted sharply, "but no one else comes into this house, mister."

A brief, sizzling silence followed her decree, and she caught a shadowy glimpse of a man out on the porch. The object of her concern, however, seemed irritated that she had interrupted. He gave her a quick glance and snapped, "This is a private discussion."

"Fine," she shot back. "I'll call the sheriff and you can have a private discussion with him."

"Maybe you should come outside, Captain," she heard the man on the porch suggest. "We shouldn't like to frighten the ladies of the house with our news."

To her surprise, the trespasser just inside the door took her by one arm. "Excuse me, ma'am. If you would be kind enough to go back to your room, we can continue our business without your interference."

Shocked as much by his presence as by his tight grip on her arm, Amanda stared at the man in openmouthed silence. A strange chill came over her. The definite resemblance to the man in the old photograph was eerie. He must be a descendant. But what the devil was he doing here in the middle of the night?

Taking a deep breath, she blurted, "I don't know you—what are you doing here?"

He looked at her closely, eyes narrowing in the dim light, and Amanda was gratified to see that she had at least succeeded in gaining his undivided attention. Her chin lifted when he raked her with a deliberately slow stare, his eyes moving from her bare feet up to her disheveled hair. Amanda resisted the temptation to glance down to see if she'd fastened the laces on the front of her robe.

The intruder drew in a deep breath, then his gaze shifted to look behind Amanda. She could hear someone coming down the main staircase, and she turned to confront a slender, fair-haired woman who gazed at her with a perplexed expression.

Amanda stared back. There was a faint quiver of recognition, though she couldn't pinpoint it. "Who are you?" she was about to demand, but it was the man who spoke.

"Deborah. Thank God. She must be one of your guests. Escort her back to her room, will you?"

Smiling uncertainly, the woman he'd called Deborah said in a soft drawl, "I didn't hear you return, Jesse. I'm glad you're safely back. Is all well?"

"I don't know. And I can't find out until this . . . this

young lady is out of here. Will you please do something?''

Deborah's voice was gentle when she suggested to Amanda, ''Why don't you come with me? The men will handle—''

''No way. If there's trouble, I should be here.'' Eluding the man in the doorway with a quick step around him, Amanda stepped out onto the porch.

But even as he uttered an angry comment and followed her onto the porch, Amanda received another shock when the swaying lantern light flickered over the mounted men in her front yard. They were garbed in Civil War costumes. On the heels of that implausible recognition came the more logical thought that this must be one of the frequent reenactments that were so common in the South. Every year, a Civil War reenactment was held to commemorate the battle at Shiloh, about two hours from Memphis up on the Tennessee River. This must be in connection with that.

''Were you men at Shiloh?'' she blurted, and the young man still on the front porch gave a grim nod of his head.

''Yes, ma'am, we were. But that was a while back.''

Sudden understanding was a relief. Of course. That explained it. Most of the men who participated in the reenactments were very serious about it. They lived in tents like those long-ago soldiers, ate the same kind of food, sang the same songs, and even tried to talk as the Civil War soldiers would have.

''Well,'' Amanda said with a smile, ''you're very believable. I suppose you're on the way to reenact that Brice's Cross Roads battle I read about.''

Instead of returning her smile, the young man only looked bewildered as he glanced uncertainly at the man behind Amanda. She felt a heavy hand descend upon her shoulder, and iron fingers dug into her skin.

"It would be much better if you were to go back inside with my sister," a male voice growled in her ear. "She'll fix you a cup of dandelion tea or something."

"Really," she began angrily, "I've had about enough of this nonsense—"

When his hand tightened, she reacted instinctively. Lifting her foot, she slammed her heel hard against his instep, and was rewarded with instant release and a muffled curse. A guffaw burst from one of the mounted men, but was quickly stifled. Amanda was aware of the amused stares in their direction, and her indignation swelled.

" 'Scuse me, miss," a deeply gruff voice rang out, "but what do you know of Brice's Cross Roads?"

Turning, Amanda saw that the man holding a plumed hat had ridden close to the porch. He leaned on the pommel of his saddle, fixing her with an intense gaze. She stared back, bewildered by another shock of recognition. The small dark beard, the deep-set brooding eyes—where had she seen that face before?

"I—I'm sorry?" she mumbled. "I don't know what you mean. . . ."

"I can say the same, miss. And I'll ask you agin—what do you know of Brice's Cross Roads? Was your husband there?"

"My husband has been dead for over a year." Her words came out in a choked whisper that had nothing to do with Alan's death and everything to do with the growing suspicion that she was being confronted by some kind of weird cult.

The bearded man with the plumed hat apparently misunderstood. He nodded gravely. "I'm deeply sorry for your loss, Mrs.—"

Clearing her throat, she interrupted. "Look, I was referring to a battle fought there during the Civil War by Forrest and—'' She jerked to a halt. Forrest. That's who this man reminded her of—the drawing she'd seen of Nathan Bedford Forrest. Blinking, she asked, ''Are you supposed to be General Forrest?''

A faint smile curled the man's mouth. ''At last muster, I was indeed thought to be named such.''

She put a hand to her temple to still the steady, dull throb. ''This is all so confusing—is it too much to hope that you're just looking for a place to camp for the night?''

''As a matter of fact, we are,'' the Forrest imitator replied in a weary tone. ''But I would surely like to know how you've already heard of the battle at Brice's Cross Roads, for we're still chasin' those Yanks back toward Memphis.''

Amanda ignored the suspicion that was fast becoming conviction and said instead, ''There's an empty field behind the house where the barns used to be. You can camp there, but clean up your mess afterward, please.''

''Excuse me, dear,'' the soft-voiced woman said at her elbow, ''but I think you're confused. Why don't you allow me to fix you a cup of tea and we'll talk?''

''I don't want tea. I don't want to talk. And I'm not confused.'' Amanda fought a wave of panic. The woman named Deborah was smiling and murmuring what were obviously meant to be reassurances, and Amanda's tension mounted. Had she somehow managed to travel back in time? No, that was impossible. Time travel involved huge machines and mad scientists, or experiments gone awry, not something as normal and mundane as fainting. It just wasn't possible. Was it?

With a hand at her throat, she asked hoarsely, ''What day is this?''

Deborah glanced at the man named Jesse, and he gave a terse nod of his head. Looking back at her, Deborah replied softly, "Why, it's June 12."

"And—and the year?"

Even more softly, "1864."

Amanda's head whirled, and her nausea increased. She reached out blindly for something to support herself, and Deborah took her arm as she swayed.

"Captain Jordan," the man she thought must be Forrest said in an authoritative tone, "it looks like this young lady's been recent witness to the violence of battle. Since she's prob'ly even met up with some of the fleeing Yanks, that'd explain her knowledge of our actions. Best let her rest a while."

"I didn't think of that," Deborah was murmuring as she took Amanda by the arm. "Poor thing—you must have been terrified. Tell us where your home is, and we'll try to get you there when you're rested enough."

Amanda managed to rally slightly. "Since I'm a Brandon, I—I suppose I still belong here."

"You're a Brandon?" Jesse Jordan repeated with a skeptical lift of his brows that was infuriating.

"Yes, but you're obviously not—"

Deborah said quickly, "Jesse's my brother from Memphis and not often a visitor here. I'm sorry no one properly greeted you, my dear, but we didn't know you were coming. Jamie never said anything about a relative arriving anytime soon. But you know how it is these days, with communication by post so slow and often impossible."

"That's true enough." Amanda tried to think of something to say that would make sense of a situation that was too fantastic to credit being real, but nothing came to mind. Shrugging, she said, "This is all so unexpected."

"General Forrest," Jesse growled, "I think this young woman should be questioned at length. It's my opinion she's a Yankee sympathizer."

"Yankee? Wait a minute," Amanda said, suddenly afraid she would end up in a Southern prison. "I was born in Holly Springs, even though I live in Memphis now. I'm every bit as much a Southerner as any of you, but—"

"Just a moment," Forrest interrupted. "You say you live in Memphis?"

"Yes. Why?"

He leaned forward, fixing her with a steady stare. "I'm well aware that Union General Washburn has severely restricted citizens' efforts to leave Memphis, save by his permission. How'd you manage to sneak from the city?"

Realizing she'd somehow blundered, Amanda shook her head. "I didn't sneak out at all. I . . . I just left."

Forrest's gaze shifted from Amanda. "Captain, your pretty relative has given me an idea. I had my doubts about your success in gaining our objective, but now I think there's a way we can do it. Join me for a discussion, while we let the ladies adjourn to the kitchen and fix us anything that resembles coffee."

The captain looked toward Deborah, who nodded and smiled. "I'll see to our guest, Jesse."

"I'm not sure I want to leave you alone with her," he said bluntly.

Amanda started to retort, but Deborah was shaking her head and saying, "If she's a Brandon, she's no threat to any of us, I assure you. I'd stake my life on that."

Jesse's wary blue gaze moved back to Amanda. "It may come down to that. I don't trust her. Holler if you need me."

"Chauvinist," Amanda muttered as Jesse grabbed a lantern and stepped off the porch. She turned to Deborah. "I have no idea what to do next. This is all new to me, and I'm still trying to figure it out, so you'll have to help."

Deborah gave her a rather startled glance and did not reply as she led the way back down the candlelit hallway toward the kitchen. Or toward where the kitchen had once been. A breezeway now connected the kitchen to the main house, not the pantry she was used to.

Amanda stood still for a moment, looking around her. An oil lamp in the middle of a small table shed a rosy pool of light. A cast-iron stove stood in place of the more familiar gas stove, and there was no porcelain sink with or even without its ancient plumbing. Some sort of pump was attached to a deep metal tub that apparently served as the sink. A brick fireplace stood at one end of the kitchen; in it a pot was slung over small flames.

Amanda closed her eyes briefly, then opened them again, hoping it would clear her vision and restore things to normal. No such luck.

"Pay no mind to Jesse," Deborah said as she put a copper kettle on the stove. "He's a bit protective since all those Yankees came through here a few days ago. We'd like to keep Oakleigh intact."

"Oakleigh—" Amanda drew in a deep breath. Oakleigh. Of course. There must be some vital information she needed to know. Maybe that was why—incredible as it might seem—she had somehow traveled back in time. She didn't know how, but if she could find out why, maybe this would all make sense and she could do what she'd obviously been sent back to do. "Are you one of the Brandons or the Scotts?" she asked Deborah.

Deborah gave her a shy smile. "Scott. That's why I'm here at Oakleigh."

Amanda nodded. "All right. That's a start—wait. Deborah—Captain Jordan. Are you Deborah Jordan Scott?"

With a perplexed smile, Deborah nodded. "Why, yes. Is your memory coming back?"

Drawing in a deep breath, Amanda murmured, "Let's just say it's coming in bits and pieces. You're from Memphis, too, then."

"Yes, but I've been in Holly Springs since right after Memphis fell to the Federals. I'm sure you understand why I had to leave Memphis."

"Yes, I think I do. If I remember my history correctly, the wives of Confederate officers were held hostages of a sort against the actions of the Rebel army."

"Well, when I left Memphis, it was before I married Michael. The Federals were well aware of my brother's activities, however, so I was often taken before General Grant to be questioned."

"Grant? I thought it was Washburn—"

"Grant was commanding officer when I was still there. As I said, I've been in Holly Springs since Jesse managed to get me past the sentries out on Pigeon Roost Road."

"Pigeon Roost? I remember—Highway 78 used to be called Pigeon Roost Road because of all the pigeons that roosted in the trees there." Aware that Deborah was looking at her curiously, Amanda shrugged and added hastily, "Your brother must be very adroit at sneaking past sentries."

"Jesse?" Deborah smiled. "He's wonderful. That's why they call him the Hawk—because he can get into and out of places that most men can't."

"The Hawk? He sounds dangerous."

"He is. General Forrest has used him many times to—well, I suppose it's common knowledge, and anyway, we need to fix them some coffee. These discussions can go into the late hours, and the general looked exhausted. No, don't try to help. You look tired, too.''

Amanda plopped down on a three-legged wooden stool that she had never seen before. Her head was still spinning, and she felt very weak. Plucking at the folds of the borrowed robe, she tried to gather her wits. She retraced her steps of the past hour, from fighting boredom and heat in the bedroom to trying on the gown in the attic. After several moments of silence, she glanced up to find Deborah gazing at her curiously. None of this should be happening. It was too incredible, like something out of a bad movie.

''Are you unwell?'' Deborah asked softly, and the question provided Amanda an explanation that sounded plausible.

''Well . . . I did faint earlier. Perhaps that's why I'm still having trouble making sense of things. Maybe I have a concussion. Or temporary amnesia. That would explain why I don't remember things so well, wouldn't it?'' Her voice trailed into hopeful silence.

Deborah took some cups from a cabinet. ''Poor thing. It would certainly explain it. Your visit here is quite unexpected, you know. General Washburn evicts ten wives of Confederate officers from Memphis every time our boys fire on one of his men, so I suppose not even widows are safe. Your journey must have been . . . quite harrowing.'' She paused delicately, as if waiting for Amanda to elaborate.

Though Amanda knew a response was expected, she had no idea what she could say. After a moment, Deborah continued as if the silence were not at all strained. ''Jamie said nothing about your arrival to me before they left to rejoin Forrest, and he is very good about keeping me informed.''

Deborah gave a slight smile. "If you've been in recent contact with him, you must know that things were rather awkward right after Michael and I were married. I suppose it's only to be expected, as I was betrothed to Jamie at one time, but still, it was a strain. I'm glad it's behind us now."

Amanda could feel her head whirl again. The clue to the reason for her improbable journey had to be hidden in the family feud. But there didn't appear to be a feud. Was she here to prevent one from happening? It took her a moment of silent struggle before she asked hesitantly, "By Jamie, do you mean James?"

Deborah nodded. "Yes. I still call him Jamie, just as I did when we were children. Oh, I shouldn't go on about my own affairs. Not when it's obvious you must have had a dreadful time. I shall give Tangie a proper scold in the morning for not waking me when you arrived. I hope she gave you the guest room, and made certain there are clean linens on the bed. Is everything suitable?"

"Suitable. Yes. Yes, of course." Amanda had no idea what she was saying. She knew a response was expected, but as everything else was so surrealistic, it probably didn't matter what she said. She stood up. "I think I'll go back to bed. Maybe if I go to sleep, when I wake up everything will be normal."

"I hope so. As normal as things can be these days." After a brief silence, Deborah said, "Forgive me, but I'm afraid I never asked your given name. I feel very foolish, for I'm sure that Jamie must have mentioned you at one time or the other, but I fear that I cannot recall it."

"Amanda."

"Oh, my, you must be one of the English Brandons. But you don't sound a bit English. . . ."

"English—oh, yes. I'd forgotten about the English Brandons. From somewhere in Somerset, weren't they?''

Deborah stared at her for a long moment. The sudden piercing shriek of the kettle broke the silence, and Deborah gave a startled jerk. ''I'll make the coffee. I think perhaps I should send for Dr. Higdon in the morning.''

''Now, wait a minute.'' Amanda paused. Her head began to throb, and she felt slightly nauseous. Maybe she should see a doctor. She didn't feel at all well. She looked up to see Deborah gazing at her with a worried frown.

''All right,'' she agreed faintly. ''I think you're right. I should see the doctor.''

''I'll light the way to your room,'' Deborah offered in a kind voice as she took the kettle off the fire. ''Candles are in rather short supply, I'm afraid. I'll bring you up some tea to help you sleep just as soon as I take General Forrest and his officers some coffee. I imagine they need it greatly, if the little I overheard is true. Poor men. Some of them are still bloodied from the battle.''

''The battle? Oh. Yes. I forgot. Brice's Cross Roads.'' Amanda allowed Deborah to lead the way to the main staircase. The handrail glowed with soft luster curving to the second floor with a gratifying familiarity. It was the same house that she'd always known, though subtly changed. The plaster frieze over the parlor door looked bright, and the wallpaper was no longer faded and dull. The wooden floors were bare and glowed with a rich, deep finish. So this was how the house had looked when it was still fairly new. She was grateful she had this opportunity to see it— and perhaps save it. All she had to do was figure out how.

The bedroom Deborah took her to was not the room she'd occupied earlier, but Amanda remained silent. As Deborah turned down the coverlet and helped her out of the robe and into bed, the story of *Alice Through the Look-*

*ing Glass* came to Amanda's mind. That's how she felt. As if she'd stepped through a mirror and into a parallel world where things looked the same but nothing was as it should be. All she needed now was to see a white rabbit. Or a Cheshire cat.

Suddenly yielding to the fuzzy edges of exhaustion that had been hovering at the edges of her consciousness for some time, Amanda slipped beneath the light counterpane on the bed and lay back on a fat feather pillow. She was vaguely aware of Deborah arranging gauzy folds of mosquito netting around the four-poster bed, and murmured her gratitude just before sleep claimed her.

## Chapter Five

"WHO THE DEVIL is that woman?" Jesse asked his sister when he found her in the kitchen. "And where did she come from?"

Deborah shook her head. She looked puzzled. "I'm not certain. Her first name is Amanda. She said she's a Brandon. I think she must be from the English side of the family, for she was mumbling things about the queen and a cat."

"Queen Victoria?"

"No, something about the queen of hearts and a cat from Cheshire." Deborah shrugged wearily. "I think fleeing Memphis must have greatly unsettled her mind. Heaven only knows what must have happened to her along the way, for she's wearing one of the old dressing gowns I put up in the attic a few days ago. I couldn't find any sign of her own garments, but the shift she's wearing looks very new and modern—"

When Deborah broke off with a faintly embarrassed smile, Jesse grinned wickedly. "Tell me about the shift she's wearing, Deborah. That sounds much more interesting than anything about a cat.''

"Really, Jesse, you're impossible. The lady's undergarments are hardly any of your business, nor any other gentleman's, I would think.''

Unable to resist the temptation to tease his sister, Jesse said, "I hope your new husband is not so ungallant as to ignore all those fine silk shifts from New Orleans that you managed to bring with you.''

"Jesse!'' Though two splotches of color stained her cheeks, Deborah's mouth quivered with suppressed mirth. "You should be ashamed to speak so boldly to a lady.''

"Ah, but I'm your brother and I've known you longer and better than anyone. Well,'' he amended, "maybe not better than Michael does.''

Rather anxiously, Deborah asked, "Has there been any word from Michael and Jamie yet?''

Jesse raked a hand through his hair, wondering just how much he could tell her. Michael and James were assigned as scouts to report on the fleeing enemy. Obviously, something must have happened. How could he tell her that? She'd only worry, when it was probable they were just delayed in their return. From what he'd just been told, the battle at Brice's Cross Roads had been long and drawn out, and in the ensuing chaos of pursuit, it was easy to lose track of time. He should know that well enough. It had taken him an extra day and a half to get back to Oakleigh because of the Yanks fleeing Forrest. The area was thick with them, and they would have been only too glad to capture the Rebel spy they'd named the Hawk. If caught, Jesse would have been hung from the nearest tree without waiting for even the semblance of a fair trial as prisoner of war.

"Jamie and Michael will be back soon, I'm sure,'' he

said evasively, and knew from Deborah's soft sigh that his answer was not the least bit reassuring. "Our more immediate problem," he added, "is what to do with our strange guest. General Forrest gave me orders to use her to get word into Memphis."

"Use her? Whatever for?"

"Forrest said she obviously knows the area, and seems rather bold for such an attractive young woman. He's convinced she must be a spy of sorts. I'd think," Jesse said dryly, "that would be enough to earn her lodging in the nearest locked shed, but Forrest is of a different mind."

Jesse lapsed into silence, thinking of the honey-haired beauty who had stared at him so long. He'd been hard-pressed not to stare back at her just as boldly. Despite her confusion, there was a vibrancy in her that intrigued him. He'd found most young women to be rather pale, insipid creatures, full of flirtatious tricks and little else. Having resisted his parents' efforts to wed him to any of the empty-headed belles they kept pushing at him, he'd been vaguely grateful when the war interrupted their marital plans.

"She isn't going alone?" Deborah was asking, and Jesse looked up at her with a faint smile.

"No, Forrest has requested a volunteer to don a disguise and accompany her into Memphis."

"At least she won't be alone. But what man would be so foolish as to take such a risk?"

Jesse grinned. "Me."

It came to Amanda in the seconds before she was fully awake, how she had arrived in 1864. Her eyes popped open. Sunlight streamed through the windows and was diffused by the mosquito netting around her bed. Of course. The portrait in the attic was the clue. This Deborah was the sad woman in the portrait. The fair hair drawn back from her forehead, the wide, honest eyes—the *gown*. It had to be the connection, the vehicle that had sent her spiraling back in time.

Nothing had happened until she'd buttoned the final pearl button of Deborah's wedding dress. Then she'd immediately grown faint. There had been a sudden gust of wind, the lights had gone out, and everything had gone black. Was that when it had happened?

Blinking at the gauzy threads of light filtering through the netting and into her eyes, Amanda put a hand over her brow. That must have been it. Somehow, the dress had been the catalyst to bring her back in time—but how could she help? Deborah had already wed Michael, and apparently the dissension between the brothers was not troublesome enough to spark murder. But where were they? Deborah had said Jamie and Michael were gone. The news article—the one in the attic that had related the details—hadn't it said something about Michael being killed by his half brother somewhere in the woods? Maybe by some miracle it was still there, and she could find out the details.

She sat up and swung her legs over the side of the bed, batting aside the netting. As she slid from the bed, a light tap sounded on the door and she called out, "Come in."

"Good morning," Deborah said as she came into the bedroom with a well-laden tray. "Did you sleep well?"

Amanda managed an answering smile, wondering how much she could ask without being considered a lunatic. Did she dare ask if Deborah had heard from her husband and brother-in-law? Of course. It was a natural enough question to ask. . . .

"I thought you might like to have a bite to eat up here in your room rather than with the others," Deborah was saying as she placed the tray on a small stool. She chatted easily as she puttered with the teacup and saucer, and Amanda managed reasonably intelligent replies.

Finally Deborah stood back, fidgeting with the folds of her dress a moment before looking up with a slightly embarrassed smile. "I hate to seem impolite, but I must ask—is your shift all you have left of your clothing?"

"My shift?" Amanda stared at her blankly, then realized that she was referring to her silk nightie. She nodded. "I suppose so. I . . . I haven't seen anything else of mine here."

She hadn't meant to say the last, but apparently Deborah misunderstood. "That's all right. I'll find clothes for you. We're just glad you were able to get here. My brother—Captain Jordan—says that Yankees are still all around us and it's dangerous to attempt travel right now. I'm sure Jamie will be pleased to know you made it here safely. Families should stick together in times of crisis, don't you agree?"

Amanda nodded and seized the opening. "Where did you say Jamie and Michael are right now?"

"They're scouts," Deborah replied vaguely. "I never know just where they are. I hope they come back safe and sound, though with all the Yankees that have been coming through Holly Springs, they'll probably have to do like Jesse did and hide in the woods."

"Is Forrest still here?"

"He rode out this morning."

"I see. Well, I'm sure your husband will return soon."

Deborah hesitated, then said softly, "I hope Michael is able to linger a day or two next time. Our hours together are so short."

"I hope so, too," Amanda said. She wished she could

recall all the details of the news article. If only her head wasn't still so achy and she didn't feel so strange. . . .

After Deborah left, Amanda went to the window and looked out. This room was at the rear, and the view should have been of empty pastures fenced with barbed wire and a few metal gates. Instead of empty pastures, there were towering wooden structures that looked permanent and weathered. Now there were two barns and a few more out-buildings scattered neatly in the field, with thick woods ranging beyond. Leaning against the window frame, Amanda had the thought that what had happened to her was like something out of *The Twilight Zone*, or even *Quantum Leap*.

When a knock sounded on her door again, she called out permission to enter without turning around. She was almost afraid to see Deborah again. What could she say? What could she ask that wouldn't make her sound insane?

''Do you always entertain gentlemen in your shift?'' a male voice drawled, and Amanda whirled around.

Jesse Jordan stood just inside her door, arms folded across his broad chest. Inexplicably, her heart leaped. She stared at him; the transition from dream man to reality hit her with all the force of a two-by-four. In daylight, he was even more devastating. What could she say? What should she do? She'd better think of something fast, she decided as his lazy glance drifted from her face down the length of her scantily clad body. Belatedly realizing that she wore nothing other than a thin silk nightie—immodest in mixed company even in 1994—Amanda stepped quickly to the bed and pulled a length of mosquito netting around herself.

''No *gentleman*,'' she said pointedly, ''would come in once he saw that I was not dressed. But I see you're ignoring that rule.''

"I take your point. Here." He strode forward, snatched up a robe, and flung it on the bed. "Put that on. We have to talk."

"I can't think of any—" she began, but put up a hand to stop him when he started around the end of the bed. "All right, all right. Give me a minute. Turn your back, since it's obvious you must be reminded to be a gentleman."

"I wouldn't be so cocky if I were you," he shot back, but turned around. "Hurry up."

Amanda reached for the robe and pulled it around herself; she recognized it as the one she'd worn the night before. "All right," she said when she had the laces fastened. "What's so important?"

He turned, eyeing her for a long moment. His mouth curved into a crooked smile that made her heart leap. It was the same smile she'd seen in the photograph. She remembered it. It was just more potent than she'd thought it would be. Combined with the slight crinkling of eyes that were dark blue instead of brown as she'd always assumed, the smile had a devastating affect on her.

"What do you want?" she heard herself ask in an embarrassingly husky voice.

To her surprise, he reached out to lift a strand of her hair in one hand. Rubbing it between his fingers, he met her gaze steadily. "That's a dangerous question to be asking me right now," he murmured.

Amanda's breath caught in her throat when she saw the glitter in his eyes. When he wound the length of her hair around his hand, bringing her closer to him, her knees suddenly felt weak.

"Captain—"

"Jesse," he corrected softly. His hand was next to her

cheek, and his thumb caressed the side of her face in a soft motion. She shivered, and the crooked smile deepened.

Putting her hand over his, she gently but firmly removed it from her face; her hair swung back against her shoulder. "I'm certain you didn't come to my room just to make small talk, *Captain*. I repeat—what do you want?"

Not seeming at all chastened by her rejection, he gave a shrug of his broad shoulders. "It's not just what I want," he said. "It's what Forrest wants."

"Forrest. Oh, yes. The man in the plumed hat."

"He's a bit more than a man in a plumed hat," Jesse said dryly, "but yes, that's the man I mean. He's come up with an idea. Would you be willing to take a risk to help your country?"

"A risk—my country? How on earth could anything *I* do help my country?"

"You apparently got out of Memphis, so you'd know how to get back in, right?"

Blinking, she muttered, "Straight up Highway 78 until it turns into Lamar at Shelby Drive sounds like the best way to me. But I guess you wouldn't know about that."

It was Jesse's turn to blink in confusion. Then his eyes narrowed and he shook his head. "You must still be unsettled. I told Forrest it wasn't a good plan, that you were unsuitable. But once he gets an idea—"

Amanda sat down abruptly on the bed, and put her face in her palms. Her words were soft and muffled. "I'm beginning to feel like Dorothy in Oz. Have there been any tornadoes through here lately?"

Jesse was silent, and after a moment she looked up at him. Of course. *The Wizard of Oz* hadn't been written yet. She sighed and quoted under her breath, "I do believe in spooks, I do, I do. . . ."

"What?"

She shrugged. "Never mind. Let's just say that I had an unconventional upbringing, if it makes it any easier to understand," she murmured. "Will that do?"

"Guess it'll have to do." Jesse raked a hand through his hair. "What's your answer? Will you assist Forrest?"

"Just exactly what is it he wants me to do? I mean, I should hardly agree to something when I don't know what it involves, should I?"

A faint smile curled one side of his mouth. "No, I don't expect you should. Since Memphis is shut off tight by the Yankees and they have sentries stationed on all the roads leading into town, not even the railroads are safe. Remember when our boys had snipers firing on the Memphis and Charleston line of the railroad, so the Yankees put prominent Memphians in the cars as targets? If we'd been able to receive word of what the Yankees had done, no innocent citizens would have been hurt. Forrest is determined nothing like that will happen again."

"I still don't understand—"

"It's simple, really. We pose as a married couple traveling into Memphis. If we make it through the sentries, I'm to deliver a message to a certain gentleman, then return here with a reply."

"Sentries. Oh, God. Do you mean like armed guards?"

"Like armed guards, yes. Are you agreeable?"

"Why do you need me? Can't you get through by yourself?"

"Posing as part of a married couple, I wouldn't be as suspect. Besides, you obviously know the way out, and we can use the same way to get back in."

She studied him for a moment. Beneath the calm veneer, she sensed tension. Her reply was important to him. And who knew—it might help Oakleigh.

Maybe that was the reason she heard herself stalling for time, saying, "Let me think about it."

A faint grin squared his mouth, and his eyes narrowed slightly as he took a step closer and let his gaze rake over her much more boldly than made her comfortable. "Go ahead and think about it. I'll give you until tomorrow morning."

His close proximity was unnerving. She leaned back to distance herself physically and mentally. "Don't wear yourself out waiting," she said coolly.

"Oh, I won't." Reaching out, he lifted a strand of her hair again, as if he couldn't resist touching it. "I can't help but wonder if you're really who and what you say you are."

Her nerves tightened. "Why would I lie?"

Releasing her hair, he said bluntly, "I can think of a hundred reasons you might be lying, and not one for why I should trust you."

"Then don't. It doesn't matter to me what you think. I assure you, if I wasn't a Brandon, I certainly wouldn't be here like this."

He frowned slightly. "Maybe not," he said after a moment. "But only time will tell the whole truth."

"If you're through mouthing platitudes," she said pointedly, getting up and moving to the door, "it's time you leave."

Shrugging, he went to the door, then paused in the opening to say softly, "You'd better be who you say you are, or I'll see to it that you're sorry you were foolish enough to pretend differently."

"Good-*bye*, Captain Jordan," Amanda snapped, and flung the door closed behind him.

It took several minutes for her anxiety to subside, and by then, Amanda knew what she was going to do next. She stood for a moment, then swung open the door and stepped out into the hall. It was quiet and shadowed. She could hear voices, but they sounded distant.

Slowly, she crept down the hallway. It looked so different and unfamiliar to her. No hall light, no bathroom, no electrical outlets. Oddly familiar, yet so strange.

When she reached the first floor, she paused. The parlor was much the same, except for the arrangement of the furniture and the absence of lamps. Candles stood in tall brass holders. Hesitating, she wondered which way to go. The sound of a voice drawing near prompted her flight toward the door at the rear of the dog-trot, or long hallway with outside doors at each end. In place of the former pantry, the breezeway leading to the kitchen was just out the back door. The attic stairs were outside, and she sped up the narrow steps, half tripping over the long hem of the robe. Why had she ever thought she could manage long skirts?

Once in the attic, she gently closed the door and leaned back against it as her eyes adjusted to the dim, hazy light. The window was open, and weak sunlight filtered over the wooden floor. The attic looked almost deserted, except for a few items she barely remembered. She searched several minutes for the newspaper she'd seen the night before. There was no sign of it. A few copies of *Godey's Ladies Book* were all she found, and she sighed with frustration. It wasn't here. She hadn't really expected to find that particular news article, but anything pertinent would have been useful. Now what did she do?

She turned toward the attic door in defeat. Then her gaze fell on the satin dress, and she moved toward it slowly. It lay in a crumpled heap over an open trunk. She lifted it, and the satin rustled. In the daylight, it looked new. None of the beautiful beadwork was missing from the intricate patterns. Did the dress have unusual powers? Had it brought her back to 1864? There was only one way to find out.

Taking a deep breath, she slid it over her head again. It fell around her in cool, soft folds. With trembling fingers, she began to fasten the buttons. A sudden wind blew through the open attic window, tugging at the dress and making her shiver. She felt slightly dizzy for a moment, then the wind died. Amanda stood in the shadowed silence of the attic and waited. Minutes passed. Nothing happened. Sliding a hand over the dress, she felt loose threads and looked down. A button was missing.

Whatever force had propelled her into the past, it must require that all the buttons be fastened. She frowned. She didn't know quite what she had expected, and was left feeling deflated. What did she do now? Look for the button? But did she really want to go back to her own time yet? Maybe she should see if she could undo the damage caused by the family feud. If she managed to prevent it, then she could go back home with a clear conscience.

When she heard Deborah's voice on the attic stairs, her head jerked up. She didn't want to be found in the dress, and she removed it hastily. She'd just tied the last lace on the robe when the attic door swung open and Deborah entered.

"Oh. I didn't know you were up here," Deborah said in obvious surprise. "I came to find you something to wear, but I see that you've already been looking in the trunks."

"Yes." Amanda flushed and added lamely, "I couldn't help noticing this beautiful gown."

"That was my wedding dress," Deborah said with a

smile as she smoothed the satin folds.

"Your wedding dress?" Amanda echoed. "It's so beautiful. What's it doing up here in the attic?"

"I hid it up here when the Yankees came through last week. Sometimes they take whatever strikes their fancy, and I have a special hiding spot. I suppose Tangie must have taken it out to clean it for me. Michael has already paid for my portrait to be painted in it. An extravagance, I know, but he was quite insistent. The artist is to arrive next week— Are you all right?"

"Yes. No." Amanda managed a smile. "I still feel a bit dizzy; that's all."

"Understandable. You must have had a dreadful time of it. I've sent for Dr. Higdon, and he should be here soon. There have been so many stragglers through here lately, soldiers with wounds from the battle, that he's been very busy. Why don't you go back to bed, and I'll find you something suitable to wear."

"Yes. I think I will. I . . . I'm feeling very odd." Moving slowly, Amanda made her way back to the room she had been given. An ominous echo reverberated in her mind— the wedding portrait had been painted after Michael Scott's death. That meant that sometime in the next week, Deborah's husband would die. Unless she could prevent it.

# *Chapter Six*

Sunlight drifted between magnolia leaves to high-light Amanda's pale hair and the steps of the front porch. Jesse stepped outside, eyeing Amanda where she sat on the top step. She didn't turn around or give any indication that she knew he was there, but remained with her arms clasped loosely in front of her. The simple cotton gown she wore had once belonged to his sister, and was almost too snug. Of course, that was because Amanda refused to wear proper undergarments, Deborah had reported with a scandalized lift of her brows. Even in these times, a corset was considered necessary. He'd always thought corsets foolish and dangerous, but then he much preferred females wearing only scanty garments.

"Are you going to just stand there staring at the back of my head all day?" Amanda demanded in a cross tone. She half turned to glance at him, and Jesse grinned.

"I'm trying to figure out your best angle," he said as he moved to sit beside her on the top step. She didn't offer to move over, and he wedged his frame into the tight space between her right hip and the porch post. He could feel the warmth emanating from her, and found it tantalizing.

She turned to look at him with a wary expression. "Have you figured it out yet?"

"Figured what out?"

"My best angle." She pushed at a loose strand of golden hair, her green eyes narrowing slightly. There was a faint spray of freckles on her nose, and he found that somehow endearing.

"There isn't a best angle," he said when she kept staring at him, and was amused by the indignant way she wrinkled her nose and glared. "If I was going to be chivalrous, this is where I would claim that all of your angles are of matching beauty and perfection, that your fair face has no equal this side of heaven, and that—"

"Rubbish," she said firmly, and some of the indignation in her eyes faded into amusement. "You really are a rogue, aren't you?"

"Among other things. And you?"

"Me? What about me?" She looked wary.

"What did the doctor say about you?"

"That I'm sound as a mule and twice as stubborn."

"My thoughts exactly."

"Liar." She looked down, then slanted him a glance from beneath her lashes. He found it extremely provocative.

"I'm still trying to make up my mind exactly how to classify you, Mrs.—"

She paled. "We were married such a short time, and now he's dead and we had no children . . . I'd feel more comfortable if you'd call me Miss Brandon."

"All right, Miss Brandon. What do you suggest?"

"Number one: Don't try and classify me."

Jesse grinned. "And number two?"

"Who said there had to be a number two?"

"It's generally required."

Her mouth curved slightly. "I see. I wasn't aware of the proper guidelines here. All right—suggestion number two: Realize that I'm just like everyone else here. I want to survive, to be happy."

"You make that sound impossible. It isn't, you know."

She looked surprised. "I find it rather astonishing that you seem to consider happiness possible, under the circumstances."

Shrugging, Jesse said, "Only a fool or a dog can be completely happy. Happiness inherently carries with it a measuring stick by which to judge other events in your life. In comparison, other incidents can be less happy, more happy, or devastating, depending upon your point of view."

"That's a novel notion. I never looked at it that way."

A slight frown puckered the delicate line of her brows, and Jesse had the overwhelming urge to smooth it away. Instead, he leaned over to rub at imaginary dirt on the scuffed toe of his boot. "It's only my opinion, you know. War makes me too introspective. At night, hiding in the woods and hoping no Yankee stumbles over me, I've got a lot of time to think."

He felt her gaze on him as she murmured, "I imagine you do. What else do you think about?"

"Women," he replied promptly, and laughed when she made a rude noise. "Well, you did ask."

"I should have known better. But I suppose men never change through the ages."

"And women do?"

When he glanced up at her, he saw her eyes widen. She stared at him from beneath the dark, lush curve of her lashes, and he was reminded of green woodland pools. Then she glanced away, the frown returning.

"No," she said slowly, "women don't change either. We want the same things now as women wanted a hundred years ago: Love. Security. Maybe even children."

"Do you want children?"

Looking rather startled, she stared at him, blonde wisps of hair clinging to cheeks that were damp with perspiration. He resisted the impulse to stroke them away as she said, "I haven't thought about it in a long time. He—he didn't want any children."

"I'm sorry. If there had been enough time, your husband may not have had a choice about children. Sometimes they come whether you want them or not."

"Oh, no, I take the pill. I mean—" She halted, cheeks flushing pink with confusion as she stammered, "I m-mean, I had to take precautions."

There was something here he didn't understand, some plane of the conversation that was on a different level. Jesse studied Amanda's face for a moment, trying to sort through the myriad of impressions he got every time he talked to her. It didn't matter what they discussed, there were always little things that caught his attention, some slight discrepancy that on the surface sounded normal, but studied closely, failed inspection. It was more than just her claim that she was from England; he'd been abroad, and had never met anyone with her eccentricities.

Looking down again, Jesse said mildly, "I see."

Amanda drew in a deep breath and blurted, "I know you think I'm odd—"

"To say the least," he muttered dryly. "But don't think you have to explain."

"I'm not a spy."

He stood up, raking a hand through his hair as he stared down at her upturned face. She looked so earnest, so—pleading, that he found himself wanting to believe her. "All right. You're not a spy. I believe you."

"Do you?" Amanda stood up, brushing down the rumpled skirts of her gown, staring at him anxiously. "I want to help. I truly do."

His eyes narrowed slightly. "Do you? Then you'll agree to show me how you got out of Memphis?"

"Oh, Lord—all right. If that's what it takes to convince you. But you won't be impressed. I keep telling you, I was just lucky."

"Maybe your luck will hold."

"I don't know," she muttered. "It hasn't been so great lately."

Unable to resist, Jesse reached out to curl a finger under her chin and lift her face to his. He heard her draw in a deep breath. As if drawn by invisible threads, he kissed her, half amazed at the strong desire to do so, and half dismayed that she didn't stop him. Instead she leaned into him, closing her eyes and breathing a soft sigh as if she had known he always meant to kiss her. It was a heady, magical moment, and he was reluctant to break the spell.

Summoning a strength he didn't know he had, he pulled away slightly and stared down at her. Her cheeks were flushed with more than summer heat, and her lashes were half lowered and languorous, her eyes a dreamy green. Dragging his thumb over the slightly swollen contour of her lower lip, he murmured, "I have a feeling your luck is about to change, Miss Brandon."

Lifting her hand, she curled her fingers around his wrist and held tightly, whispering, "I hope you're right."

\*   \*   \*

Balanced atop her mount and moving along a narrow dirt path the following morning, Amanda wondered how on earth she was going to get them past sentries when she had no idea where they were. And why on earth had she even agreed to this ridiculous scheme? It was a harebrained notion that only a desperate man—or woman—would concoct. If not for the fact that Jesse had mentioned the possibility of meeting up with Jamie and Michael along the way, she would have changed her mind despite his electric blue eyes and devastating kiss.

"Careful," Jesse cautioned, and she jerked her attention back to her surroundings, pulling a shawl more closely over her head even though the early morning sun was already beating down with a vengeance. Heat shimmered up from the hard-packed dirt ruts of the main street of town. Holly Springs looked nothing like she knew it—no library, no familiar country café across from the courthouse, just brick buildings far apart and recently burned. She breathed a sigh of relief when they passed through the town without incident and were once more in the shaded, cooler environs of the woods.

Turning to look back at her, Jesse grinned. "Now all we have to worry about are Yankee patrols."

And that was another problem—Jesse. The mystery man of her dreams finally had a name. And a completely different personality than she had once envisioned.

Instead of being the strong, silent type, the Jesse of reality had a more forceful nature. And he was so distrustful. If she thought about it, she could hardly blame him for wondering about her. She could only imagine what he must be thinking, in light of the remarks she had been making and the unfamiliar references in her speech.

Smothering the sudden impulse to burst into laughter,

Amanda studied Jesse's back. He rode just ahead of her, clad in the rough cotton shirt and tan butternut trousers of a backwoods farmer. He carried a heavy pistol stuck into his belt, an uncomfortable reminder of possible danger. Instead of horses, they rode mules, as more befitting farmers than soldiers. Or spies. She shuddered. If she remembered correctly, spies were usually hung if they were caught. Did that stricture apply to females as well? She wished she'd paid better attention to her local history.

Afternoon shadows deepened as they rode along the track Jesse apparently knew well. Hazy sunlight filtered through tree limbs. It was hot, but grew cooler the deeper they rode into the woods. Jesse said little to her, other than a few directions or a warning of low-hanging limbs, leaving Amanda alone with her tortured thoughts. Was it possible that a lifetime of dreaming and wishing had somehow engineered this phenomenon? If dreaming about a man could transport her to the past, perhaps so. In retrospect, she'd come to the conclusion that she'd somehow started this incredible journey by a combined desperation to save the house, a wish that she could change history, and a decision to put on a wedding dress that had been lost for a hundred and thirty years.

Jesse suddenly jerked his mule to a halt and hissed a command for Amanda to be still, startling her. She swallowed the urge to demand an explanation. Dark shadows stretched in the deep woods on each side of the road. Motionless in the shrouded silence surrounding them, she strained to hear what had made Jesse come to such an abrupt stop. It took several moments, but then she heard it, too—the unmistakable sounds of horses and men.

Silently, Jesse gestured for her to dismount, and Amanda did so with shaking hands. She held tight to her mule, putting a hand over its muzzle as she saw Jesse do to his, and followed him from the road into the woods. Sunlight wavered, revealing little more than hazy shadows. Hiding behind her mule in a thicket, Amanda was waiting nervously for something dreadful to happen when she saw Jesse draw his pistol and stand behind a tree.

Closing her eyes, she shivered with apprehension. When a hand fastened on her arm, she gasped, eyes jerking open. Jesse put a hand over her mouth.

"Hush. A Yankee patrol," he said with his lips against her ear. "Stay still and keep your mule quiet."

Nodding wordlessly, Amanda tried to still her wildly thumping heart. This was insane. What was she doing out here? Would she end up dead long before she'd ever been born? Did it work that way?

As the patrol drew close, Jesse seemed to sense her growing panic. He took her hand, giving it a slight squeeze. She held tightly, as if he were the only link to safety and sanity. Leaves crunched underfoot, and occasionally a small twig or fallen branch would snap as the patrol passed by close enough for her to see individual features on the men. Though garbed in blue uniforms and carrying weapons, the majority looked to her like boys instead of the hardened soldiers she'd always envisioned.

Recent rains had soaked the earth, and in the deep woods the sun had not yet dried the roads, leaving them quagmires that sucked at wagon wheels, men, and beasts. It seemed to take forever for the patrol to pass by, and Amanda fretted that at any moment, they would be discovered.

When at last the Yankees had gone and only the echoes of tramping feet and rattling wagons could be heard in the distance, she breathed easier. "I thought one of them looked directly at me once," she murmured. "I just knew we were goners."

Realizing that Jesse was still holding her hand, she turned to look at him. He regarded her with a strange intensity as he released her hand.

"You could have called out, you know," he said softly.

"Why would I do that?"

He shrugged and said, "The Yankees would love to get their hands on me. They've been chasing me for two years now, ever since Memphis fell. There's a price on my head."

"I told you—I'm not a Northern spy. I have no intention of betraying you."

Jesse studied her for another moment, then looked away and said, "Not even if I tell you that the Federals call me the Hawk?"

"Really. Then I'm in famous company, I see. Should I be impressed?"

A faint smile tucked in one corner of his mouth, and the suggestion of a dimple creased his cheek. "You should be. Are you?"

"Very. I can truly say I've never before met one of Forrest's raiders."

"Rangers," he corrected with a grin. "And I hate to disappoint you, but I'm a free agent for the South. I work for whoever needs me most. Of course, since I'm pretty familiar with Memphis and northern Mississippi, I'm most effective here. When Forrest conducts his campaigns in Georgia and Alabama, I give whatever services I can to the next Confederate commander in this area."

"Ah. A man of versatility, then."

His eyes narrowed slightly, and she could feel a subtle

change in the way he turned to look at her. "I can be very versatile," he murmured.

Amanda caught her breath. The rush of fear she'd felt when danger was near didn't compare with the sparks that vibrated between them now. She didn't quite understand it, but there was electricity in the air, almost as if a bolt of summer lightning had struck nearby. Never before had she felt this way, not even with her late husband. There had been none of the tension, the feeling as if she were a delicate instrument strung too tightly—the feeling that if she didn't somehow gain release, she would explode.

"Jesse," she said tentatively, her voice a whisper, "I can't explain what's happening to me anymore. Everything is so—so strange."

Filtered sunlight flickered through tree limbs to cast shadows on his face as he studied her for a long moment. "Strange?" he repeated. "Or just different?"

"Different, I suppose. No—strange as well. Oh, not just you. It's more than that."

"I don't suppose you could explain that a little bit better," he muttered, but the cynicism she'd half expected was absent from his tone.

"I wish I could. If I told you what has really happened to me, you'd be shocked. You wouldn't believe it. I'm not sure I do."

Reaching out, he curled his hand beneath her chin and lifted her face so that he could look into her eyes. "There are times things happen to people through no fault of their own. I would never condemn someone for what they did not do of their own free will."

Realizing that he thought she meant something else, Amanda opened her mouth to explain, but Jesse leaned forward and kissed her. Her instant reaction to the kiss took her so by surprise, she could not think. His lips were warm and firm on hers, and she couldn't help the surge of response that made her lift her arms and put them around his neck.

Before she quite knew what was happening, she found herself clinging to him in a passionate embrace that left her breathless and aching. Jesse kissed her mouth, then the line of her jaw up to her ear, bunching her hair in his fist to hold it, his breath heated against her skin. Amanda shivered and clung to him as if drowning.

It was like drowning. The tides of overwhelming reaction left her floundering, and she was helpless to do more than curve her hands over his shoulders and hold on when he trailed kisses down the arch of her throat. He was holding her up with one arm behind her back while his other hand tunneled into her hair to hold her head. The neat coils of hair she'd put atop her head that morning loosened, tumbling around her shoulders in a disorderly mass.

"This is crazy," he muttered, lips moving against the pulse at the base of her throat. His arm tightened behind her, pulling her hard against him. "We're likely to be shot if we don't pay better attention to what's going on around us."

Through a foggy haze, Amanda heard herself say, "Yes. You're right."

But neither of them relinquished the other. Her fingers were tangled in the material of his shirt, caressing his muscled back. Heat and humidity only added to the inferno that raged inside her, and she wondered vaguely if she'd truly lost her mind. This was even more unbelievable than finding herself in another century.

When Jesse finally pulled away, his chest was rising and falling rapidly and there was a pinched look on his face.

"It will be dark soon," he said thickly. "I know a place where we can camp for the night."

It was crazy and she knew it, but her entire world had careened out of control. Amanda shivered. Sexual tension only added to the physical strain of hours of unaccustomed riding. It felt as if every muscle in her body were protesting, and all her internal organs were in revolt. She briefly closed her eyes.

"Are you all right?"

Amanda glanced up to find Jesse's night-blue eyes resting on her. She managed a smile. "I'm fine. I can keep up."

"I've no doubt of that," he replied in a murmur. "You seem to be full of surprises."

"I'm not nearly as fragile as you may think. I take all the proper vitamins, read all the right magazines—never mind. I'm fine."

Giving her a half smile, Jesse turned his attention to the narrow road a short distance ahead. He seemed to be waiting for something or someone, standing still and silent in the shadow of a huge elm. Finally he motioned for her to remount and follow him. Wagon ruts were the only indication that it was some sort of road, and Amanda could barely see them in places. Apparently, Jesse knew exactly where he was and where he was going. She only wished she did.

# *Chapter Seven*

NIGHT WAS CLOSING in around them, and Amanda had no idea how far they had gone. Jesse seemed to be taking a circuitous route, weaving in and out of thickets, back onto the road, and then into the woods again. None of which added up to a feeling of security. Or did it? Odd, but she felt safe with him despite the gravity of their mission. Even when she'd seen the Yankees, she'd not felt as threatened as she should have. As a child she'd sensed strength and promise in the handsome man in the photograph. That impression of the man in her dreams was not lessened by the reality of him. Jesse Jordan exuded a strong sensuality and strength of will that could never have been totally captured by mere photographic equipment or even imagination.

"This is where we'll camp for the night," Jesse said finally, dragging his mule to a halt in a small thicket surrounded by well-laden blackberry bushes. He dismounted with an agile leap, apparently suffering no ill effects from their daylong ride.

Amanda dismounted stiffly, silently cursing the uncomfortable, restrictive clothing she was forced to wear. Of all the things in the twentieth century she missed, shorts and trousers were at the top of the list. How had women ever managed to get around in long skirts and these wretched undergarments? The pantalets went to her knees, and Deborah had been so horrified when she'd suggested cutting them off she'd quickly said she was only teasing. Now here she was in the middle of the woods in hot summer weather wearing enough layers of clothing to smother her mule.

Jesse eyed her with a lifted brow, apparently misreading her discontent. "I know this isn't exactly the Gayoso House, but it'll do."

"Gayoso House? Oh, I remember. It's the nineteenth-century equivalent of The Peabody."

As he reached for her reins, Jesse gave her a speculative glance from beneath the thick bristle of his lashes. "I never heard of the Peabody. Is that a Memphis hotel?"

"It will be the South's finest one day," she replied with an amused smile. "Don't look so worried. That's just a prediction."

Resting one arm across the saddle, Jesse studied her in the late light. His face was dark and shadowed, highlighted only by a hazy glow from the setting sun. "A prediction," he repeated slowly. "Are you saying that you can predict the future?"

"Let's just say that there are certain things I may be able to predict correctly. And I don't need a crystal ball or pack of cards." She stretched her arms to ease cramped muscles, well aware of his intent gaze. How much should she say and how much should she let him discover for himself? He probably wouldn't believe her if she said the Southern cause was doomed, and might even consider her a traitor. No, best to allow him to think whatever he wished.

After a moment, Jesse began to silently remove the saddles from both mules, and Amanda took custody of the food sacks Deborah had prepared for them. Along with cornmeal cakes, there were pieces of dried fruit and some kind of salted meat. She arranged the crude meal on the top of a rough wool blanket she spread over a tree stump, looking up when Jesse joined her. "No fire, I presume," she said as he sat down, and he nodded.

"No fire. Can't risk the smoke. It's too hot, anyway."

Jesse ate silently, flashing her an occasional piercing glance that she found extremely unsettling. The light had dimmed, and it was difficult seeing much beyond a few feet in front of her. The black silhouettes of trees and brush slowly blended into an anonymous, blurring line.

"So tell me," she said when the silence threatened to stretch into uncomfortable infinity, "how long have you known the Brandon family?"

"Most of my life." Jesse ate the last of the wild blackberries they had picked, then washed them down with water from a leather flask. "Our fathers attended the same university as young men."

"You know," Amanda said slowly, "I've always been confused by the relationship of Michael Scott and James Brandon. I mean, I know they're half brothers, but I cannot recall who came first."

Jesse shrugged. "It's simple enough. James Senior wed Clare Scott, a widow with a young son named Michael. She gave birth to Jamie the next year. But it was always Jamie who was his father's heir, not Michael."

"And that obviously made no difference to Deborah," Amanda mused.

"Obviously," Jesse said lightly, "my sister married for love."

After a moment, Amanda asked, "If the unthinkable should happen and the South loses this war, what will you do afterward?"

"Do?" He looked startled. "I hadn't thought that far ahead, though I have to admit there are times I wonder just how long the Confederacy can hang on without ammunition factories. Our only hope is to convince England to support our cause. After we win, I'll go back to my studies at the university, then maybe finish my grand tour."

"And if we should lose? What will happen to you?"

"Why the sudden curiosity?" Jesse leaned to one side, propping up his weight on an elbow. "Do you have any suggestions? Or are you predicting that the South will lose?"

She looked down at her clasped hands, then up at him. "Let's just say morbid curiosity prompted the question."

"I see." A patch of pale light shifted, falling across his face and casting it in muted shades of dark and light. A faint smile curled his mouth. "Go to South America, I guess. I've heard it's almost like the South. A man can make his own life down there."

So that was what had happened to him after the war, why he'd disappeared from family history along with most of the Scotts. Amanda drew in a shaky breath, wondering if she was doing the right thing. What if she failed? What if she couldn't prevent the feud from happening?

"All right," Jesse said, "I've answered your questions. Now you answer mine. Who are you really?"

Amanda hesitated. Did she dare tell him the truth when she wasn't even certain what the truth was anymore? "I really am a Brandon," she said vaguely, "but distantly related to Jamie. It's a long, boring story, and it's hard to untangle all the bloodlines."

"All right," Jesse said after a moment, "I guess I believe that. What about your late husband? Was he a Yankee? Is that why you prefer going by your maiden name?"

"No, he was from Memphis. I suppose I've just always considered myself a Brandon. And I've always loved Oakleigh, so I want to see it stay in the family. It's my belief that Grandfather James did leave a portion of the land to Michael as well as to his own son. Is that true?"

"Yes. Of course, once the war started, Michael had to put off his plans to build his own house on his portion. He and Jamie got along well enough until—"

He broke off, and Amanda said softly, "Until Michael wed Deborah. Now there's tension between them. Is that what you didn't say?"

"Yes, damn you. But don't go blaming my sister. It was something planned by our parents, not her. Jamie never did say anything one way or the other. Who knew he'd take it so hard?"

"There have been words between Jamie and Michael?"

"Once or twice." Jesse sat up and ran a hand through his hair. "They'll work it out. There's more to think about now with the war. The Yankees hold Memphis, and if they have their way, they're going to keep Forrest busy protecting the Mississippi grainfields and supply lines when we really need him to strike Sherman's flanks."

"So Jamie and Michael are both riding with Forrest?"

"Yes," he answered slowly. His eyes narrowed in sudden suspicion. "I thought you knew that."

"I just wondered why neither of them were there when I—I arrived, that's all. I'd certainly like to meet Jamie. Again. Meet him again, of course. It's been a long time since we've seen each other."

After a moment of taut silence, Jesse shrugged and said,

"So many Yankees have been coming through Holly Springs lately that it's too risky to spend much time at Oakleigh."

"Deborah said several patrols have stopped at Oakleigh, but at least they left it standing."

"After they'd cleaned out the larder and livestock. Good thing I ran across one of the supply wagons they abandoned when they were running from Forrest."

"You did?" Amanda laughed. "That's sweet revenge."

Jesse grinned. "Very sweet. None of the Yankees were able to get close enough to catch me, and they chased me almost all the way back to the Coldwater Bottoms."

*Coldwater Bottoms.* Why did that sound important to her? Amanda fell silent, trying to remember. Wait—that was it. The news article in the attic had said Michael Scott was killed in the Coldwater Bottoms. But had it specified when Michael died? Her head jerked up suddenly. "What is today's date?"

"It's June the fourteenth. Why?"

Her heart leaped into her throat. The news article she'd found in the attic flashed in her memory with wrenching clarity: *June 16, 1864.* Now it was June 14—two days before Michael Scott died exactly one hundred and thirty years ago. She could stop it. She could keep Michael from being killed and prevent the feud between the Scotts and the Brandons. Oakleigh would remain in the family.

Surging to her feet, Amanda said urgently, "We have to find them. We have to find Michael and Jamie before it's too late!"

# *Chapter Eight*

"WHAT THE DEVIL are you talking about?" Jesse snapped, rising to his feet and grabbing Amanda by her shoulders. She shrugged free and took a step back. A loose strand of pale hair fell over her forehead and into her eyes, and she shoved it back. Her eyes in the dim light were wide and dark as jade. He recognized the anxiety in her expression. Her words tumbled over one another, and she put out a hand as if to keep him there.

"Jesse, I know you don't understand, and I don't really, either, but I know something terrible is going to happen. We have to find them before it does. . . ."

"For the love of—I was right. You're deranged." Jesse shook his head, wondering what he was going to do with her now. This went beyond simple shock from fear. Now she'd crossed the boundaries into uncharted territory that was far beyond his first suspicions. How could he help a woman who claimed to predict the future, yet knew little about her own past?

"Please believe me," Amanda was begging. "I know it

sounds too fantastic to be true, but it is. They're in danger. Michael Scott will be killed if we don't intervene, and James Brandon will be blamed for it.''

"Would it be too much to ask just how you know this?'' Jesse asked skeptically. "Unless maybe you know a lot more about the Yankees' plans than you've said, I don't know how you'd know Jamie and Michael are in danger when we aren't even certain where they are.''

Amanda drew in a deep breath, and the hand she had on his arm tightened. "Look, I told you I could predict certain events. What if I told you that I know Forrest plans to ride directly into Memphis in an attempt to take it back from the Federals?''

Jesse stared at her. Though Forrest had indeed mentioned that aim several times, it was only a distant hope, not an actual plan. He managed a careless shrug.

"Then I'd say you know what just about everyone else in northern Mississippi and western Tennessee can guess,'' Jesse said grimly. "It would be more of a surprise if he didn't plan to take back Memphis.''

"But he will attempt it in August, and his brother will ride his horse straight into the lobby of the Gayoso House,'' Amanda said with convincing fervor. "A Yankee general will run away in his nightshirt, abandoning his pants and his wife. The legend will live a lot longer than Forrest, I promise you that.''

"How do you know all this? You sound very sure of your facts.''

"I am sure.'' Amanda drew in a deep breath, fastening her gaze on him, and he felt a twinge of uncertainty. "I told you I can predict certain future events. You'll just have to trust me, Jesse.''

He smiled faintly. "That's asking a lot. Would you trust

me under the same circumstances?''

''Probably not,'' she answered more honestly than he'd thought she would. ''But this is very important. I know you have been given a mission, but so have I. If we find Michael and Jamie, we can prevent a family disaster. Think of Deborah's happiness. She's your sister. Will you risk her being made a widow?''

''Amanda—'' Jesse paused helplessly. She sounded so damn certain. It was possible that she could actually predict future events, he supposed, but much more probable that she had somehow come across vital information concerning the two Forrest scouts. Could he take a chance that she was giving him the opportunity to save them for whatever reasons?

''Are we near the Coldwater Bottoms yet?'' she asked.

Jesse's eyes narrowed. ''We're on Hurricane Creek. Why?''

''Because there are Yankee soldiers hiding there, and that is where you'll find Michael and Jamie. We have to get there in time, Jesse. Please.''

Her urgency penetrated his resistance, and Jesse heard himself saying, ''I guess another detour won't hurt. If you're wrong, we still won't be too far out of our way.''

Amanda smiled, and in the fading light of dusk, he recognized a lot more in her eyes than just concern for her family. He took a deep breath and reached for her, and she came into his arms willingly.

For several minutes, he held her to him. He could feel the rapid thud of her heart, and the gentle rhythm of her breathing. Her hair smelled of flowers, tickling his nose as he rested his chin on the top of her head. For the life of him, he couldn't understand how he'd been drawn to this woman so quickly. It was as if the first meeting of their eyes had been the thousandth, and he'd felt a jolt that even her sharp words had done nothing to erase. He'd heard of falling in love at first sight, but until now had never believed it was possible.

Finally releasing her, Jesse said gruffly, "We have to let the mules rest. Get some sleep, and I'll wake you in a little while."

She smiled up at him. "Thank you for believing me."

"I don't suppose," he muttered, "that you have any notion of exactly *where* in the swamps they'll be? It might help us find them a lot quicker."

"I'm afraid not," she said with obvious regret. "But I do know that if we don't find them in time, we'll all be sorry."

Amanda woke with a sudden jerk, trying to remember where she was. Then her memory returned in a rush, and she peered through the dark shadows toward Jesse. He was rolled up in his blanket a foot away, and she could hear the steady rhythm of his breathing. As her eyes adjusted to the absence of light, she could make out small details.

Jesse's arm was bent beneath his head as a pillow, his body too long for the blanket. The dull gleam of his pistol was barely discernible at his side. He was taking no chance, she saw.

"What are you looking at?" Jesse asked softly, startling her.

When her heartbeat slowed, she said, "I didn't know you were awake."

"Do you think I could sleep knowing there are a few hundred Yankees prowling around?" Jesse sat up, folding his long legs in front of him. "You didn't sleep long. Why are you awake?"

"It could be because I'm rested."

"But it's not."

"No," she said. "It's not."

There was the rustle of damp leaves as he moved closer to her. His hand cupped her cheek, warm and strong and hard. She shuddered at the contact, and he pulled away.

"Scared?" he asked softly, and she nodded.

"Yes. Terrified. I wish I were asleep. At least my dreams aren't quite as scary."

He laughed. "What do you dream about?"

She was tempted to tell him the truth, that as a child she had dreamed about him, but she didn't. "Right now, fried chicken," she replied, and her stomach growled audibly.

Chuckling, Jesse lay down next to her. For a moment he fumbled in his pocket, then drew something out and held it up. She strained to see in the dim light. "Here," he said. "It's not fried chicken, but it may help."

To her surprise, it was a stick of hard candy. "Where did you get this?"

"I've been saving it for an emergency. This qualifies, I guess."

Amanda broke it in two, thrusting a piece into his palm. "My conscience would sting if I hogged it all. I insist we share."

"Sounds fair to me."

For several minutes they lay quietly, then Jesse asked, "Did you eat yours already?"

"Yes."

"I thought I heard you crunching. I like to savor mine for a while, make it last." His voice lowered huskily. "Are you always in such a hurry to enjoy things?"

"Sometimes." She took a deep breath. "And sometimes I like to make things last."

She was expecting it when he rolled to his side and pulled her into his embrace, expecting his kiss. What she wasn't expecting was the depth of her fiery response. Maybe it had been too long, maybe it was the heightened sense of being in danger, or maybe it was just Jesse: but whatever it was, Amanda knew she was lost.

And he seemed to know it too.

Caressing her, hands skimming lightly over her face, arms, and then shifting to her waist, Jesse stroked her quivering body with skillful touches. Amanda wore no stays or corset, and he found that out quickly. His fingers deftly undid the buttons of her shirtwaist and slid inside to stroke her bare skin, and Amanda caught her breath. Still kissing her, Jesse put a hand on her breast.

She arched upward, unable to think clearly, unable to do more than react. Once, he lifted his head to gaze down at her through lowered lashes, his eyes a hot, narrowed blue, but Amanda could barely think by then. Nothing mattered at this moment but Jesse, his touch and kiss and the way he was murmuring soft endearments to her, telling her she was beautiful, that he'd waited for her all his life. She believed him because she wanted to, because she needed to hear it from him.

And when she gave herself to him, it was completely, wholly, body and mind and soul. With Jesse inside her, nothing in the outside world could touch or hurt her. The aching tension grew higher and hotter until the world seemed to explode around her and she was drifting earthward like a feather, twisting and turning and as light as air. Jesse's voice was against her ear, breathless and hoarse, muttering her name as he buried his hands in her hair and collapsed atop her.

Drowsy, holding him in her arms and feeling his warm,

damp body next to hers, she thought that no matter what else ever happened to her, she would have this memory to hold close.

Riding through knee-high water that soaked her dress and made her uncomfortably aware that slithery creatures still inhabited the swamps, Amanda kept her gaze fastened on Jesse's tall silhouette. They had ridden part of the night and all day. She'd thought when she woke again that she would feel shy with him, but his easy smile and the light in his blue eyes had quickly eased her fears.

The sense of urgency was on them now, as it was dark again. The mules were weary and plodding. At least the rain that had plagued northern Mississippi in the past weeks had stopped. There was an almost full moon to provide light. Tree stumps and sluggish pools smelling of rotting wood and stagnant water were everywhere. Dry land seemed a thing of the past.

"It hardly seems likely the Yankees would come this way," Amanda ventured to say once, but Jesse pointed out what were to him obvious signs of their recent passage.

"The water here has been stirred up with a lot of mud, which indicates horses and men have passed through within the last few hours. It takes a while for that much mud to sink back to the bottom of the swamp."

"I don't know how you can tell the difference," Amanda said, peering at the cloudy water. Patches of moonlight on the water's surface were distorted and murky.

It was a relief when they finally reached comparatively dry land, and she slid from the mule onto the marshy bank with a sigh. One of the mules shook much as a dog would do, spraying her with foul-smelling swamp water. Looking down at her borrowed dress, Amanda had the rueful hope that it was not one of Deborah's best. It was certainly ruined now. If she'd known that their trip would entail sloshing through swamps, she'd have insisted upon borrowing men's trousers instead of the dress. She was grateful she'd refused the corset and most of the petticoats as being too uncomfortable and cumbersome. Maybe modern clothes didn't have the romantic appeal of the nineteenth century, but they were definitely more practical.

"Here," Jesse said, holding out a hand, and Amanda put her hand in his strong clasp as he helped her up a steep bank. There was something to be said, however, for the definite romantic appeal of the men in the nineteenth century, she decided when he swept her from her feet to lift her over another water-filled gully.

She took advantage of his gallantry by putting her arms around his neck and holding tightly, and he laughed softly. "If I didn't know better, Miss Brandon, I'd think you were a delicate creature."

"What makes you think I'm not? Just because I have endurance doesn't mean I'm not as fragile as the next woman."

"There's nothing fragile about you," Jesse remarked as he stopped and swung her to her feet on solid ground. "You have a determination that would put most men to shame."

"Do I?" She looked up at his shadowed face, and saw that he was smiling. "Why do you say that?"

"If you didn't," he replied softly, placing a finger under her chin and lowering his head to brush his mouth against hers, "I sure wouldn't be traveling through the swamps in the middle of the night on a wild notion."

"Don't you believe me?"

He kissed her again, then said, "Let's just say that I'll

reserve my final judgment until later.''

"Then you're doing this for me, not because you have any faith in my prediction." When he frowned and started to reply, she put a hand over his lips. "No. It's all right. I find it very gratifying that you have enough regard for me to agree to do this even when you don't really believe it."

Jesse stared at her in the dappled moonlight. "You're an odd little thing," he said after a moment. "You almost make me believe in destiny."

"Almost? Don't you believe in fate?"

"No. I believe man controls his own fate by his actions. Or I did until I met you, that is. Now I wonder if there aren't sometimes inevitable conclusions."

Amanda asked, "Do you mean kismet? Preordained destiny? One man for one woman? That kind of thing?"

"You must admit," he said wryly, "that there could be few other explanations for our ending up in the swamps like this. It's not exactly a rational thing for me to do, and I used to think I was a very rational man."

"This is very rational. You're going to keep your brother-in-law from being killed." She glanced up when a cloud passed over the moon and shadows darkened the night. "We must hurry. I'm not certain exactly when it will happen, but any time after midnight tonight is a risk."

Jesse helped her mount the mud-covered mule and looked up at her. "You know that if you're wrong, Forrest will probably have me shot for disobeying orders."

She smiled. "No, he won't. For one thing, I'm not wrong. For another, Forrest would never be foolish enough to shoot a valuable soldier for such a trivial thing—though he might not mind giving you the very devil for a while."

"If that's intended to be comforting," Jesse muttered,

"it's not. I've seen Forrest's brand of chastisement, and it holds no appeal for me."

Amanda laughed, but she couldn't help feeling a twinge of self-doubt. What if she was wrong? Or they didn't find Michael and Jamie in time? All manner of things could go wrong, and she might be risking a lot more than Jesse's pride. As she had been reminded earlier, these were perilous times. Anything could happen. She might even end up being a footnote in history: the death of a mysterious woman in the Coldwater River Bottoms at the hands of the Yankees. It was hardly a comforting thought.

Doubts plagued her as they rode along in silence and the moon drifted in and out of clouds, providing fitful light for them to see their way. They'd reached Panther Creek when Jesse jerked his mule to a halt and put up a warning hand. Amanda's heart lurched into her throat.

Through the trees ahead of them, she could see the faint flicker of a fire on the opposite banks of the creek. Shadows grouped around the flames, but she could not discern if the men were Federal or Rebel. Her heart thudded painfully against her ribs when Jesse motioned silently for her to dismount.

He'd drawn his pistol; moonlight gleamed dully along the long, lethal barrel. Amanda reached his side, averting her eyes from the weapon. It was a too vivid reminder of their danger.

"Who are they?" she whispered when the tension grew too heavy for her to bear.

He glanced at her, then turned his attention back to the campfire. "Yankees," he said softly. "No sentries that I can see, but those men sitting right in front of the fire are prisoners that you should recognize."

"I should?" She stared at the fire, slowly able to detect

the firelit forms of two men with their hands bound in front of them. It struck her who they must be. "Michael and Jamie," she breathed softly, and Jesse nodded.

"Yes. You were right, it seems. I'll do what I can to get them out of there before the Yankees kill them. I want you to stay here—"

"No." Her quick response made him jerk his head around with a frown, and he glared at her.

"I refuse to allow you to be endangered any more than you already are. For the love of God, don't be stubborn."

"It isn't stubbornness. It's determination, remember?"

Jesse swore softly, then growled, "I suppose we don't have time to argue about this. Can you fire a weapon?"

Startled, she said, "If I have to. I took a course at the shooting range at the penal farm."

"These are not wooden targets, but live ones. If nothing else, I suppose you can at least put the fear of God into them," Jesse muttered as he withdrew another pistol from beneath his shirt. "It's loaded and fires to the left. Try to remember that. Pray the powder has stayed dry and the cartridge isn't jammed."

Gingerly hefting the heavy pistol in her right hand, Amanda took a deep breath. "What's your plan?"

"I don't have a damned plan," he said grimly.

She grabbed his sleeve. "We can't succeed without some kind of plan. Damn—what would MacGyver do?"

"Tsk tsk. Your language—who the devil is MacGyver?"

"Never mind. Wait—I know. Do you have any extra bullets and powder?"

"These pistols would be rather useless if I didn't," Jesse pointed out.

"Good. I have an idea. . . ."

# *Chapter Nine*

SWEARING SOFTLY TO himself, Jesse had to admit as he snaked his way through the underbrush on his belly that Amanda had a pretty good idea. It was a variation of one of Forrest's favorite tricks, and it just might work. And it seemed as if she'd been right in feeling that Michael and Jamie were in danger. From the looks of things, they were in a dire situation.

Seated on the ground with their hands tightly bound in front, the prisoners had ropes looped from their wrists to the bonds around their ankles. Trussed like Christmas geese, Jesse mused as he paused beneath the thorny branches of a blackberry bush. He'd have to be ready and work quickly when Amanda provided the necessary distraction.

Stickers pressed painfully through the material of his shirt, pricking his skin as he reached into the pouch at his belt for the extra bullets. With Amanda's clumsy help, he'd loaded them with extra powder, packing it tightly into the metal cartridges. In crossing the creek, he'd had to hold the powder bag high above his head to keep it dry. Now he hid in the brambles and waited for Amanda to accomplish her goal.

One of the Yankees around the fire rose and stretched, then walked toward the two Rebel captives. He stood for a moment grinning down at them. "Old Forrest gave us hell at Brice's Cross Roads, but you Johnny Rebs will do the payin' for it when we git you back to Washburn in Memphis."

Michael Scott glanced up, and Jesse winced when he saw his brother-in-law's battered face. Through split lips, Michael said, "You Yanks only got what you deserved."

"Is that right? It wasn't us who started this damn war, it was you Southern hotheads."

Michael glared at him. "You're standing on Southern land; what did you expect—a warm reception? Well, I hope we gave you damn Yanks a hot enough welcome at Brice's Cross Roads. . . ."

Crouching down, the soldier glared at his prisoner. "My brother died in that battle, Reb. As far as I'm concerned, I'd just as soon shoot you now as wait till we git you to Memphis."

"Untie me, and we can settle up with pistols at ten paces," Michael shot back. "Or are you too scared?"

Jesse smothered an oath. Young fool. What did he think he was doing, prodding the enemy into retaliation? He could understand preferring death in the swamps to one at the end of a rope, but as long as he was alive, there was hope. Where the devil was Amanda? What was taking so long? If she didn't hurry, that hot-tempered brother-in-law of his was going to talk this Yankee into shooting him before he could be rescued.

Glancing at Jamie, Jesse saw that he was staring at his

half brother with narrowed eyes. Finally Jamie said, "Let it go, Michael. Leave the Yank alone before you make him cry."

Furious now, the Yankee soldier stood up and drew his pistol. Jesse tensed. He had to do something quickly. But what? He wasn't near enough to the fire yet, not with the Yankee only a few feet away and too close to risk doing anything.

"Damn Rebs," the soldier was snarling as he thumbed back the hammer on his Navy six, "I'd just as soon see you all in hell. . . ."

Jesse cocked his own pistol and took aim on the Yankee. Sweat beaded his forehead and dripped into his eyes, stinging. Suicide. That's what this was—suicide.

Just when it seemed as if he'd have to shoot, a loud explosion shattered the night. Men shouted and leaped from their blankets, scattering as they fumbled for weapons and prepared to meet an assault.

The soldier about to shoot Michael and Jamie jerked around in surprise, and Jesse squeezed the trigger of his pistol. It bucked in his hand, and he was scrambling to his feet even as he saw the Yankee clutch his chest and fall backward. Michael and Jamie had instinctively hit the ground, falling to one side as best they could. Jesse ran to them in a crouch, praying the Yankees wouldn't see through the ruse until he had them free.

Slicing through the ropes binding them with his sharp knife, Jesse just grinned at their obvious surprise when they recognized him. "Run like hell," was all he said before turning to toss his powder-packed bullets at the campfire. In the confusion, he managed to run back into the thick woods just as the bullets began to explode, adding to the general chaos.

Ahead of him, he could see Michael and Jamie running through the woods toward Panther Creek. When Michael stumbled and fell, Jamie paused to help him up, half dragging him as they fled. Jesse paused to set off a few more bullets, hoping the damp ground wouldn't keep them from exploding.

Reaching the edge of the creek, he paused, breathing hard. Amanda ran to the edge of the opposite bank, her moonlit face anxious as she called across the water, "Where are they? Did you free them?"

Unable to catch his breath, he pointed, and she turned to see the two men approach. Bruised and battered but very much alive, they grinned when they reached Jesse.

"If we had time," Jamie drawled, "I'd kiss you."

"Save it for the ladies," Jesse shot back. "Let's put some miles between us and those Yanks. They're going to be mad as hell when they figure out you're gone and there ain't no more Rebs in sight."

They wasted no time in floundering into the murky water of the creek. Recent rains had swollen it, and the current was swift. Jesse held his pistol up in the air to keep the powder dry, cursing the drag of water against his body. It seemed to take much longer to get back across than it had to cross the first time, but finally he clambered up onto the bank.

Breathing hard and dripping muddy water, he gave a mild protest when Amanda flung her arms around him. "Hey, you'll get wet. . . ."

"I don't care," she said in a half sob. "You did it. You freed them. Now Michael won't die and Jamie won't be accused, and there won't be a family feud and Oakleigh won't be torn down for a McDonald's—"

"Hush, hush," he said, reaching out to hold her against

him. "You're hysterical. We don't have time for this. Michael's hurt. We'll have to let him ride one of the mules back to Oakleigh. And we sure can't stand here congratulating ourselves, or the Yankees will have us all. Now come on. You can get reacquainted with Jamie when we get back home."

"Oh—yes," she said softly, and he gave her a sharp look. Moonlight gave her face a pale glow, but her eyes were shadowed.

"What's the matter, Amanda?"

"There's something I must tell you," she began, but was interrupted just then as Jamie and Michael reached them.

Dripping and exhausted, they sank to the muddy banks, and Jesse knew they'd never all be able to make it away with only two mules. He made a swift decision.

"Jamie, you and Michael take the mules. Don't bother to argue. Amanda and I will walk back. The Yanks won't be looking for an old farm couple. They'll be looking for two Rebs. You and Amanda can catch up on family history later."

"Amanda?" Jamie echoed, lifting his head to look up at Jesse with a puzzled frown. "Who's that?"

A chill shivered down his spine, and Jesse turned to look at Amanda. She met his gaze steadily, but offered no explanation or defense. He looked back at Jamie and said, "Don't you have a cousin named Amanda?"

"Not that I know about. Why?"

Jesse drew in a deep breath. "It doesn't matter right now. What's important is getting you two safely out of here. The mules are tethered over in that grove of cottonwoods. Take the levee road around. You're less likely to run into any patrols that way, as Morton and Forrest have pretty much got the Yanks on the run."

Rising to his feet with an effort, Jamie reached down to help his brother up, then turned back to Jesse. He gave a wet, weary smile. "See you at Oakleigh."

"Yeah. See you at Oakleigh," Jesse said flatly. He stood watching them disappear into the shadows, unwilling to even look at Amanda. What could she say? What explanation could she give for her lies that would be believable? And what reason would she have for lying in the first place, unless she was the enemy.

Closing his eyes, Jesse had the miserable thought that he would hardly care if she was Lincoln's daughter. He still wanted her, and that inescapable fact was as galling as the knowledge that it went against everything he'd been fighting for these past three years. . . .

Oakleigh was just ahead. Amanda could see the chimneys rising above the tops of the trees. In the uneventful day and a half since they'd liberated Jamie and Michael, Jesse had said very little to her. Beyond an occasional comment or general direction, he'd been remote and aloof. She had tried to explain once, but he'd just looked at her with shadowed blue eyes and said he didn't want to know.

Now they were within sight of the house and she knew she would have to tell him everything or lose it all. She'd thought—hoped? feared?—that like Sam Becket in the *Quantum Leap* television series, once she had accomplished her mission and saved Michael, she would be transported elsewhere. Or at the very least, wake up in her own bed at home. But it had not happened.

She was still here, and she didn't know quite what to do now except tell Jesse the truth. Then he'd probably have her committed to the nineteenth-century equivalent of an insane asylum, and she'd spend her final days knitting wool caps in a padded cell. If she knew another way, she'd take it. But she didn't.

"Jesse," she said when they reached the edge of the woods bordering the pasture behind the house, "I have to talk to you."

He jerked to a halt, his back stiff and straight. Afternoon sunlight glittered in his black hair, making it glisten. "I told you. I don't want to hear it."

"But—"

He whirled on her, and she was surprised at the fury and pain in his eyes as he snarled, "It doesn't matter, damn it. Do you understand that? It doesn't matter to me who you are."

Grief clogged her throat and brought tears to her eyes. "Why not?" she whispered. "It matters to me who you are."

"God." Jesse closed his eyes for a moment, and she saw his hands clench and unclench at his sides.

Moving to him, she stood on her toes and pressed a kiss on his jawline. His hands flashed up to grab her, and his fingers dug painfully into her upper arms. He looked down at her through the thick brush of his lashes.

"It doesn't matter, Amanda," he rasped. "If you tell me you're in league with the devil or the Yankees, I don't care. God help me—I don't care."

His last words were a groan, and she felt a flash of hope. For the first time since she'd awakened on the attic floor, she caught a glimpse of promise.

"Jesse—are you saying you love me?"

"I don't know if it's love or obsession, but whatever it is, you're all I think about." He looked despairing, and Amanda pulled free of his grasp and put both her palms on each side of his face.

"I love you, Jesse," she said softly. "I think I've loved you since I saw your face in a photograph when I was ten."

His brows knit in a frown and he shook his head. "I've fallen in love with a madwoman. I suppose they'll lock us up together one day."

"They may," she agreed, "especially if I ever tell anyone what I'm about to tell you."

"Amanda, I don't think I want to hear this."

"But you must. We have to be totally honest with one another. And if I don't tell you, you may always think I'm just crazy." She laughed shakily. "Or once I tell you, you may be convinced of it. Please? Let me tell you?"

Jesse gazed down at her for several moments before saying with a sigh, "All right. But I warn you—if you tell me things I think my commander should know about, I'll reveal them."

"No national secrets, I promise," she said. "Although what I intend to tell you may cause you pain, fortunately I don't know enough to influence the war either way."

Leaning back against the broad trunk of a tree, Jesse crossed his arms over his chest and regarded her steadily. "As long as we understand one another, you may say what you like."

"I know this will sound rather silly, but do you mind if we go up to the attic when I tell you? I think perhaps it will be easier there."

"The attic? Oakleigh's attic?"

She nodded. "Yes. I don't know why, but it all started there with your sister's wedding dress and a news clipping. Maybe it will be easier to explain if we go there."

Shaking his head, Jesse muttered, "None of this is going to make any sense, but I guess I've already committed myself to the deed."

She put a hand on his arm. "I want us to be alone when I tell you."

A faint smile curved his mouth. "I wonder just who will be more at risk?"

# *Chapter Ten*

"THIS IS IT." Amanda draped the wedding dress over the open trunk and glanced up at Jesse.

He was regarding her with a stunned, disbelieving expression. "So you're saying that one minute you were living in 1994, and then you put on that dress and traveled back in time?" he repeated slowly.

Amanda managed a smile. "Basically. I know it sounds crazy. It would to me, too. But that's the only conclusion that I can reach. One minute I was in 1994, and then I fastened that last button, and the wind blew out the light and I got dizzy, and when I regained my senses, I was here. I don't know how else to explain it."

Jesse frowned. "Forgive me, but I find that very hard to believe."

"How do you think I knew about Michael and Jamie? There was an article in the Memphis paper dated June 19, 1864, telling how a Holly Springs man had been killed only six months after his wedding to a Memphis woman. The Yankees claimed Jamie was responsible. That suspicion ended up dividing the Brandon family, and in 1994, Oakleigh would be sold. By preventing the feud, maybe we prevented the house from eventually being made into a mall.''

Rising from the crate where he'd been sitting, Jesse walked over to the wedding dress. He didn't say anything for a long time, but stood looking down at the satin dress as if afraid to touch it.

Amanda watched silently. She wouldn't blame him if he didn't believe her. It was too fantastic for anyone to believe.

Finally, Jesse looked up at her. "So what will happen now? Do you put the dress on again and go back?''

''Go back?'' she echoed. She'd already thought of that, of course. If the dress had gotten her here, it would probably take her back. All she would have to do is find the missing button, and she would be back home where she belonged.

Or did she?

Did she really belong there? She'd never felt like it. Jessica had been right when she'd said Amanda had been born in the wrong time. But could she adjust to living a hundred years too soon? The twentieth century was filled with marvels and timesaving conveniences. She remembered enough history to know that times in the South would be much harder before it was all over with. After the inevitable fall of the Confederacy, there would be Reconstruction and carpetbaggers and endless struggle.

But in 1994, there was also war and hunger and poverty. Times didn't really change, only people did. There had always been war, always been hunger and hard times. Until mankind figured out a way to avoid war and the other evils of the world, nothing would really change.

Here, there would be love and hope. And here there was Jesse. . . .

"Amanda?"

She looked up and took a deep breath. "What do you think I should do, Jesse?"

"What do you want to do?" he countered. "It's your decision to make." He rubbed a hand across his face and mumbled, "God, what am I saying? I'm not even sure I believe any of this, and I'm acting as if putting on that wedding dress will whisk you a hundred years into the future." He took a deep breath and said flatly, "Deborah wore the dress to be married in, and she's still here. Why would it only work for you?"

"Maybe because Deborah has found her true love. She's already in the right century." Amanda slid one hand over the satin folds of the gown. "One of the buttons is missing," she murmured. "I think I recall losing it the night I wore the dress. It would have to be found if I wanted to go back. . . ."

When her voice trailed into silence, Jesse asked harshly, "Is that what you want? To go back?"

Throat aching, she looked up at him. "Do you want me to stay?"

"I want you to do what you feel you must," he said shortly. "Whatever it is, I'll understand."

"I think," she said after a moment, "because I spent so many years dreaming of you, fate took pity on me and brought us together."

Hot tears unexpectedly stung her eyes, and Amanda was vaguely surprised to see sudden damp splotches mar the ivory satin of the wedding dress. She dragged her hand over her cheeks to wipe away the tears.

"Amanda," Jesse said gruffly, and reached out to pull

her into his arms. "I won't lie and say I don't want you. You know I do. But I want you to be happy. If you truly think we're meant to be together, we will be, even if it's only in *my* dreams. You must have family that will miss you if you stay here. Maybe you should go."

She looked up at him, shaking her head. "They're all dead. I'm the last Brandon."

"But won't you miss anyone?"

"Maybe Jessica. But we haven't stayed close. She'll think I just couldn't bear losing the house, and left town." Amanda laughed shakily. "Somehow I think she'd approve. She always said I was born in the wrong time."

His arms tightened. "Are you saying you want to stay?"

"Yes. I want to stay."

"Thank God. I don't know what I would have done if you said no . . ." He kissed her fiercely, and Amanda knew she had made the right decision.

When Jesse finally lifted his head, he was breathing hard. "I see that I'm going to have to ask Forrest for leave to get married, so I can make an honest woman of you."

"Married? You mean—"

"I don't know how they do it in the twentieth century," Jesse said dryly, "but in 1864, people in love get married to each other." He glanced at the dress, then added, "Just please don't decide to wear that particular dress."

Caught between laughter and happy tears, Amanda said, "I won't. I promise. Now that I have found the man of my dreams, after all this time, I have no intention of taking any chance of losing him."

It was a quiet wedding, and due to the urgency of war, a brief one. Jesse wore his best gray uniform, and Amanda wore a simple cotton gown that Deborah said was elegant in its simplicity.

"But I still don't understand," she said with a sigh, "why you refuse to borrow my dress. Don't you like it?"

"Oh, yes," Amanda said with a smile, and her glance at Jesse was so mischievous he had a hard time not laughing. "I have to say it's my favorite dress. I just wanted something of my very own. I hope you understand."

"I suppose so. It barely fits me now. Why, when I put it on to have my portrait done, I could hardly get all the buttons fastened."

"That," Michael said, "is because of your condition."

Deborah blushed and protested, "No, it's because one of the buttons is missing. I've looked everywhere for it but can't find it. I guess it just popped off somewhere."

"I'm sure that's it," Amanda agreed. "It's a shame Jamie couldn't be here for the wedding, but I understand that General Forrest has taken him with him to Tupelo."

Michael, his face healed now, grinned. "He's not sorry to go. If there's anything Jamie likes better than fighting Yankees, I don't know what it is."

Jesse smiled as his gaze drifted back to Amanda. Maybe it was wrong, but he'd helped her convince Jamie that she was a distant cousin from England. Fortunately, there were enough cousins that Jamie wasn't really certain which side of the Brandons she came from, and they'd been purposely oblique. One day they might tell them all the truth, but not now.

The war occupied their minds these days. The summer of '64 had started out with high hopes, but Jesse suspected that Confederate advantages wouldn't last long. He'd finally completed his mission into Memphis—without risking Amanda. As she had predicted, General Forrest staged a daring raid into Memphis. His brother Bill had ridden into the lobby of the Gayoso House on his horse, and Forrest's other brother Jesse had driven Washburn from his quarters in the wee hours of the morning. All of Memphis had rocked with laughter at the Yankee commander publicly fleeing in his nightshirt.

Even though she offered to tell him, he'd not allowed Amanda to reveal the ultimate end of the war. He believed in his choice, and he wanted to feel free to give it his all.

"Jesse?" Amanda said softly, and he looked down at her and smiled. "I love you," she whispered.

"Then come with me."

"To the attic?" she protested when she saw where he was taking her, and he grinned as he shut the door behind them.

"It's the most private spot in the house right now. Besides, I feel like this is where it all began for us."

Glancing around, Amanda nodded. "I feel the same. There is something special about this place, though I think it was the gown that brought us together—Jesse, look."

"What is it?" he asked when she bent and picked up a small white object and held it up to the light from the open window.

"I think it's the missing button to Deborah's wedding dress."

Jesse took it from her when she held it out. It rested on his palm, pale and luminous and dangerous. Time hovered in his hand, beckoning. Looking up, he met Amanda's steady gaze and saw the question in her eyes. He took a deep breath, then strode to the open attic window and flung the button out into the yard. He turned around, half expecting Amanda to be angry.

She was smiling. "Does this mean you think I might be

tempted to leave? Not a chance, Jesse Jordan. You're stuck with me forever.''

He grinned. ''I can think of worse fates.''

Then she was in his arms, and as he bent his head to kiss her, he had the thought that he had to be the luckiest man who had ever lived in any century.

# Bride's Joy

### Elda Minger

*Do all the good you can,*
*in all the ways you can,*
*to all the souls you can,*
*in every place you can,*
*at all the times you can,*
*with all the zeal you can,*
*as long as ever you can.*

—John Wesley

> *It is never too late to be what you might have been.*
>
> —George Eliot

# Chapter One

### Lindsey House, present day

On the third floor of the guest wing, with a light spring rain streaking the windows of the English manor house, Amelia Jamison thought about destiny.

"Pick a card," her friend Penny Bickham urged. She laughed. "Any card." The tarot deck was fanned out on the Oriental carpet, shadows from the flames in the fireplace dancing over the intricately patterned wool.

Amelia's hand trembled only slightly as she finally settled on one. She trusted Penny completely, since the day they'd first met as college roommates. Since that time, they'd gone in separate and very creative directions. She to England because of her work in manuscripts at the British Museum, and Penny to fame and fortune in New York as an incredibly talented floral designer.

Amelia slowly turned the card over and immediately regretted it. The Death card in the Waite deck stared back at her, the dark skeleton astride his white warhorse, the battlefield littered with bodies.

"Appropriate for the night before a wedding, don't you think?" She tried to put a humorous spin on the whole thing, desperate not to reveal how terribly apprehensive she was about marrying Hugh.

"It's not what you think it is." Penny pushed her dark, chin-length hair behind her ears and leaned forward, studying the card. "If it had been the Tower—"

They both stopped, aware of someone else in the room.

"I brought you some tea," the maid announced as she came in, tray in hand. "Mrs. Edwards thought you might like a little something before retiring."

"I do love the Brits," Penny muttered as she gathered up the cards. "There's nothing a cup of tea won't cure."

"Tell me about that card," Amelia insisted. She stood, dusted off the seat of her skirt, then sat in one of the chairs flanking the fireplace.

"Total transformation," Penny said as she sat down in the overstuffed chair across from Amelia. "Which, considering that tomorrow you'll be a married woman, is entirely appropriate."

"But it doesn't mean anything bad."

"No. People just get all creepy when they see the word 'death.' It can represent the death of one sort of consciousness and its replacement with another."

"Hmmm." Amelia busied herself cutting slices of the rich chocolate sponge cake, then pouring them both cups of strong black Indian tea.

The maid hovered in the doorway. Amelia, aware of her presence, didn't have the heart to ask the young woman to leave. She'd been in service to the Lindseys for several years, and had been assigned the task of helping Amelia get ready for her wedding day.

Which was tomorrow. Her classic bridal gown, carefully

pressed, hung in her bedroom closet. The caterers had their elaborate preparations under control, the calligraphers had long since finished with the place cards, and the musicians were hopefully getting a good night's sleep and would do their very best tomorrow.

Penny would be in the garden at dawn, carefully selecting the most perfect blooms for her bridal bouquet. Penny's designs were exquisite, and this one would be a masterpiece. Calla lilies, French tulips, and full-blown peonies. She would also pick sweet peas and violets, hand wiring them into the all-white bouquet Amelia had decided upon, then carefully braiding narrow white satin ribbon over the stems.

"Which will look lovely with your fair coloring," she'd assured Amelia. "Hugh will be absolutely enchanted with you; I'm so glad you chose white flowers."

All was ready for the morning. Now the great house slept, with numerous guests tucked into their rooms, of which Lindsey House had plenty. Almost a hundred and twenty.

Everyone seemed to be sleeping quite peacefully. Except Amelia, who was panicking.

"It's not a bad card, Amelia, honestly. Now, if it had been the Tower—"

Amelia shot her friend a look, and Penny, sensitive to a fault, instantly stopped talking.

"Is everything all right, Annie?" Thank God she'd remembered the girl's name. An American, Amelia had trouble adjusting to the concept of her own maid. It just wasn't the way things were done across the Atlantic.

"No." The girl took a deep breath, and Amelia could see the effort it cost her to speak out. "No. It—it makes me nervous, miss, the talk of these cards and speaking of the tower.''

''Why?'' Penny asked, clearly fascinated.

''There's a—history to this house,'' Amelia began.

''Centered around the tower?''

Annie hesitated. ''Yes, miss.''

''You know about this, Amelia?''

''Hugh told me about it.''

''Tell me.'' Penny settled back in her chair, cup of tea in hand. Her expression was interested, but she certainly wasn't the sort of person who took delight in misfortune.

''An earlier descendant of Hugh's . . . forced to marry a man she didn't love, she—'' Amelia hesitated.

''She took her own life, she did,'' Annie finished for her as she cut another piece of the chocolate sponge for Penny. ''Hung herself in the tower room. Couldn't go on.''

''Lovely,'' Penny muttered. ''And this is appropriate conversation on the eve of your wedding?''

''I don't look on it that way,'' Amelia said. When she'd first come to Lindsey House, it had been to authenticate a series of letters. John Lindsey, Hugh's grandfather, had called the museum in London where she'd been working. They'd farmed the assignment out to her; she'd taken the train up and fallen in love with John, the great house, his dogs and horses, the garden, Mrs. Edwards's teas, everything.

Then John had called his grandson home, and Hugh had fallen in love with her. So much so that he'd asked her to marry him. And here she was.

She loved him. That wasn't the problem. It was simply that Amelia didn't have a whole lot of faith in the institution of marriage. ''Forever,'' when your mother had gone through six different husbands, didn't have a whole lot of meaning.

But marriage to Hugh Lindsey would be forever. He was a strong man, and his grandfather had told her the story of how his beloved grandson had brought the family out of destitution through his financial wizardry. Hugh worked in London, and had almost killed himself in order to make the money to keep Lindsey House in the family. Not for him, the practice of taking in boarders, making a bed-and-breakfast out of the estate. He also refused the idea of giving tours or opening a gift shop.

What he'd done was far more difficult. He'd exhausted himself, working at a frantic pace, using his skills to the fullest, taking the last of the Lindsey money and turning it into a small fortune. Enough to bankroll the bigger fortune he still planned to make.

The only thing missing from Lindsey House was a bride for Hugh. A mother for the children whose shouts and laughter would soon fill the halls. The continuation and rebirth of a dynasty.

"Something happened," Amelia said quietly. "No one is entirely sure what. She couldn't go on; he couldn't go on without her. He took his own life two years later."

"It's sort of romantic, in a macabre sort of way," Penny mused. She shuddered. "But it gives me the creeps. Where is this tower room?"

"In the south wing," Annie answered. She'd started to gather up their tea things, and Amelia took a last hasty swallow of the strong tea before setting the fine bone china cup on the tea tray. The maid was clearly uneasy at the turn this particular conversation was taking.

"I'd like to see it before I leave," Penny said.

"That can be arranged."

"You'd better get some sleep, or you'll look like death in the morning—no reference to the card intended."

"I know. Can you find your way back to your room?"

"Easily. I'll see you in the morning."

Amelia retired, but couldn't sleep. Close to midnight, she left her bedroom and headed toward the south wing, and the tower room.

She'd never been afraid of the room, even given its rather grisly history. John had converted it into a small library, where he indulged his passion for tracing the Lindsey family history. He was the archivist, he'd told her when she first arrived. It mattered to him, to know where he came from—and what had happened to all the Lindseys throughout time.

Now, knowing exactly what she wanted to find in the tower room, Amelia sped swiftly along the hallway, her slippered feet making no sound.

Inside the small, circular room, she went to its center, to a massive teak table with a wooden box on the right side. Opening it, she stared at the packet of letters. Letters that had belonged to Jane Stanton, and the man who had loved her, Jonathan Lindsey.

That last letter. She'd read them all, feeling there was one letter missing, the one in which Jane should have explained why she hung herself. Impossible, that she should take her own life, cause so much pain, and not even offer a reason why.

She'd never given Jonathan any explanation, but from the letters he continued to write to her after her death, it was clear he knew. Yet he never alluded to it directly.

The last letter Jonathan wrote, in which he laid bare his soul to the woman he loved, a woman dead two years, was the one that had finally broken her. She'd been moved to tears.

The elderly John Lindsey had watched her reaction as she'd sat with the letters for the first time, and had smiled as she'd looked across the room at him through her tears.

"Quite a man, wasn't he?" he'd said. "Like my Hugh."

She'd nodded, overcome with emotion. Even now, before taking that final letter out of the wooden box, she knew its contents, had read it so many, many times that it was committed to memory. The words had been burned into her soul.

*My dearest Poppet,*

*I find that I cannot go on without you. Though I've never considered myself a weak man, life no longer has any meaning without you to share it with me. I'm tired, and I want to go home. To you. I'd thought I would come home to you each evening, but instead the nights at Lindsey House are not to be borne. You are everywhere, my darling, yet nowhere.*

*God will forgive me for what I am about to do. It is said He never sends us more than we can bear, but I find I have reached my limit. I want nothing more than to be with you, and the thought of you waiting for me beyond death is the only thing than enables me to even contemplate such an act.*

*Soon, my darling. Soon.*

*Your devoted servant, in this life and the next,*

*Jonathan*

What could it be like, to love like that?

Amelia traced her fingers over the fine writing, wondering at the state Jonathan Lindsey had to have been in to

271

even contemplate such an act. According to the family legend, he'd recreated Jane's suicide, hanging himself in the tower room. His manservant had found him and cut him down. The family had mourned for weeks, and that particular Lindsey line had died out.

Hugh had told her more about it, as she'd continued to work with the letters. She'd helped his grandfather preserve some of the older letters, which were crumbling with age. Jonathan and Jane's letters had been remarkably well-preserved in their small wooden box. She'd read them all in one sitting, had recognized Jonathan's passion, Jane's reluctance. Somewhere along the line, she felt the girl had either seen a marriage go bad, or been ill-used. She was not a woman who had planned on going to the marriage bed quietly.

Jane had led Jonathan on a merry chase, but he'd loved her, had tried to show her how deeply countless times. Then there had been an oblique reference to another man; then after Jane's suicide, countless letters Jonathan had written, trying to understand how he might have prevented the tragedy.

She'd read them all, many times. She'd called the museum, telling her superior that there was a lot more material here than they'd first suspected. Three months later, she'd had almost all of it cataloged.

Three months later, she'd been engaged to Hugh.

She'd never gone back to London.

Amelia ran her fingers over the packet of letters, then gently plucked the last one from the box. She closed it, then sat down in John's large leather chair. It smelled like him, leather and sandalwood, dogs and horses. He was a generous old man, and she felt he'd recognized a kindred spirit when she'd gotten off the train in the village.

He'd come to pick her up himself in an ancient, battered old Range Rover. She'd recognized his determination immediately, and been comfortable with it. Here was a man who really did want to get to the bottom of various family documents.

There had been other passengers that day, as well. An ancient Alsatian, a spaniel with only three legs, and a tiny Jack Russell terrier who sat in the front seat with the two of them the entire drive home.

"Arthritis?" she'd guessed, looking at the little dog. Though his dark canine eyes danced with mischief, his movements were stiff and painful.

John had nodded, never taking his eyes off the road. He drove fairly fast for a man his age. "Charlie's having a bad day. The vet says I'll have to be making my mind up about him soon."

Then there was nothing more to say until they reached the house.

It had astounded her, Lindsey House. Though her parents came from a certain amount of money, she hadn't dreamed such places existed. Her first glimpse of the estate had been in the late afternoon, close to dusk. The mist had been rolling in, and as they'd turned into the huge circular drive, she'd been overcome with emotion.

"You like it?" John had asked her.

"Very much."

"We'll get you settled in. No use looking at the letters until tomorrow—"

"Oh, I'd like to start right away, if I could."

She'd seen the delight in his face. They understood each other, after all.

Dinner had been in the kitchen, near the warmth of the Aga. She'd insisted on no fussing; she wanted him to maintain his usual routine. That first dinner was incredible. Homemade soup and freshly baked bread, thick with butter from the nearby dairy. A salad made with herbs and greens from the garden.

"Kind of a wreck these days," John had confided over the split-pea soup. "The deer get in and eat everything. What they don't eat, they trample. Hugh sent me the money for a brick wall, but I like to see them in the morning."

She nodded. This was the house of her dreams. A large, marmalade-colored cat lay dozing by the fire, and John's damaged dogs were everywhere.

"You live in a village where they know you have a soft spot for dogs, and you end up with the ones the others don't want."

She'd nodded, leaning down to scratch Charlie behind his ears. The little terrier was fiercely protective of John, but he'd decided to accept her. Knowing the temperament of most Jack Russells, Amelia was grateful.

The menagerie of animals living outside was quiet now, as night had fallen, but she could hardly wait for the morning, when she would come to know them all.

The kettle sang, and Mrs. Edwards, the cook, made them tea.

"We can take it up to the tower room," John informed her. She agreed. One of the handymen had already put her bags in one of the many bedrooms, and now all her attention was focused on the letters and what they might contain.

Several hours later, over yet more tea, she'd been moved to tears by Jonathan Lindsey's life.

"What happened after he died?" she asked John.

"He left the entire estate and all its holdings to several distant cousins. That's where my side of the family comes in. We took over Lindsey House, and quite a state it was in, let me tell you.''

''What had happened?''

''The folks around here said Jonathan went a little mad before he died. Burned the west wing to the ground, along with the garden. He'd been quite the gardener; he'd even created a flower distinctly his own. It's in some of his sketchbooks and journals, the details about all that.''

''Could I see them?'' Now that she'd read Jonathan Lindsey's most intimate letters, she felt compelled to get to know the man through his work.

''I'd be delighted to show them to someone who's interested. Not many are, in these parts. Not many who understand exactly what it is I'm trying to do.''

''And that is?''

''Break the curse.''

That stopped her cold, but she schooled her face into acceptance and decided to give this delightful old man a chance to explain himself.

''A curse.''

''The Lindsey curse. It's been hanging over this house since Jane took her life, and I'm determined to see it put to an end before I die.''

She hesitated, aware that his full attention was on her.

''Come now. Tell me what you felt when you came up to this room. After the letters.''

She wondered how honest she could be with John Lindsey, then decided to go for broke. The worst that could happen was that he'd pack her off on a train to London the following morning.

She swallowed, suddenly nervous. ''That you all have a ton of money but can't find happiness.''

''My point exactly. Now, my Hugh has started breaking

the curse, though he doesn't know it. It all started when he refused to let the house go.''

She'd heard of Hugh, his single-handed attempt to keep the creditors at bay, his financial work in London. He was a regular Scarlett O'Hara fighting to save Tara, but with a lot more ethics than that particular fictional character had possessed.

She didn't get to sleep until almost five in the morning, and woke at nine, the sun streaming in the large bedroom windows as a maid opened the heavy drapes.

''I didn't mean to wake you. Just thought you might like some air.''

Amelia didn't want to waste a single day of her great adventure at this house. She got out of bed, showered, dressed, then headed for the kitchen. Taking a scone and a mug of tea at Mrs. Edwards's suggestion, she left the fragrant kitchen and approached the cow stalls, now dog kennels.

She found John there, working with a heartbreakingly thin, sad-eyed sheepdog.

''You have a way with them,'' she said, keeping her voice low. It wouldn't do to startle the poor animal.

''I do. I wanted to study veterinary medicine, but we didn't have the means. Now I simply try to do what I can.''

They spent the morning exercising the dogs, then had lunch at a table by the garden. Afterward, they retired to the tower room, and Jonathan Lindsey's life. They worked nonstop for several hours, then John walked her through one of the hallways in his part of the great house.

Black-and-white photos adorned one wall, and Amelia made her interest known. John identified the various relatives, frozen in time in the photos.

One, of a little boy taking tea with his teddies and his

obviously adoring mother, caught her eye.

"My daughter, Frances, Hugh's mother. That's Hugh, around three. He was an only child, though she wanted more."

"And she lives where?"

John paused, and Amelia was immediately sorry she'd asked.

"She was killed. A riding accident. Her husband was in a car accident shortly thereafter. He never got over losing her."

"And Hugh?" She thought of the little boy in the picture, with no parents or siblings to take comfort in.

"Came to live with me. I raised him, but it wasn't the same for him. He missed them terribly."

"How old was he?"

"Twelve. Not a good age to lose one's parents."

She placed her hand on John's arm, offering him comfort. "I don't think there's ever a good time for something like that."

Her days fell into a routine. Walking the dogs, exercising the two old horses that still lived in the stable. Enjoying tea every day at five. Working on the letters and journals. Enjoying Lindsey House and all that its eighty acres contained: the dovecote, the boathouse, the flower beds, the library and sitting room, the fresh herbs from the kitchen garden, Hugh's mother's watercolors, the sleepy river with its pair of swans.

The soft roll of the lawns. The beautiful misty mornings. A crackling fire on a cool day, the afternoon tea table set with beautiful china. Feeding the goats and rounding up the chickens. The distinctive scent of the lavender furniture polish the maids used. The exquisite smells of baking from Mrs. Edwards's kitchen.

She began to understand Hugh on a deeply emotional level, and why he'd fought to keep all this in his family. But nothing could have prepared her for actually meeting him.

She'd been breakfasting in the garden, throwing crumbs from her scone to one of the starlings, when she looked up and saw Hugh Lindsey in the kitchen doorway. He was studying her, and had the oddest expression on his handsome face.

He came forward quickly, offering her his hand.

"You must be Amelia. I can't thank you enough for the time you've spent with my grandfather."

She started to rise, but he gestured her back. He sat down in one of the other chairs, a mug of hot tea in his free hand. He was still holding hers.

It happened that instant. To both of them. But he was more honest than she was. She tried to deny it.

"It's fascinating work," she said quickly as she disengaged her fingers from his. She knew she was about to babble, but she didn't care. Anything to put some distance between them.

He was a glorious man, strong in both body and face. Hugh possessed the same dark coloring that had fascinated her in Jonathan Lindsey's portrait in the great hall. The two men looked rather alike, with their high, strongly defined cheekbones, fiercely intelligent blue eyes, and longish dark hair.

He seemed to read her mind.

"Yes, I do resemble him. I hope Grandfather hasn't bored you to tears with his ideas about the Lindsey curse."

"You don't believe in it?"

"No." He set his mug of tea down on the wooden table, leaned back in his chair, and studied her intently. "But I do believe we're here for a specific reason.''

"I do, too." She felt slightly more relaxed with him—slightly—and took another sip of her morning tea.

"But I don't agree with Grandfather. I believe we are our own destiny. Through who we are, the choices we make day by day. What we show our children, what we pass on to them. We're constantly creating and molding the future all the time.''

He fascinated her. He frightened her. She was due up in the tower room in less than fifteen minutes, yet they talked nonstop for over two hours. When Amelia finally realized the time, she glanced up toward the window of the tower room, which was clearly visible from the kitchen garden.

John, that rascal, was sitting in the window. He laughed out loud as he waved to them.

Hugh's proposal was swift in coming. Within days, he'd shipped a fax machine, several computers, and a modem to Lindsey House, telling all who would listen that he wanted to spend a little more time with his grandfather.

Unspoken was the fact that he spent most of his time with Amelia.

He could be heartbreakingly romantic, and they took long walks with the dogs over the rolling green hills. John worked on in the tower room alone, not minding this particular interruption one bit.

They were having a picnic down by the boathouse one afternoon when it happened. They'd both finished Mrs. Edwards's sumptuous repast, and were lying on the blanket Hugh had spread beneath the huge walnut tree.

"I love the swans," she said drowsily. "They're always together and they look so graceful.''

"They mate for life, you know." Something in his tone

made her turn toward him. The minute she saw his face, she knew.

"Hugh—"

"Marry me, Amelia."

How like Hugh. Not *will you marry me*, but *marry me*. Then she saw the uncertainty in his blue eyes, and her fear lost its edge.

She did love him. Attraction had been instantaneous, passionate, out of control. What had happened in the weeks that followed had deepened that first feeling into something much more. Something she'd never felt before. Something she couldn't have described if she'd tried.

"Yes."

The joy that lit his eyes made tears come to her own.

"Don't be frightened," he said into her hair. He'd taken her into his arms, and they lay like that, content with each other. She wished she could be as strong as he was, as sure. But she wasn't that way, and no amount of wishing could make it so.

"I'm not—I am." She laughed into his shirtfront, dangerously close to tears.

"I'll show you every day, for the rest of my life, how much I love you. You'll come to believe it."

"Yes," she whispered again, against his strong chest. Against the rapid beating of his heart. "Yes."

Amelia sat in the leather chair, listening to the silence of the tower room. She had to get back downstairs to her bedroom and try to sleep. But she had a feeling she would just lie in her bed, willing the morning to come and put an end to her feelings of apprehension.

Why couldn't she just marry Hugh and be done with it? Why did she have to go through such emotional agony over a decision countless young women made every day? She knew, on an intellectual level, why she was scared. Her father had been seriously ill before she'd reached her seventh birthday. He'd died when she was nine. Six marriages had followed for her mother, and Amelia had stopped trying to get close to any in the long succession of stepfathers a long time ago.

She still missed Max Jamison terribly. The only memories she had left of her father were the home movies her mother had transferred to video. There was the father she remembered, frozen in time. Leading her pony as a four-year-old Amelia practically screamed with joy. On a carousel, riding the prancing wooden stallion next to hers. Sharing an ice cream cone at the beach.

Would life have been better, emotionally, if he'd lived? Would she have these terrible fears of ultimately being abandoned?

Her fingers traced the delicate paper of the letter.

*My dearest Poppet* . . .

To love like that. So fearlessly. Passionately. Suddenly depressed, she wondered if she'd ever really been in love. Even with Hugh.

A cloud passed over the moon, and the tower room was plunged into darkness. Amelia was afraid for only a second, then she felt her eyelids drifting shut, the letter slipping from her fingers. The leather chair was so soft, and she was so tired, she'd rest just for a moment . . . a moment in time. . . .

*When one door is shut, another opens.*

— *Miguel de Cervantes*

## Chapter Two

The sharp rapping sound awakened her.

Amelia struggled to consciousness, wondering who would be up in the tower at this time of night. The moon was still obscured by clouds, the night still dark.

Someone was trying to get into the tower room.

Perhaps John. Maybe he was having trouble sleeping as well, and wanted to escape to the past, to his study filled with letters, journals, pressed flowers, and sketches. She understood the older man and his fascination with history.

"Let me in!" whispered a voice.

Strange. She didn't recognize it. Amelia got up from her chair. Her back ached, and she wondered at that. The leather seat had grown cold and hard as she'd slept in it. Well, it was nothing like a bed.

She found the doorknob in the dark, then turned it. The door stuck.

*How odd.*

She tried again. Pulled harder.

"Open this door!" a female voice demanded.

"I will; give me a minute—"

With one last yank, the door yielded. It felt as if the wood were swollen within the frame, and that was strange because it was a door that normally opened without any trouble at all.

The clouds parted, and a thin, cool moonlight slipped through the window, illuminating a scene Amelia knew she would remember throughout eternity.

Jane Stanton stood in the doorway—Amelia recognized the girl from the engagement portrait she'd seen. And this was no simpering chit who couldn't cope with what life handed her. This was no coy miss who simply gave up. She was furious.

"I suppose this is your way of saying you're not coming with me!"

Amelia couldn't answer as shock assailed her, a peculiar roaring in her head, a weakening in her limbs. She steadied herself, a hand grasping the rough stones in the tower wall. How could it feel the same? How could it look the same?

But it didn't. John had put in carpeting. This stone floor was bare; she could feel it through her shoes.

*Shoes. No. Slippers. I was wearing slippers.*

She didn't have her nightgown on, either, but a wool dress that itched against her skin. All she could see of herself was her hands, and they were broad and square, with freckles on the backs.

She'd never freckled in her life.

"Where am I?" she whispered, then looked at Jane as she started to tremble.

"Stop it! Come back right now, Emma! I won't have you going off in one of those trances like your aunt. Now, you agreed to help me and you shall. Come."

Jane grabbed her hand and started away from the tower

room. Though her hand was small, it was surprisingly strong and warm. Vital. Alive.

*Alive. No, no, Jane is dead, she hung herself. . . .*

Terrified, Amelia pulled her hand away, but Jane grabbed it again and dragged her further down the stairs.

"Stop it," she hissed. "If you get us caught, I'll make your life a living hell, I swear it!"

*Alive. Jane Stanton is alive. I have to be dreaming. This has to be a dream. I've just gone a little mad. . . .*

She almost missed the bottom step, and the sharp pain that shot up her shin was no dream; this was no dream, this was real, and she had no idea where Jane was leading her, or why, or how she'd come to this place. . . .

For it was Lindsey House, but not the Lindsey House she'd come to love. This was a strange, dark manor house, and she knew with a sharp instinct honed purely by survival that she'd never been to *this* house before.

A light, misty rain had started to fall as the two women approached the great front door.

"Quiet! Someone may still be about." Jane let go of her hand, then grasped her upper arm with steady fingers. This woman knew exactly what she wanted and how to go about getting it.

"Here." She handed Amelia a cloak and she put it on gratefully. The weather was bitterly cold and damp, and even the wool dress didn't offer her much in the way of protection.

Then they were outside, running across the grounds, dashing and slipping over the wet grass, away from the dark, silent house. Amelia had no idea where they were headed, but as she moved she suffered yet another shock. Her body didn't feel like hers—it was shorter and considerably plumper. Sturdy. Unfamiliar. Strange.

She'd always been thin as a child. Wiry. Miserable because she'd been one of the tallest in her class, almost always the last ever asked to dance. Now she was eye level with Jane—and Jane was not a tall woman.

Was she running away to marry Jonathan? Was that where they were going? As she followed Jane further away from the manor house, Amelia thought furiously, tried to remember every detail of the story John Lindsey had told her.

She couldn't think. The shock was too great. Her breath came in great gasps; her lungs hurt from the cold spring air. She stumbled, and Jane jerked her upright.

"Come on, Emma! Once they know we've gone, we haven't got a chance."

She was a tough one, Amelia thought. Tough and strong and smart. She was a survivor; that was the first thing she'd thought upon meeting her.

*What has happened?*

She concentrated on putting one foot in front of the other. One after the other. Breathing through her nose because it warmed the cold night air. Trying not to let the cloak whip open and the frigid wind crawl up her legs.

They reached the main road, and Amelia was struck by how absolutely black the night was. Even when she and Hugh had taken evening walks with the dogs, they'd come back to see the windows of Lindsey House ablaze with light. Not now. Everything was black, except what little was silvered by the new moon.

She stopped, and Jane was yanked back by the force of her strength.

*New moon. No. Not new, the moon was full. . . .*

The truth began to close in all around her. She couldn't shut her mind off to the final possibility, the only possibility, the reality of what had happened to her. She'd fallen down the hole, like Alice after the White Rabbit, only this was real, this was *real*. . . .

"Emma! The carriage!"

And there it was, at the end of the dirt road. The road she and Hugh had just walked this evening, three of the house dogs at their heels, Charlie in her arms because his legs were too stiff, Hugh's arm around her . . .

Tears blurred her vision, but her legs kept moving because she didn't know what else to do.

She assisted Jane into the carriage, then climbed in after her. There was nothing for her here at this Lindsey House, more than two hundred years in the past. She'd been flung back in time, and who knew if she'd ever see anyone or anything familiar again?

The horses started up, and the carriage bounced around horribly. Amelia gritted her teeth, then gave up on that idea when a bone-jarring jounce almost caused her to bite off her tongue. Though she and John were both fascinated and passionate about history, neither had ever romanticized it, and she longed for the safe confines of the Range Rover.

"It won't be much farther now," Jane whispered. She sounded so very pleased with herself.

"Until what?"

"Oh, Emma, don't go off like that again! Jonathan's mother would have let your aunt go had she not been so terribly accurate with those visions." She sighed, then sat back on the seat. The small lantern on the one side of the carriage illuminated her animated face. "I must confess, I'd love to see what the future has in store for Robert and me—"

"Robert?" Her tongue suddenly felt thick, her head filled with cotton wool. "Robert? I thought you loved Jonathan—"

The look on Jane's face stopped her cold.

"Jonathan? Jonathan? To marry him and live that carefully planned out, boring life in that huge old house? Oh, no, not for me! I want more than that, I told him—"

"Does he know about—"

"Robert?" Jane laughed, then glanced out the carriage window, eager to see where they were in their journey. "No." Her expression grew thoughtful. "Even though I didn't want to be Jonathan's wife, I couldn't bear to hurt him. He thought we were betrothed, and I let him continue to think it until tonight. Tomorrow, once he realizes I'm gone, he'll find another girl, much more suitable than I am."

Amelia was quiet, thinking of the letters. Of that last letter. Those passionate words. Jonathan had loved this Jane Stanton, no matter how hard-hearted and cold she seemed to Amelia now.

She ventured a guess. Perhaps this Emma, this woman whose body she'd appropriated, would have known both men.

"I think you're tossing away a good man."

Jane gave her an incredulous look that instantly told her she'd overstepped her station in life. The girl had an incredibly expressive face; it registered her emotions quite clearly.

Once again, Amelia found herself an American misunderstanding British customs. Obviously, this Emma was a maid. Jane's maid. Amelia, in the first shock of tearing through time, had overlooked the plainness of the wool dress she was wearing. But now, seeing the way Jane related to her, there could be no doubt concerning her station in this life. She couldn't meet her mistress's expression and glanced away, embarrassed.

"I'll thank you not to trouble me with your opinion on this matter."

"As you wish."

But now a sense of foreboding grew, a sense that their carriage was racing toward a more sinister future than either of them could anticipate. Amelia stared out the carriage window at the dark forest flashing by; she swayed in rhythm with the drumming of the horse's hooves. It was almost hypnotic, what that sound did to a body.

Something was very wrong. Jonathan had never alluded to what had happened to Jane, what had driven the woman he'd loved to take her own life, but Amelia had a horrible feeling that she was going to watch Jane's life unfold in front of her as if it were some sort of program on television.

What was it Hugh had said to her that day in the garden? *I believe we are our own destiny. Through who we are, the choices we make day by day.*

She had the strangest foreboding that Jane was about to make a choice that could possibly cost her her young life.

Was this Robert a murderer? Would he make it look as if Jane had committed suicide? And why was there never a mention of a maid named Emma in all the work she'd gone through, the letters, various correspondence, the journal, the estate records? She didn't remember an Emma; it was as if the servant had never existed.

*But now you don't exist, except in her body. And perhaps in time your consciousness will fade, to be replaced by this woman's. . . .*

She didn't know what to think.

The rain was coming down harder now, lashing the carriage, pounding on its roof, causing the driver to whip the reins down on the horses' rumps, urging them faster. Amelia tried to rid her mind of the thought of the carriage overturning; the idea of a broken bone or worse in the eighteenth century didn't bear thinking about.

She closed her eyes, trying to shut everything out.

"Do you have the sight?"

It took her a moment to realize that Jane was speaking to her. She had to be referring to Emma's aunt.

"Can I see the future, do you mean?"

"Yes."

"No. I've never had a vision in my life." *But I get feelings, and I have very bad feelings about this night, Jane, about what's going to happen to you—and to Jonathan.*

She thought of all the novels she'd read about time travel, how she'd lazed afternoons away speculating what she would do if she were ever able to leap through time. Now that she was actually doing it, there were two things she was sure of. One, that a person was never ready for such an experience. And, two, that it wasn't as terrific as might be expected. Time travel was as romanticized as the past.

"Do you wish you could? See into the future, I mean."

"No." And Amelia realized what she said was true— she knew the future now, and felt the impossible burden of knowing what was to come and being unable to stop or alter it in any way. For you couldn't alter the future, you couldn't make people's choices for them, of that she was sure.

And even as headstrong and fiery as Jane was, she'd come to like her in a strange way. She didn't want to see her die. The portrait artist who had captured Jane on canvas hadn't captured her spirit, her strength, her determination. If someone could have shown her how to channel all that energy before tonight, if someone had taught her how to make decisions more carefully . . . .

The carriage slowed, and Amelia realized they were pulling into an inn. She didn't recognize where they were; the actual building must have been torn down before she was born. She and Hugh had ridden the horses for miles; she would've recognized this place.

The carriage horses clattered into the stable-yard, and she and Jane were inside the inn shortly, standing by the main entrance, assaulted by the smells of smoke and burning grease, roasting beef, the sour tang of ale, the aroma of too many unwashed bodies.

Jane went forward boldly, and the innkeeper's wife seemed to know what she was talking about. She showed them upstairs, and the two of them entered the small room beneath the eaves. A young girl started a fire, and Amelia stood silently by, not sure if she would be allowed to warm herself by the flames. The night was starting to catch up with her; she could feel exhaustion stealing into her bones.

More than anything, she wanted to go to sleep and wake up in the present, in her bed at Lindsey House, with the most pressing worry on her mind the thought of whether her makeup and hair would do for her wedding day.

That existence seemed so long ago. Time was relative; it could swirl and flow like a river, elongating some moments and throwing others into sharp relief. As long as she had her own consciousness, she could remember, she could keep Hugh and her father and John and even the terrier Charlie alive in her mind and heart.

''Go on,'' Jane said quietly as the innkeeper's wife and the young maid left the room. ''You can sit by the fire.'' She had taken off her cloak, and now, with more light than she'd had all night, Amelia got her first real look at Jane Stanton.

She was beautiful.

Amelia could understand Jonathan's passion for this woman. Her skin glowed with vitality, her red-gold hair seemed to have a life of its own. Her green eyes were alive with emotion, slightly tilted at the corners like a cat's. Her lips were full, her bones elegant, her body small but lush. Vibrant. Energetic. Filled with passion. Jane Stanton was a woman any man would want. Why hadn't she wanted Jonathan?

"Robert should be here shortly."

"What do you plan on doing?" Amelia heard herself saying. She could already guess.

"We're going to run away and be married." Jane smiled at the thought, lost in her dreams. "I couldn't marry a man simply because it was arranged." Her voice caught fire with urgency. "No one asked me what I wanted. No one thought of how I might feel."

"Not even Jonathan?"

This stopped her, and Amelia knew that Jonathan Lindsey had cared what this woman thought. How she felt. He'd been an extraordinary man in an extraordinary age.

"He—did. He asked me once, what I thought about our being betrothed to each other."

"Did you tell him?"

"I couldn't find the words. But he should've known!"

"How did he feel about you?"

Jane smiled then, and Amelia could sense genuine affection in her expression. "He told me he'd loved me since we were children, and looked forward to our marriage." Now she sounded uncertain of herself and her plans, and Amelia seized the moment.

"And Robert?"

Jane seemed to glow with emotion. "He loves me; I know he does. I can't describe to you the way I feel when

I'm with him; it's as if I burn with a rare fever—"

Amelia wondered if anyone had ever bothered to tell this young woman the difference between sexual desire and love, for it was clear she'd confused the two. She did remember reading about Jane's upbringing. Her parents had died, and she'd been shipped off to live with two maiden aunts for the remainder of her childhood.

Not the best way to receive any instruction in life.

They'd probably been relieved to be rid of her, glad of the arranged marriage. Unmarried women without means had to struggle to stay alive, and Jane would have been perceived as just another mouth to feed. The young woman was woefully unprepared for what her future held.

Amelia decided to try. She couldn't live with herself if she didn't. Perhaps if she could make Jane come to the decision by herself, think it was her own, it wouldn't technically be changing the past by much.

"You're sure you don't love Jonathan?"

Jane almost faltered, but Amelia could see the young woman pull herself together. It was a heartbreaking picture, that stubborn little chin rising to the challenge.

"Quite sure."

"Where did you meet Robert?"

"We met at the—"

The sound of booted feet could be heard on the stairs, and Jane hurriedly smoothed her hair, then the front of her skirts.

"Emma, how do I look?"

"Splendid."

The door swung open, and Amelia's heart sank as she got her first glimpse of Jane's Robert. She felt as a mother might feel, with her darling daughter caught in the clutches of a truly bad boy.

"Emma?" Jane indicated the door with a little nod of her head.

Amelia knew she was to sleep outside the door, as was the custom. But how could she leave Jane alone with this man? He looked exactly like Dickens's description of Bill Sikes in *Oliver Twist*—big, bad, and coarse. A brute. How could Jane not see it?

"You wish to be alone with him?" she whispered, not liking the look Robert was giving her from beneath his heavy-lidded eyes.

"Yes. Robert won't hurt me. We're to be married in the morning." Jane turned toward the man, and the look on her face, shining innocence and anticipation, tore at Amelia's heart.

"I'll be right outside the door," she offered, but neither of them was listening to her.

Once outside, she curled up into a small ball on the hard wooden floor. Her cloak served as both pillow and blanket, part of it bunched beneath her head, the rest covering her from the chill night air.

It was quite cold, away from the warmth of the fire.

A noise like a kitten crying drew her out of a deep sleep. Half awake, she listened, almost relaxed again, then heard it. Louder. Then a deeper, masculine murmur.

A sharp cry. A slap. Amelia sat up, completely awake. All thoughts of sleep flew from her mind. She stood, arms and limbs protesting, then approached the thick wooden door.

The sounds of a scuffle. Another slap. A deep, cruelly amused masculine laugh. Then a howl of pain, and then a scream.

Enough. Amelia didn't care what century she was in. If

she didn't have a whole lot of time left in Emma's body, she'd give the stout little maid a new consciousness before the end of the night. It was about time eighteenth-century England heard of women's rights.

"Stop it!" Her voice sounded loud and authoritative in the low-ceilinged hallway. "Let go of her."

Another scream, then Amelia was pounding at the door.

"Quiet down!" someone called.

"Give it to her, mate!" another voice called from another room.

Jane was screaming, fighting; the sounds of the fight seemed to go on forever. Amelia pounded on the heavy wood, clawed at it, not even noticing the splinters that gouged her broad, freckled hands. Her only thought was to get to Jane before the bastard murdered her.

It seemed forever before he finally opened the door.

"Little bitch," he said, looking down at her. "Making that kind of noise. Who do you think you are?" With that, he slammed his fist into her face.

Blood spurted from her nose, filled her mouth. She fell like a stone, heard Robert's laugh, felt the bite of his boot in her ribs; then he was clattering down the stairs and away.

She couldn't breathe, the pain in her side was so bad. But she thought of Jane, and crawled toward the room she'd shared with Robert. She didn't want to see, couldn't bear to see; she'd have to cut her down; what if Robert had—

The small feminine figure was huddled beneath the bed linen. Shaking. Crying. Sobbing as if her heart had been broken, as indeed it had.

"Jane," she whispered, wiping her split lip with the cuff of her dress as she made her way to the bed. She winced as the rough wool abraded the tender flesh. "Oh, Jane."

That beautiful face was bruised; the life was gone from

those vibrant green eyes. Instead she stared at the shadows the fire threw on the slanted ceiling, her expression lifeless. Except for the tears. They kept running down her face.

"Jane." Not knowing what else to do, she gathered the weeping girl in her arms and simply held her while she sobbed. And thought, irreverently, that Emma's broad, cobby little body was perfect for this type of nurturing.

Jane's dress was torn, her face bruised, her lip split. Her eye would be black by morning; it was swelling shut. What should have been the happiest day of her life had turned to a nightmare.

A white-hot rage burned in Amelia's heart as she rocked the girl, back and forth, whispering words of comfort, remembering what her father had said when she'd skinned both knees trying to learn to ride her first bike. Only this was so much worse.

By the time Jane let her peel the covers back, Amelia already knew what she would find. Blood was flecked on the linen, Jane's chemise, her thighs. Blood that signified her virginity. Robert had taken that, as well.

Perhaps it was more of Emma's consciousness coming through her, but Amelia knew what they had to do.

"We're going back to Lindsey House, Jane—"

"No! Oh, no!"

"Come on. Let me make the decisions for now. You're in no condition."

In the end, their decision was made for them by the innkeeper and his wife. Rushing upstairs after the commotion was safely over, they both demanded to know who was going to be responsible for settling up the bill.

Jane just stared at the two of them, her lifeless green eyes dull and uncomprehending.

Amelia decided to bluff it out. Neither of them looked

that tough, and what could they do that would be any worse than what Jane had been through? Throw them out?

"He took base advantage of the lady," Amelia said quietly as she gathered up Jane's bag, her few possessions. "We'll both be leaving now, and not troubling you further."

"But what about the money?" the innkeeper's wife demanded. Jane started to sob again, and Amelia realized that the innkeeper was cowed by his overbearing wife.

She addressed her comments toward the wife. "As God is my witness, you should be ashamed of yourselves for what you allowed to transpire beneath this roof tonight." Before she was halfway through her statement, she was pushing Jane out the door and toward the stairs.

Something happened when the young woman started to move. It was as if part of her came back to life. Her pace quickened, and even though Amelia realized she was barefoot, she didn't dare try to go back for her shoes.

"I want my money!" the innkeeper's wife demanded. "Filthy little whores!" Her face was turning an ugly mottled color, and Amelia hoped they could get out the door of the inn without her trying to pull their hair out by the roots.

The rain was still coming down in torrents when both women dashed out the front entrance and toward the road. Amelia put her arm around Jane and supported her, trying to keep her upright. Her bare feet kept slipping and sliding in the oozing, sticky mud.

Lightning arched and crackled through the night sky, illuminating everything around them. Amelia counted to three, then heard the deep rumble of thunder. Too close. And here they were in the middle of a forest with immense trees, perfect lightning rods, all around them.

Jane turned her face up to the rain, and it was as if the heavens wept with her. Her vivid hair, already soaked, streamed wildly down her back. Her left eye was almost completely swollen shut now, her lower lip a grotesque puff.

She worked her bloody lips clumsily, trying to speak.

"Don't say anything," Amelia began.

"I heab you—at dah dor."

*I heard you. At the door.*

Amelia nodded, signifying understanding.

Jane's fingers tightened on her arm, only this time she wasn't forcing her to follow her. This time she was merely trying to keep her balance.

"Tank you, Em-ma."

"You're welcome."

Jane Stanton started to cry again, but she kept walking.

*Know the true value of time; snatch, seize, and enjoy
every moment of it.*

                                    —Lord Chesterfield

# Chapter Three

SHE FELT AS if the world were coming to an end.

Rain poured down, slicing through the dark sky. Amelia
kept her arm firmly around Jane's waist, forcing the girl to
take step after step as they made their torturous way along
the side of the muddy road. And it wasn't as if Jane dragged
her down. The woman was a fighter; she wouldn't give up.
Though Amelia had her doubts as to whether Jane wanted
to go back to Lindsey House. She rather doubted it. Jane
probably wanted to put as much distance between herself
and those odious innkeepers as possible.

The one thing Amelia hadn't counted on was meeting up
with any sort of danger.

She sensed the hoofbeats before the riders came into
sight. Acting purely on instinct, she dragged Jane into the
shelter of a nearby tree, hiding them behind its massive
trunk. Several riders, seven or eight of them, came into
view, their horses galloping clumsily through the mud.
From what Amelia could see of them in the rain and darkness, they seemed to be dressed in a rather ragged fashion,

and she surmised that their mounts were probably stolen.

What men like these would choose to do to two women, alone on the road, was anyone's guess. She just didn't want to find out. Her breathing sounded loud to her own ears, but she knew they couldn't hear her over the fury of the rain and wind. The sheeting water also obliterated any tracks they might have made.

The riders galloped past, and Amelia resolved to watch the road, both ahead and behind them. No one was going to get a chance to hurt Jane again.

They walked further down the road, alone for the next hour, before she heard hoofbeats again. This time, both she and Jane dove for the nearby underbrush, seeking the safety and shelter of the thick forest.

But the rider, a lone man on a black stallion, looked strangely familiar. As did the horse. Amelia's heart started to race as she recognized them both. And she should have—she'd spent so much time in the great hall admiring his portrait, astride that same stallion.

Leaving Jane in the shelter of a giant oak, she ran out into the road. Lightning split the heavens, illuminating their small stretch of highway, as she screamed into the night sky.

"Jonathan Lindsey!"

Somehow, despite the noise and the rain, the thunder and lightning, the weakness and exhaustion of her voice, he heard her. The stallion wheeled, controlled by his master's hands. The great animal galloped in her direction, and had barely come to a stop before Jonathan vaulted down out of the saddle and was standing beside her.

Amelia had to look up into his face, and his resemblance to Hugh absolutely overwhelmed her. For a moment she couldn't speak as she took in the sight of his face, his eyes, his dark hair plastered back from his face, soaked by the rain.

Those eyes, so fierce and dark and blue. Intent and passionate and worried.

"Jane?"

"Right over here."

She wondered how they were all going to get back to Lindsey House on one animal, then surmised she was probably in for the longest and wettest walk of her life. After all, Jane was still in shock, after what she'd been through. The girl needed immediate attention.

"Jane!" When he reached her, he went down on his knees, pulled her into his arms, and held her against his strong chest. Jane began to weep as Amelia remembered another time, by the boathouse, when Hugh had held her in his arms and promised to show her every day how much he loved her.

*You'll come to believe it.*

She hadn't. She'd let doubts and old fears come between them, get in the way, and now the closest she might ever come to seeing Hugh Lindsey was in the face of his ancestor.

It didn't bear thinking about.

"I've got a carriage coming," Jonathan informed her as he and Jane stood up. She seemed to have lost that glowing vitality again, that will to fight, and now leaned on him, giving over to him, seeming to draw strength from him. As Amelia watched the two of them, she thought Jonathan Lindsey a thousand times the man Robert ever had been.

What disastrous judgment Jane had exercised in this matter. But what could have been expected, when all she'd been instructed to do was to look to everyone else in her life to give it meaning? That was women's real tragedy in the past, and even in Amelia's present. The hardest lesson growing up was knowing you were the captain of your own ship, and that some decisions had to be faced head on.

Actions most certainly had consequences.

Yet how was Jane to have known this, when she'd never been given the right to make any but the most frivolous of choices?

The carriage came into view, looming up in the mist and rain like a giant ship. Jonathan flagged it down. He helped Jane inside it, out of the rain. Then Amelia. He tied his mount to the back of the vehicle, then climbed inside, shut the door, and rapped smartly on the roof with his fist.

The carriage started its jouncing, rocking motion forward, and Amelia thought she'd never been as pleased with any particular mode of travel in her life. The Range Rover be hanged—at least this contraption would get them all safely back to the shelter of Lindsey House.

Yet the roads were still dangerous at this time of night, and in a storm such as this. She'd noticed the pistol Jonathan had tucked inside his waistband, and Amelia had utter confidence that he would protect both her and Jane, with his life if necessary.

*How like Hugh he is. How Jonathan would have loved to have met him, just for a moment.*

She thought how extraordinary it was, to see both people come to life, step out of the mists of history, become living, breathing spirits. They sat on the narrow seat across from her, their faces illuminated by the shifting light from the small lantern. Even in such irregular light, she could see the deep concern on Jonathan's face; the way he looked at Jane was so unbearably intimate that Amelia had to glance away.

Jane had started to cry again, and seemed to be trying to

tell him what had happened. It crossed Amelia's mind what an extraordinary thing that was in itself, that she should trust this man with all a woman possessed in this century—her reputation. But this was Jonathan Lindsey, not your ordinary man. He soothed her to silence, and Amelia found comfort in his deep, rich voice.

Soon Jane quieted, her agitation ceased. Amelia leaned back against the seat, her eyes closed, feeling as if she were invading a most private moment but so glad she was out of the driving, chilling rain. Jonathan hummed to Jane; Amelia was sure the man was rocking her in his arms the way a father would tenderly hold his most beloved, wayward child. He talked nonsense into her ear, and at one moment Amelia even heard what sounded like a breathy, exhausted laugh.

Then silence. Jane was asleep, or had fainted from exhaustion, she wasn't sure which. The interior of the carriage was silent as it rocked along the muddy road.

Amelia thought both of them were probably sleeping, or at least Jonathan would have his eyes closed when she chanced a peek. And that moment was the one she knew would be burned into her soul for the rest of her life. She'd remember this, even if Emma's spirit subsumed hers completely and all her former memories left her.

Jonathan rested his chin on the top of Jane's fiery hair. She was asleep, curled into his chest like an exhausted kitten, her small fingers gripping the front of his white shirt and waistcoat. What was so extraordinary about this particular scene was that Jonathan was crying.

The tears coursed down his cheeks, and it seemed as if all the pain in the world were mirrored in his eyes. A pain so deep it seemed to have shattered him.

Amelia couldn't look away. At that moment, she realized

the depth of his love for Jane, that he felt her pain as if it were his own, as deeply as she had. He knew her, he could see inside to those most secret recesses of her soul. He knew what tonight had cost her, and it was tearing him apart.

He wasn't thinking about what Jane's folly had done to him, to his dreams, to their impending marriage. He simply empathized, felt her pain, knew her fears. He loved her.

She must have made a slight noise, for somehow Amelia knew she'd alerted him to her presence. His gaze swung to hers, their eyes met, a long frozen moment in time. Amelia almost shrank back, for she knew this certainly had to be a breach in behavior, a most serious offense.

She wasn't even aware of the tears running down her own cheeks.

"We will not speak of this night to anyone," Jonathan said, his deep voice breaking.

Amelia didn't say a word. Couldn't.

"Do you understand?"

She nodded her head.

"We have to protect her."

She found her voice. "Yes."

He wiped at his eyes with the back of his hand.

"Tell me what happened."

With a certain sort of person, you left out the details, sugarcoated the facts. With Jonathan Lindsey, Amelia sensed that nothing could be left out. He was an extraordinarily sensitive man, but strong as well. He could and would be strong this evening, for both himself and Jane.

Briefly, but with as much detail as she could remember, Amelia recounted their evening.

"And you did not think to come to me?"

"The—this plan came up suddenly. She—she threatened

to leave without me. I thought the most prudent course of action was to go with her. To protect her. I had no idea . . ." She faltered as tears filled her voice and her nose stung painfully. "I had no idea of what that man intended to do to her."

The silence in the rocking, creaking carriage was agonizing.

"I believe you," Jonathan said quietly. "And I thank you, for protecting Jane as best you could." His eyes welled with tears as he looked down at the bright head, nestled so trustingly against his chest. "You acted accordingly."

High praise indeed, from Jonathan Lindsey.

She'd had no idea that Jonathan would have to fight his own father before this long night was over.

The carriage took them to the main entrance of Lindsey House, and Jonathan stepped out first, then swung an exhausted Jane up into his arms. He started up the front steps after giving the driver swift, careful instructions for the grooms. He wanted his horses looked after.

Amelia followed close behind him, knowing where her protection lay. She was so very tired, but filled with the knowledge of what an extraordinary evening this had been. And it was still far from over.

"Get her out of here!" The angry voice came from an old man, sitting in a chair by the fire. Now he rose to his full height and Amelia recognized Edward Lindsey, Jonathan's elderly father.

Jonathan simply kept walking toward the staircase. Amelia followed him, practically running on her short, stubby legs to keep up with his long-legged stride.

"You, young woman. Stop. I won't have this going on in my house."

She knew he was addressing her, knew she was a mere servant and in service to this man's family, but Amelia kept her attention on Jonathan's back. If he continued to move, so would she.

"No, Jonathan!" Now Edward made his final move, and it was quite remarkable for a man of his years. He blocked Jonathan at the foot of the stairs, refusing him entry to the rooms upstairs.

"I won't welcome that whore into my house."

"Step aside, Father."

"You cannot be serious—"

"Get out of my way."

Two strong-willed men, clashing over a woman. Amelia stepped back, knowing she had no place in this particular battle. And sensing that it had been an ongoing one.

"You bloody fool, you'll never know whether your children are your own—"

"If she wasn't in my arms, I'd come after you—"

"I will *not* have her presence in my house!"

"It's my house as well, old man."

The silence stretched interminably, the only sound the pattering of the rain. Its force had lessened, but still it fell outside, sheeting the garden and vast lawns.

She saw the implacable strength in Jonathan's face, and already knew who the winner in this battle would be. The two men faced off, the younger already the winner in this particularly deadly game of one-upmanship.

"I'll fight you for it, old man. And I'll win. Now, let me by, or suffer the consequences of your foolish actions."

Edward struggled with it, rage apparent on his wrinkled face. He struggled, then finally stepped aside, furious in his defeat. Jonathan started up the stairs, Jane in his arms, Amelia right behind him.

"You fool! You great big bloody fool! She's got you by the bollocks and you can't even see it—"

Amelia heard the sound of another voice, a confused murmur. But she didn't look back as she followed Jonathan up the stairs and through the dark manor house toward the master bedroom.

Apparently he was already the master of Lindsey House, for he occupied its main bedchamber.

Jonathan didn't waste any time. He summoned other servants, and a hot bath was prepared in front of the massive fireplace. He undressed Jane tenderly. She fought him, seemingly caught up in remembering the earlier nightmare.

"Jane," he said as he held her. "Jane, it's all right. I'm not Robert. It's Jon, it's me, darling. You're safe."

Amelia's eyes stung as she watched him help the girl into the bath. Jane cried out in agony as the hot water touched her frozen body. She'd been barely dressed beneath her cloak, and barefoot as well, much more prone to exposure than Amelia had been. Jonathan stayed by her side, talking to her, bathing her, washing the mud and twigs, the leaves and dirt out of her glorious red-gold hair.

He dried her with linen towels, then sat her by the fire and toweled her hair. He helped her dress for bed, in a nightgown and warm wrapper. He rubbed an herbal salve one of the maids brought into the bruises on her face, his ministrations so gentle. Amelia saw a muscle jump in his jaw as Jane reacted to his touch with pain.

She'd tried to stay out of his way as he administered to Jane. Amelia had stood as close to the fire as she'd dared, attempting to get warm. Now that she had a moment in time that was relatively calm, she had to start thinking about what she planned to do with the rest of her life. Perhaps there was a way back to Hugh. She'd come forward in time, she could find a way back. It might simply have to do with the tower room. . . .

She didn't know how this whole process worked, but she knew she had to find a way back to Hugh before she forgot who she really was and where she'd come from.

More than anything, she wanted to go home.

"There's additional hot water coming," Jonathan told her. "I'll be going downstairs shortly. You may take a bath, if you wish."

"Thank you." The man was extraordinarily generous.

"I have to settle things with my father," Jonathan said quietly, his eyes on Jane in his huge bed. She'd fallen asleep as soon as she'd laid her head on the lace-edged pillow. Amelia sensed Jonathan didn't look at Jane as a conquest to be taken to his bed but more as a frightened woman who needed time to adjust to what had happened to her.

"I understand."

"You will not speak of what happened with him this evening."

She smiled up at him. "We will protect her, sir."

Some of the worry was starting to leave his eyes.

"Yes, Emma, we will."

It pleased her that he knew her name. How she wished she could have heard that voice, so like Hugh's, say her name.

*Amelia.*

But it wasn't to be. She might never hear her name spoken again. It was a sobering thought, to feel that a major part of her identity might only survive within her own mind.

Two maids came back with more buckets of steaming hot water, which they added to the tub. Taking the sliver of French soap and a few of the linen towels, Amelia prepared for her first bath in the eighteenth century.

It was rather like camping. Roughing it. The hot water felt so heavenly, she didn't even care that it had already been used by Jane.

She'd felt fat and clumsy while running from the house earlier this evening, but now Amelia realized she wasn't fat, simply built differently. Stocky and short. Compact. Curvy. Quite a neat little package, if she did say so herself. And breasts! She finally had breasts!

*I had to travel back in time to get cleavage.*

The thought made her laugh, and it relaxed her. She continued the physical inventory as she bathed. Tiny waist, flaring hips, strong thighs. No saddlebags on this woman. Short legs and small feet. All in all, very nice.

She scrubbed herself until her freckled skin glowed, then stepped out of the tub, close to the fire. She'd taken her hair out of its severe bun, and the straight brown length of it reached to her waist. Amelia wrapped it in one of the linen strips, turban style, then dried her body and slipped on a nightgown and wrapper.

Thick hand-knitted socks and warm slippers completed the outfit. One of the maids must have gone to her quarters and brought a few of her things to Jonathan's bedroom.

She knew he expected her to stay with Jane and look after her until he returned. As she didn't quite know what her regular duties entailed, she was relieved by this particular turn of events. Soon enough, she would have to make sure no one realized she was a twentieth-century woman inside an eighteenth-century body.

She sat by the fire as she dried her long hair, wondering

for the first time where Emma's consciousness had gone. Where was the woman? Had she just awakened one morning and realized she had no body? Was her soul flitting around, waiting for Amelia's own consciousness to leave?

"I'm sorry," she whispered into the silence of the room. The only sound was the snapping and hissing of the fire. She couldn't hear Jane breathing, could only see the barely discernible rise and fall of her chest. "I'm sorry, Emma, for what you had to go through because of me."

She wondered what Emma had to learn from this whole experience. What she had to learn.

*I do believe we're here for a specific reason.*

She could almost hear Hugh's voice as he said the words. It was one of her favorite memories, the day they'd met by the garden. That long first talk. John laughing in the tower window. Later that evening, she and Hugh had walked the dogs, and though he hadn't taken her hand, hadn't even touched her, she knew she'd met her destiny that day.

Only to have it taken away.

*No. I can't believe that. For if I believe that, I have nothing left to live for.*

She thought of Jane, taking her own life. They seemed to be past the worst of it. Much could be repaired by a good night's sleep. She was nodding off herself, almost hypnotized by the dancing flames.

*We're here for a specific reason. . . .*

If only she could figure out her own. Why had she been sent back in time? Her mind refused to believe it was a symptom of random chaos, with no reason or structure behind the entire event.

There had to be a reason. She'd find it, and in doing so, she'd find a way home. Her spirits lifted, and feeling much more awake, Amelia checked Jane, then turned, catching ight of another person in the room.

Not a person. Her reflection.

The large mirror was not a good one by twentieth-century standards. The glass wavered slightly; it was a bit pitted. But it was certainly enough to enable her to see the face she'd been given for this trip back in time.

Emma—what was her last name?—stared back at her.

Long, straight brown hair. A round face. Irish, if she had to put a nationality to it. Smooth, clear skin, except for the scattering of freckles.

She looked at her reflection more closely, moving toward the mirror. What she saw caused her to take in a sharp breath and hold it tightly.

Her eyes. Emma had her eyes. Or she had Emma's. The eyes were the same. Large, gray, flecked with the smallest amount of green. Darker around the edge of the iris.

Surrounded by thick lashes. She'd always been proud of her eyes, considering them her best feature. Now it was disconcerting to see them staring back at her from a different face.

More than anything else, that small physical resemblance convinced her that she and Emma were linked in a way she couldn't yet figure out.

"I'll bet you want your body back, too."

No answer.

It could get extraordinarily lonely, talking to oneself.

She thought about the body she'd left, the shoulder-length blonde hair, the slender shape, the tall stature. She'd liked her hands. They hadn't been square like Emma's, but they'd been strong and capable.

Her palms tingled, and she remembered what it had felt like, a sense memory, touching Hugh's sleeping face with her finger one day, then flicking a rose petal off his cheek.

They'd been lying together in the gazebo, enjoying the late afternoon. One of the scarlet petals from the climbing rose-bush had fallen, he'd wrinkled his nose in sleep, and she'd gently brushed it off, waking him. . . .

The memory made her unbearably lonely.

"Sleep," she said to herself quietly. "You need to sleep just like Jane." She didn't think Jonathan would be angry with her if she slept for a little while. Jane wasn't likely to wake soon, and Amelia knew he would have his hands full with his father.

She curled up on the foot of the massive four-poster bed, opened the bed curtains slightly to catch some of the heat from the fire, and closed her eyes.

As Amelia drifted off to sleep, her last conscious thought was that she might not ever be able to tell Hugh how much she loved him, for he wouldn't be born for almost two hundred years.

> *It is one of the most beautiful compensations of life
> that no man can sincerely try to help another, without
> helping himself.*
>
> —John P. Webster

## Chapter Four

LATER, SHE COULDN'T remember what woke her.

The fire had burned low; the bedchamber was filled with deep shadows. Someone had tucked a warm wool blanket around her, and as Amelia sat up in bed she wondered why Jonathan's return hadn't wakened her. Funny—now she was waking up in the eighteenth century and that seemed perfectly normal.

She glanced around the bedchamber, trying to take it all in and immediately noticing that something was wrong.

Jane. Gone. Her mind raced frantically. Where was she? Had Jonathan come to get her? Had they gone for a walk? Of course not; Jane was in no condition to go anywhere.

She remembered the Lindsey legend, the story that had been passed down for countless generations, and as Amelia leaped off the bed and started out the door, she prayed that the house hadn't changed that much. She could still make it to the tower room from Hugh's master bedroom in about three minutes.

How long did it take a young, frightened girl to suffocate? If she did it right, her neck would snap instantly and her pain would be at an end.

Amelia's side hurt as she raced up the circular stairs, praying Jane hadn't thought to lock the door, hoping against hope she wouldn't find herself helplessly pounding on another strong wooden barrier. Had anyone else suspected? Had anyone else tried to save her the other time? Jonathan hadn't thought she was in such a state; his letters had revealed as much.

Was he still calming his father? Perhaps he and Jane had slipped off somewhere to be together. No, they would have merely asked her to leave the room had they wanted their privacy, for whatever reason.

She climbed the last of the high, narrow stone steps, her breath coming in burning gasps. Her heart pounded, she felt slightly nauseous, but Amelia pressed on, and as she entered the tower room, her worst fears were confirmed.

Jane stood, a silhouette in the moonlight, on a wooden chair. A rough noose lay around her slender neck, the thick rope securely fastened to a cross beam. Once she kicked the chair over, the deed would be done.

For a moment, Amelia couldn't say a word; she simply stared. Shock had almost rendered her immobile. She watched as Jane's split lip moved; the girl seemed to be talking to herself. Her eyes were closed. Amelia wondered if she'd simply gone mad. Then realization struck.

*She's praying.*

Jane was asking for forgiveness for what she was about to do. And Amelia, no stranger to despair herself, knew the depths a soul had to reach to contemplate such a desperate act.

"No."

Her voice sounded loud in the quiet room, and startled

Jane out of her almost meditative state.

"Emma." Her tone was that of a mother asking her disobedient child to go back to sleep. "I want you to leave this instant."

"I can't. You know that. Now, I want you to come down from that chair, but first you have to take that rope from around your neck—"

"Don't you come near me!"

Amelia stopped midstride. She'd approached Jane as carefully as she could, as one might come close to a deer in a forest glade. Jane had that same wild, frightened expression. Though Amelia had thought her so strong, this woman had reached the end of all hope. There was nothing more for her, and Amelia could see it in her eyes.

*Stop her.*

She couldn't consider any other action. She knew it was wrong, to force destiny to alter itself, to bend in upon itself. The repercussions of this action would be felt for centuries, but Amelia was powerless against the strong tide of emotion assailing her at the thought of this vibrant young woman ending her life.

*Stop her. Whatever it takes.*

Telling the truth would be a good place to start. Amazing, how lives were altered when the facts were exposed.

"He won't be able to live without you."

That stopped her, just as a small slippered foot almost stepped off the wooden chair.

"You're lying." But her voice had the slightest tremor to it.

"No. I'm not. You see, I finally had a vision."

Jane didn't answer, she simply stared at her.

"Like my aunt."

She continued to stare.

"You can't do this to him, Jane. He loves you so."

"No." Her voice broke on the one word, but Amelia was far too concerned, too wary, to believe she'd gotten through to her. Yet.

"Yes. He ends his own life two years after this date, on the anniversary of your death. He comes up to the tower and re-creates your act." She was hurting Jane and she knew it, but she had to hurt her, to shock her, in order to get through to her.

"His manservant comes up and cuts him down—"

"Stop this! I demand it!"

"—and he is buried next to you, out in the family grave-yard, as he wished. He wanted the two of you to be together for all eternity."

"I don't want to hear this! I can't!"

"Do you love him, Jane?" Amelia was shouting now, edging a little closer. Trying to get close enough that if Jane did take that fatal step she could grab her and keep the rope from closing around her neck long enough for help to arrive. She shouted to attract Jonathan, knowing how voices could carry from the tower. She'd loved the Lindsey House of the twentieth century; there wasn't much about the old estate she hadn't discovered while working with John and falling in love with Hugh.

Now it would all work to her advantage.

She watched Jane carefully. Calculated the distance between them. Her chest hurt with the effort.

"Do you love him?" she shouted again, praying the entire time that the sound would attract Jonathan. He would know what to do. He would help her. Once Jane saw him, she wouldn't be able to leave him this way.

"*Yes!*" The word came out an almost feral snarl, and Amelia knew Jane hated her for forcing her to admit what she'd finally learned during this long night.

"Then take that noose from around your neck. Now."

Jane hesitated, and Amelia fired her final shot, the only ammunition she had left.

"I see the letter," she began quietly, praying the entire time that her voice would hold up. "He wrote you almost fifty letters after you took your life, Jane."

"No!"

"He needed to talk to you, to finish it—"

"No, I will not hear this!"

"Yes, you will." Amelia was fully aware of the consequences of her decision. Ensuring Jane's survival meant that Hugh would never be born. She knew that, and just as surely as she loved him, she knew what she had to do. John's words echoed in her mind.

*He left the entire estate and all its holdings to several distant cousins. That's where my side of the family comes in. . . .*

That side of the family had been close to starvation when they'd inherited Lindsey House. Now, if she succeeded, they wouldn't. Hugh's branch of the family wouldn't survive. She'd never see him again, whether she managed to make it back to her own time or not.

Amelia hesitated for one agonizing moment, but once she started, her voice never faltered.

" 'My dearest Poppet—' "

That stopped Jane cold.

"How do you know—"

" 'My dearest Poppet, I find that I cannot go on without you.' " The words rushed out of her mouth, words she'd committed to memory over countless readings of that particular letter. Words she had wondered at, wondered how any one mortal could feel so deeply, could be willing to sacrifice their life because of another.

Now she knew.

"Stop it! I won't tolerate this!"

" '—I'm tired and I want to come home. To you. I'd thought I would come home to you each evening—' " The pain in her chest was tremendous. This had to be what a heart felt like when it was breaking.

"*Don't!* You have no right!" But life was back in those green eyes, that vivid presence that had struck Amelia at the inn, by the fire. Jane was angry. Jane was back.

They were screaming at each other like fishwives, and Amelia almost laughed out loud. Whoever couldn't hear them had to be deaf—and Jonathan Lindsey was many things, but hard of hearing wasn't one of them.

" 'You are everywhere, my darling, yet nowhere—' "

"*Damn* you!"

*Oh, Hugh, forgive me. I love you.*

" 'God will forgive me for what I am about to do—' "

"*No!*"

" 'It is said that He never sends us more than we can bear, but I find that I have reached my limit.' " She took a deep, steadying breath. "I see him writing the words, Jane! You cannot cause him such pain!"

"Emma, *stop* this!"

She could. So easily. If she stopped right now, before Jonathan reached them, if she let Jane sink into the despair that made such an act possible, she might see Hugh again, and John, and her old life—

Impossible. Amelia knew she could never live with herself if she made such a decision.

*We're constantly creating and molding the future all the time.*

She saw Hugh in her mind's eye. That first meeting, in

the garden over breakfast. Somehow, in the strangest way, Hugh had known the truth all along.

"Oh, Jane!" Something of the despair in her heart colored her tone. Their gazes locked, and Amelia knew this was her last chance to get through to her.

"Jane, to love someone like that! I used to think it was beyond me, until I let it go! I doubted it could exist and I lost it! Don't you understand—you have a chance to have something most people never get to experience! Please don't make the mistake I did!"

Jane faltered, and Amelia knew she almost had her.

"I can't. He—he won't want me when—"

"Damn you—you're so much more than your virginity! You're more than the physical body I see before me! And if you cannot believe that, then why were you praying?"

She had her. Almost.

"He *loves* you, Jane. Really, really loves you. And if you're selfish enough to take your life because of the shame in a foolish mistake, then I—" A sharp pain squeezed her heart, and she grabbed her right arm. It felt decidedly odd.

She struggled on.

"If you're selfish enough to lose what most people only dream about—damn it, I want you to stop thinking about yourself and think about him!"

"How do you know all this? It's not just that vision, is it?"

*Right the first time out, Jane. Smart girl, got it in one.*

"No. I'm . . . not from here." The pain in her chest was excruciating. Like being in the grip of a giant, grinding jaw. She was starting to sweat; she felt the sick dampness along her temple.

"Where?" The green eyes were lit with a feverish glow. "Where are you from?"

Her eyes rolled up, her head lolled back as the pain claimed her. Crushed her. Pain like she'd never felt before. She steeled herself against it. From a great distance away, she heard booted feet on the tower stairs.

*Help. Jonathan. Help me.*

"From . . . a long way . . . far away . . ." Her vision started to cloud over. Dear God, her heart wasn't breaking, it was failing. She was suffering a heart attack.

"Emma!" And Jane, impetuous as ever, forgot the rope and stepped down to help her.

It seemed to happen in slow motion. Amelia fought for one last surge of strength. It propelled her beneath Jane's slight body, just long enough to prevent the rope from snapping her slender neck. Her short, stubby arms grasped the slender, flailing legs, and as Jane felt her support, her struggles ceased.

"Emma, no, put me down! The noose is off, it's off I tell you! Please, *please* put me down, I don't want you to—"

She didn't hear the rest of the words. Her vision dimmed, then faded to black.

*Hugh. Oh, Hugh. I love . . .*

The last sound she heard was that of a woman crying.

Those who bring sunshine to the lives of others cannot keep it from themselves.

—James M. Barrie

# Chapter Five

SHE WOKE SLOWLY, to the sound of birds chattering and singing. To the softness of the English country air. The light was diffused as it entered the tower room, and for a moment as Amelia blinked and tried to orient herself, she didn't quite know where she was.

Or who.

*Hands.* Her hands. Slender and pale, not a freckle in sight. She pulled at her hair as she sat up, and saw strands of the lightest blonde, not Emma's brown—

Everything stilled within her.

"What an extraordinary dream," she whispered, then touched the floor of the tower room. Carpeted. Just like before. John had been so very proud when he'd described how he'd brought the little room back from its rather dilapidated state. It was his sanctuary, his hideaway, his place of peace where he came to be renewed.

*Such a powerful dream . . . almost real . . .*

She sat very still in the comfortable leather chair, so happy to be back. Now, through what she'd experienced during that one wild night of her imagination, she realized she'd lost all her fears concerning her upcoming marriage. She would marry Hugh; they would have children; they would contribute to the Lindsey line and make their lives matter. She would teach their children to live each day to the fullest, to love one another, and to never, ever take anything—or anyone—for granted.

She glanced out the window. Still early in the morning. Still time. She closed her eyes and a powerful peace washed through her.

*Thank you. For letting me see so much through that dream. For giving me that realization, that awakening. Thank you for letting me see how much I have, how blessed I am, and how Hugh was right. We do constantly create our own futures, through our thoughts and actions. . . .*

She finished the short prayer, then thought of her father and how much she would miss him on this day. She'd asked John if he would walk her down the aisle, and the older man had been delighted. But, still, secretly, she would miss her father's presence on this day.

A sound at the door made her turn her head.

"Miss?" Annie's voice was cautious as she studied her. "Whatever are you doing, sleeping up here?"

"I had—I had the most extraordinary dream, Annie." She found that she had to tell someone. "Do you believe the soul exists apart from the body?"

"I do."

"Well." She laughed then, still delighted to find herself back in her present life. That dream had been so vivid, for a moment upon waking she'd actually thought she'd traveled through time. "I dreamed—I was with some of the older souls of Lindsey House." Somehow, she knew Annie wouldn't make fun of her.

"Really." A pause. "Lady Jane?"

A prickle of unease worked its way up Amelia's spine. How had the girl been so quick to guess?

"Yes. And Jonathan."

Annie nodded her head. Her face was expressionless, but her eyes, those gray eyes, were decidedly animated. Filled with delight.

Strange.

"Probably because we were talking about the tragedy in the tower last night. I remembered it, came up to the tower room, and was thinking about it before I fell asleep."

Annie remained silent.

Something wasn't quite right, and Amelia didn't know what.

"I'm sure that's it, Annie."

"Of course. Now, you must come with me. We have a lot to do, getting you ready for your wedding day." Annie approached her, held out her hand.

How strange. The young maid had seemed so standoffish the night before, while serving tea. Now it was almost as if she were truly welcoming her into this great house.

"Come." Annie took her hand, pulled her to her feet. "I'm glad you slept so well, dreamed so deeply. You'll need your strength for what's to come this day."

She followed the maid back to her bedroom. Everything was as it should be: her bridal gown, her veil, her satin shoes, gloves, and wedding purse. Everything laid out, just as it had been the night before, but it didn't feel right.

Something was . . . different.

"I'll go get you a cup of tea, and then we'd better run your bath." And Annie was gone, as swiftly and silently as she'd arrived.

*She reminds me of Emma. . . .*

She wondered where Hugh was, and was filled with an overpowering urgency to see him. But she couldn't; he was charmingly superstitious about such things, and they'd agreed not to see each other on the morning of their wedding. Where could he be at this hour?

Probably in the garden. He was passionate about the grounds surrounding Lindsey House, and would certainly want them to be immaculate for his wedding day.

She approached the window and thought about calling down to him, the maiden in the tower to her prince, when she saw . . . she saw . . .

This shock was greater than any her dream had produced. Flowers. Everywhere. Lilies, that particular lily, she'd only seen it one place before, in Jonathan Lindsey's sketchbooks. . . . Creamy white, with the palest pink center, he'd called the flower Bride's Tears, after his Jane, after the woman he'd loved.

*But he burned that part of the garden to the ground; he leveled it, would have sown salt into the earth if he'd thought of it. He couldn't bear to see the flower he'd created. He wanted it over; he burned the garden to the ground right before he hung himself. . . .*

Before her mind even consciously realized what she was doing, she was racing out of the bedroom, across the great hall, down the curving staircase, out the double front doors, and toward the flowers. . . .

*Hugh. I have to see Hugh.*

George, the gardener, was busily raking the path through that part of the garden when she approached him. If he looked a little startled to see a wild-eyed woman in her nightgown and robe at this time of the morning, he had the good grace not to show it.

"Good morning, miss."

"George." She put a hand over her heart to still its frantic racing. "George, how did this flower get here? Why is it here? Isn't it Bride's Tears?" As she spoke, she snapped a slender stem and brought one of the blooms up to her cheek. The velvety petals brushed her skin, seemed to ground her. She was here, she wasn't dreaming. . . .

"Bride's Tears?" He stopped his raking, then leaned on the gardening tool. "No, miss. Bride's Joy, it's always been called. Your friend Miss Bickham should be here shortly to gather them for your wedding bouquet." He cleared his throat. "Unless, of course, you'd be changing your mind and wanting those red roses. Or maybe the apricot. I can let her know—"

"No. No, of course not. Penny will know what to choose, of course she will, but—that is—do you know where—where is Hugh? Have you seen him?" She knew how she had to appear to him, her hair uncombed, still in her nightgown and robe, but Amelia was confident he'd attribute her wild behavior to bridal nerves. She couldn't possibly confess what she'd really been up to.

But she had to tell Hugh.

"He's on the other side of the garden, miss, taking his morning walk."

She lifted the skirts of her long gown and robe, then raced in the direction he'd indicated.

Hugh was walking in the garden, and when she saw him, she stopped just before the path and simply filled her senses with him. He'd never looked more beautiful to her. He was here. It was enough. All would be well.

"Hugh!"

He looked up, then smiled. But it seemed a rather shaky smile to her; thus, she approached him quickly, took his hand, kissed his tanned cheek.

"Hugh, I know we agreed not to see each other before the wedding, but there's something quite extraordinary I have to tell you—"

"You've changed your mind?"

"I—no, why would I do that?"

He took both her hands in his, then turned so he was facing her. "I know you've had your fears, Amelia, and I'd hoped you'd overcome them with time." The expression in his dark blue eyes was so like Jonathan Lindsey's that it gave her another of those queer little ripples up her spine.

"But I *am* all right with it; it's part of what I came to tell you. Nothing could stop me from marrying you. I remember what you said. 'I'll show you every day, for the rest of my life, how much I love you. You'll come to believe it.' I do, Hugh, I do!"

His face slowly changed, lit with a cautious happiness, then all anxiety vanished. "Then that's what you came to the garden to tell me?" He looked at her and laughed, and she joined in, knowing how she had to look. "I still don't want to see you in your gown before the ceremony, darling, if that can be arranged."

"No. There's something else. The most extraordinary thing happened to me last night—"

"Master Hugh," the gardener called. "Master Hugh, your grandfather is back, along with Miss Amelia's father, and they—"

She didn't hear any more. Hugh's face swam in front of her eyes, and she, who had never fainted in her entire life, knew she was about to do just that. . . .

"Hugh?" She gripped his arm tightly, the blood roaring in her ears, her pulse thundering. Her father? How could that be? *He'd been dead for years.* . . .

\*    \*    \*

"Daddy," she said shakily as she came to.

"You gave us quite a scare in the garden, Ami."

Her eyes filled at the sound of the familiar endearment. Max Jamison was sitting on the edge of the huge four-poster bed, holding her hand. She remembered the feel of it, the way he'd held on to her hand while she'd ridden her first pony, so long ago.

She couldn't stop herself from staring at him. Though she'd never forgotten how he looked, he'd been frozen in time in photos and films. Now that same dear face was in front of her, a little more weathered, a few more lines, a sprinkling of white hair at the temples. But he was still her father. Max Jamison was alive.

"I'm sorry."

"No need to be. Bridal nerves." He grinned, and Amelia felt the tears start to run down her cheeks. He had a grin just like Clark Gable's in *Gone with the Wind*. Cocky and self-assured. And full of such love for her.

No one had ever loved her like her father had. Until Hugh.

"Now, Ami," he said, his deep voice so suddenly familiar. "Sure you want to marry this man? You can tell me otherwise up until we get to the altar, and after that it's in God's hands."

She sat up on the bed, wiped away her tears, and threw her arms around him, hugging him close, so close she felt as if she might crack his ribs.

"I do," she whispered. "But he'll never take your place in my life."

"He isn't supposed to," Max replied, his voice sounding only a little gruff. "But marriage is serious business, darling. Once you make that commitment, you can't back out.''

''I know.'' She wanted to ask where her mother was, but didn't know how. But he answered that question soon enough.

''Your mother's in London, doing some last-minute shopping. Something came in that she'd ordered for you and Hugh. You know how mad about shopping that woman is.'' He laughed, his gray eyes alive with mischief. ''I thought about picking her up at the train station and telling her you and Hugh eloped!''

''You wouldn't!'' But she giggled, and remembered her mother as a different woman when she'd been married to her father. She'd laughed a lot more.

Amelia couldn't wait to meet her.

''Up to any more visitors?''

They both turned their heads, and saw John Lindsey standing in the bedroom doorway, a wriggling Charlie in his arms.

''Of course!'' How she adored that old man.

He let the terrier go, and the little dog bounded out of his arms, hit the ground running, then leaped up on the bed and began to prance all around Amelia, barking and trying to get in a few swipes on her face with his tongue.

*Charlie's having a bad day . . . the vet says I'll have to be making my mind up about him soon. . . .*

This little dog was in perfect health.

''Charlie.'' She picked him up and hugged him, and his wiry doggie body squirmed with delight. ''Oh, Charlie.''

Then she burst into tears.

She went with her father to the train station. Amelia recognized her mother instantly, but not the tall, striking woman with the dark auburn hair and intelligent hazel eyes who was with her.

"Amelia," she said, "I left my car here at the station. Would you ride back with me?"

She looked to her parents, unsure.

The hazel eyes were sympathetic. "I don't mean to take you away from time you'd like to spend with your mother—"

"Oh, it's all right, Frances," her mother said. "We'll have plenty of time once we get back to the house."

*Hugh's mother . . .*

"Oh, dear," Max said. "Does this mean we can't stop off for a quick kiss at the lake like I'd planned?"

"Maxwell!" But Catherine Jamison patted his cheek as she said it.

"No, it's fine. I'll ride back with you." As she got into the familiar battered old Range Rover, Amelia wondered how long she'd actually known Hugh's mother.

Maybe she wanted to have a private word with her before the ceremony. After all, he was her beloved only son.

After today was over, nothing would ever surprise her again. How strange were the ways of the Universe. And how wise.

They were a third of the way to Lindsey House before Frances Lindsey spoke.

"I'm probably overreacting . . . and Hugh would throttle me if he even suspected what I was up to."

"It's all right." Amelia had a feeling she knew what was coming. She could handle it.

"I just . . . are you *sure,* Amelia? Really sure? My Hugh has never fallen in love before, and I don't want to see him hurt. I know he seems rather formidable and . . . something of a terror at times, but he has the softest of hearts. I know him as only a mother can.''

Frances was having a hard time of this, but she plunged on and Amelia admired her for it. It was such a demonstration of love for her son.

"So if you have any doubts, please voice them now.''

What a fierce mother hen, protecting her only chick.

"I'm sure.'' Her voice was perfectly steady. How much Jane had taught her. She'd needed to go back through time, needed to see things through different eyes, through a different and very courageous soul, in order to find peace within herself.

She would never, ever forget Emma. Though her health had been frail, the tiny woman had possessed the heart of a lion.

"Personally, I think the two of you are perfect for each other,'' Frances continued, her eyes on the road. "I knew from the moment you came to the house. Amelia, I never had any doubts, but there were times when I sensed you were afraid.''

"I was. I'm not anymore.''

"Good.'' Frances smiled, then reached for her hand and gave it a brief squeeze. "Don't think of me as an ogre of a mother-in-law, will you?''

"Never.''

"I know I'm being overprotective, but Hugh is my first-born, and holds a very special place in my heart. I know that must seem strange, what with seven other children, but—''

Amelia didn't hear any more; she turned her head ever so slightly so her future mother-in-law wouldn't see the sheen of tears in her eyes and misconstrue them.

*She had eight children, not just Hugh.*

Amelia remembered that day with John, when he showed her the family photos lining the walls. Hugh's teddy bear tea, how Frances had wanted more children, that awful fall from her horse. She'd bet there were many more photos along that wall now.

*You'll have seven sisters and brothers now. And who knows how many nieces and nephews.*

She sat forward in the car seat, and glanced at her future mother-in-law. Amelia had the feeling they were going to get along just fine.

"Anxious to get back?" Now Frances was smiling.

"Yes."

She was ready to be married.

The wedding took place in the middle of the garden, in the early evening. The weather was gorgeous; everyone commented on it for weeks afterward. The garden was alive with starlings, sparrows, dogs, and cats. Children laughed and an excited anticipation seemed to grip the guests.

Amelia approached the heart of the garden with her father, along a walkway Penny had made through the grounds by draping and knotting white satin ribbon from tree to tree. Tiny white lights sparkled among the branches, making the garden seem magical, inhabited by fairies. The overlapping white runner, scattered with rose petals, protected the hem of her gown.

They reached the arch that Penny had designed, twined with more of Jonathan's lilies, and also gardenias, lilacs, and roses. Hugh looked so dashing in his cutaway suit, trousers, and wing-collar shirt. The expression on his face when he saw her approaching in her bridal finery made her glad he hadn't seen her in it before this moment in time.

Amelia and her father reached the altar, and she found

331

this particular good-bye wasn't difficult at all. He squeezed her hand, then gave her over to Hugh with a wink that seemed to say, No backing out now. She smiled at Penny, her maid of honor, who was trying valiantly not to cry. Then Amelia handed her the bridal bouquet.

Peace filled her heart as she and Hugh faced the minister. Their wedding ceremony began.

Afterward, she tried to find Annie, but couldn't.

"Where did she go?" she asked Hugh as they danced in the grand ballroom of Lindsey House. One of the advantages of marrying into an extremely wealthy English family was that you didn't have to worry about renting a hotel or a country club. The family estate was just fine.

There were a couple of tense moments, when she'd met up with a few of Hugh's former girlfriends, but nothing too harrowing. They were all congratulatory, a few even openly envious.

The day went by as if part of a dream. The toasts, the sit-down dinner, the dancing. She'd opted for candlelight, as it suited Lindsey House. The bride's table had been decorated with more flowers, and even the candelabra were trimmed with miniature white roses at the base of each candle. Penny had been allowed to go quite wild inside the estate, and staircases, columns, mantels, and archways were festooned with greenery. And flowers. Everywhere, Bride's Joy, symbol of the day and what it meant to the Lindsey family both past and present.

The reception would last far into the night, but she and Hugh planned to retire early. They were leaving for Barbados in the morning for a monthlong honeymoon, and had to get off to an early start.

She threw her bouquet, and Hugh's younger sister, Olivia, caught it. Amelia took off her gown in the upstairs bedroom, with another maid's assistance. She dressed in a simpler outfit, then picked up the smaller going-away bouquet Penny had created for her and went back downstairs.

Amid showers of birdseed, rose petals, and congratulations, the couple left Lindsey House and walked across the moonlit lawns toward the small cottage on the edge of the woods that had been prepared for them.

Once inside, Hugh directed her toward the fireplace. He started a fire with swift economy, then handed her an elaborately wrapped package.

"Your bridal gift. It's late, I know. Your mother did me the favor of going into London this morning and picking it up. I had it re-covered for you."

He was running on; he was nervous! Hugh Lindsey was actually nervous! She remembered what his mother had said in the Range Rover that morning, about his sometimes formidable demeanor concealing the softness of his heart.

She'd never seen anything but that heart.

Her fingers trembled as she set down her bouquet and unwrapped the package. The lovely paper fell away, and she stared at the large, leather-bound book.

Before she even opened it, she knew what it was.

"Jonathan's journal," she whispered.

"Do you like it?" There was just an edge of apprehension to his voice.

"I love it; it means ever so much to me." She threw her arms around his neck and kissed him, and when they finally came up for air, he grinned and cocked a rather arrogant eyebrow at her.

"Weddings. Bloody awful, aren't they?"

"Yes!" She laughed, and then he kissed her and everything faded away to be replaced by both love and desire, made stronger and more poignant for her because she knew in her heart how close she'd come to losing him.

He carried her to the bedroom, nudging the door open, and she cried out in delight. Penny had done her magical and transformative work here as well, with red rose petals showered across the bed, and flowers and candles everywhere.

"Champagne?" Hugh asked, and she saw the absolute delight in his eyes at her reaction to his surprise.

"Oh, Hugh . . ." She couldn't find the words.

"I just let her loose to do what she does best," he said, pouring the pale, sparkling liquid into one of two crystal flutes. He took a deep breath as he handed her the champagne. "I want you to be happy, Amelia."

"I am." She knew he was still worried about her doubts, but now she saw her fears for what they were, and they no longer had any power over her. That darkness had been lifted forever.

They sipped champagne, then kissed. Hugh lit a few more of the candles, then helped her out of her clothing, slowly, seducing her, kissing her, whispering words of endearment. She loved him for taking time with her, creating a moment she would remember all her life.

Because it was different now.

He joined her on the bed after shedding his own clothing, and emotion overwhelmed her. She felt as if she truly belonged to him. There would never be anyone else; there would never be any barriers between them. She gave herself to him with no reservations, no hesitations, knowing this was right, that they were right for each other.

That they were meant to be with each other at this exact moment in time.

She was lying on top of him when she suddenly cupped

his face in her hands and kissed him, remembering the fear and her feelings of darkness and despair, not that long ago. Remembering that horrible feeling of not knowing if she would ever see him again. Realizing he might never be born.

A tear slipped out from beneath her lashes.

"Amelia?" Everything stopped as Hugh tightened his arms around her, holding her closely. "What's wrong?"

"I thought . . ." Her voice trembled. "I thought I'd lost you."

"Never." He kissed the single tear away. "Never in this lifetime, my darling."

"I know that now," she whispered against his chest. "Oh, Hugh, can you forgive me for being so frightened?"

"There's nothing to forgive."

She raised her head and looked down at him, saw such love in those dark blue eyes that she caught her breath.

"I knew," he whispered, touching her cheek, "the minute I saw you in the garden. That first day."

She nodded her head. "I did, too."

His eyes narrowed as he studied her. "Then why were you so frightened?"

She thought of the past before she'd gone back, and didn't know if she'd ever be able to explain it all to him. Someday. Not now. She didn't want to sacrifice this moment to any explanation.

"I couldn't explain those fears, even to myself." She kissed him then, and felt his hands in her hair as he moved against her, up over her, pressing her down into the bed. And mere seconds before they became one she gave a silent, thankful prayer that the Lindsey men were such passionate, understanding lovers, that they cherished their women even when they lost their way.

And that they had faith enough to sustain a marriage into eternity.

Later that night, Hugh fast asleep in their marital bed, Amelia crept down the stairs. The fire had burned low, but there was still just enough light left to read Jonathan's bold handwriting. She searched through the journal until toward the end, where she found the passage she needed to read.

*Quite an extraordinary act, what Emma did. She restored my Jane's faith in the goodness of people. Her death had a shattering impact on Jane, both good and bad. It changed her forever, the way she looked at life. Including the way she looked at me.*

*Perhaps I have Emma to thank for that, as well. We were married only days after her death, and father fought me on that. I insisted Emma be buried in the family cemetery, and the old man fought me on that one, as well. But I won, and Emma was laid to rest. I wrote to all her relatives, but no one ever came for any of her things.*

*I wondered at that.*

*We don't speak of Emma, though I know both of us think of her daily. Jane might have been killed, or could have succeeded in taking her life had Emma not intervened.*

*There was one evening when Jane insisted she'd been in the presence of a heavenly being. She told me Emma had said she was from a long way away, and my Jane took that to mean Heaven. An angel, a heavenly creature, she told me, visited this house and blessed its occupants.*

*I don't really know. I don't know if it matters. All that matters is that Jane and I have each other, and the children. She is a different woman from the headstrong, scared, and selfish little creature I had the good fortune to fall in love with. She was profoundly transformed that night, convinced that a merciful God sent an angel in the form of a plump little serving girl to help her see her life. What it was meant to be. What it could be.*

*Thus, my darling, headstrong, romantic girl has taken it upon herself to single-handedly rescue any unfortunate member of my family. She says that as she has none, this gives her something to do. Just this morning, we arranged for some cousins from the North to come live with us. . . .*

Amelia stopped reading, her question answered. Hugh had been spared, but she hadn't known why. Now she did. In saving Jane's life, she had put an extraordinary chain of events into action, all of them good.

Why had she assumed it was a bad thing, to try and change the past? Why had every novel she'd ever read assumed that fact? She turned several of the journal's pages, enjoying the feel of the paper, studying Jonathan's bold handwriting, until another phrase caught her eye.

*Thus we were taught the ultimate lesson. That faith, if shared, creates faith. That hope, if encouraged, creates hope. And that love, once given, creates an infinite form of that emotion, so that no one need ever want for it.*

How true. There were only a few paragraphs left, and Amelia scanned them quickly.

337

*My only regret in this life is that I never had a chance to thank Emma. I did so for her part in bringing my Jane safely home, but she died before I had a chance to tell her how thankful I was she fought Jane's misguided will and kept her alive.*

*Had I but one wish, it would be to have the chance to thank her. To let her know what she meant to me, what her actions meant to my family. I take lilies from the garden to her grave each Sunday. My way of doing penance, I suppose. . . .*

Here the journal ended.

Amelia closed the book. Gathering up her robe and slippers, she knew there was one more thing she had to do before she and Hugh left on their honeymoon in the morning.

She picked up her small going-away bouquet and smiled at Penny's choices. Red roses for love. Rosemary for faithfulness. Hyacinth for constancy and bachelor's button for hope. All qualities that brought Emma to mind.

Outside, the spring air was gentle and cool. So unlike that cold, rainy night when she and Jane had escaped to the carriage. She walked steadily toward the graveyard.

Hugh had pointed it out to her, but she'd never wanted to see it before now. Graves and their occupants had always left her with a rather creepy feeling, and she'd wanted nothing to do with them.

She wasn't afraid anymore. She'd been in much darker places.

Once inside the gated property, she turned on the flashlight and started studying the headstones and their inscriptions. She would've guessed Emma was buried on the outskirts, but wasn't surprised when she found the headstone toward the center of the family plot.

"Emma," she whispered, sinking to her knees. She placed the small bouquet on the grave. The inscription below the single name was brief. A LOVING WOMAN, A NOBLE SERVANT WITH THE HEART OF A LION. MAY SHE FIND PEACE.

"Emma," she whispered again, then touched the moss-covered stone. She knelt silently for a while, enjoying the feel of the night air, and somehow knowing that Emma and Jane and even Jonathan were close by. Would always be close to the house in spirit. Would possibly even choose to come back, through their children.

She began to speak, the words clumsy and halting, though they came from her heart.

"Emma, I wanted to thank you, for . . . showing me what I had, and what I might have run from. I could've thrown it all away, I was so frightened. Until you showed me what it meant to step outside yourself and truly love another person."

She paused. Amazing, how right it felt to talk to a dead person, buried beneath the ground.

"I'll come and see you when I get back. I'll bring you flowers. And I want you to know, Emma, what you meant to Jonathan, and to Jane. And especially to me."

She wiped away the tears gathering in her eyes.

"You won't be forgotten. I won't let that happen. John and I will gather up all the papers, the family history, and write a book about the history of this house. You'll be prominently mentioned—"

She laughed then, and the sound carried on the night wind. How funny. The type of person Emma had been, she wouldn't have given a fig about being included in a family history. But Amelia didn't want the little maid to be forgotten.

"I'll always consider you a member of my family. I'm going to name my firstborn daughter after you. And your memory will always live on in my heart."

She stood, then remained silent for a few more moments until she sensed another's presence. She turned and saw Annie, in a dark cloak, standing to the side.

"Annie. I didn't see you at my wedding."

"You went back, didn't you?"

She saw no reason to lie.

"Yes."

"And had the courage to change it. Thank God."

"Yes."

"My mother had the sight. She told me, before she died, that a woman would come to this house and set things right. The day you came, that night I had a dream. I knew it would happen, but I was scared for you. That you might not have the courage to change things. That you might get stuck back there, and die."

"So I did go back."

"You know you did."

Amelia nodded. "And everything is finished now?"

Annie smiled. "Lindsey House casts a strange spell over people. There are more writings that will be found. Perhaps by you, perhaps by your children. They might open up the way for others to do what you've done. I don't know. I only know that my work here is finished."

"I'd like you to stay. To remain in service here. To take care of the children."

"Will you tell your husband?"

"I don't like keeping secrets from him."

"But some things . . . we have to find on our own."

She nodded her head. "You think I should keep this to myself."

"Yes."

"Would you stay if I asked you to? So that I might have someone to talk to?"

Annie hesitated, and Amelia could sense the conflict within the girl.

"For now, I can't. But I can promise you, should you ever need me, I'll come back."

It had to be enough. "Thank you."

The girl suddenly grinned. "Get back to that husband of yours and keep him warm."

"Oh, I intend to."


She stood in the cottage's small bedroom and watched Hugh sleep. The love she felt for him overwhelmed her, and she thought of all their marriage would entail.

She would do her best to be a good wife. To help him, comfort him, love him. To stand by him, no matter what life might send their way.

The flowers in the bedroom filled the air with their sweet scent. Amelia closed her eyes and thought of her wedding, remembering each moment, treasuring it, knowing it might never have occurred.

She would save those memories. Penny would have a duplicate bridal bouquet waiting for her when she and Hugh returned to Lindsey House from their honeymoon. Amelia wanted to press the flowers, put them in their wedding album along with the satin ribbon. She wanted to create several pressed flower frames for the wedding pictures that would soon join the others on the walls of Lindsey House.

She would take one bloom and put it, pressed, inside th locket Hugh had given her with their wedding date en graved inside.

She would travel through time with those memories, an when this life came to an end, she would pass those mem ories on to their children. And suddenly she didn't want t wait for a baby. If she could have held their firstborn i her arms this minute, she would've wished for it.

Hugh wanted children right away. She'd been more cau tious with her heart. Not anymore.

When she slipped back into bed, Hugh woke up.

"Where were you?" he murmured, drawing her close She put her arms around his neck and melted into th warmth of his lean body. If she had her way, they woul start trying to bring another life into the world this ver night.

"Reading the journal. The end made me cry."

He was silent for a moment.

"Have you read it?"

He nodded. "I felt as if I knew Jonathan, the way h thought, the things he observed—"

*More than you will ever know . . .*

"It's extraordinarily sad," Hugh continued, "how h never got a chance to thank that woman, to let her know how much her courage meant to him. She changed hi world. She changed everything for the Lindseys."

"I know. But you know what? She knows."

He smiled, then pulled her closer. "How can you be s sure?"

She kissed his cheek, then whispered into his ear, "Yo just have to have faith in these things, darling." She kisse him again, told him she'd changed her mind about havin child right away, then laughed out loud at his expression of total joy.

> *In memory of my father.*
> *I'd bring you back if I could.*

# TIMELESS

*Four breathtaking tales of hearts that reach across time—for love...*

*Linda Lael Miller*, the *New York Times* bestselling author, takes a vintage dress-shop owner on a breathtaking adventure in medieval England—where bewitching love awaits...

*Diana Bane* unlocks the secret love behind Maggie's taunting dreams of a clan war from centuries past...

*Anna Jennet*'s heroine takes a plunge into the sea from the cliffs of Cornwall—and falls back in time, into the arms of a heroic knight...

*Elaine Crawford* finds time is of the essence when an engaged workaholic inherits a California ranch—a place she's seen somewhere before...

## \_\_0-425-13701-5/$4.99

Payable in U.S. funds. No cash orders accepted. Postage & handling: $1.75 for one book, 75 for each additional. Maximum postage $5.50. Prices, postage and handling charges may change without notice. Visa, Amex, MasterCard call 1-800-788-6262, ext. 1, refer to ad # 654a

Or, check above books    Bill my:  ☐ Visa  ☐ MasterCard  ☐ Amex _____
and send this order form to:                             (expires)
The Berkley Publishing Group    Card#_____
390 Murray Hill Pkwy., Dept. B                    ($15 minimum)
East Rutherford, NJ 07073    Signature_____
Please allow 6 weeks for delivery.    Or enclosed is my:  ☐ check  ☐ money order

Name_____    Book Total    $_____

Address_____    Postage & Handling  $_____

City_____    Applicable Sales Tax $_____
                                   (NY, NJ, PA, CA, GST Can.)
State/ZIP_____    Total Amount Due  $_____